A

CANDLELIGHT REGENCY SPECIAL

CANDLELIGHT ROMANCES

Bride of Torquay

Lucy Phillips Stewart

A CANDLELIGHT REGENCY SPECIAL

Published by
Dell Publishing Co., Inc.
1 Dag Hammarskjold Plaza
New York, New York 10017

Dell ® TM 681510, Dell Publishing Co., Inc.

ISBN: 0-440-11000-9

Printed in the United States of America

First printing—July 1979

CHAPTER ONE

It was certain that the family of the Marquis of Weldon shared a love of country life. Every summer saw them in Brighton, as surely as fall found them in London, but once the Christmas season was upon them they lost no time in escaping to the fastness of Cornwall, and Weldon Hall. The fact that few families of note resided in the neighborhood troubled them not at all. The Marquis and Lady Lenora much preferred each other's company to that of the larger world, and neither Lydia nor her brother, Gerald, looked for companionship beyond the family circle. Once Lydia became a debutante, however, they were obliged to alter the pattern of their lives, remaining in London until each social season drew to a close.

On the whole Lydia enjoyed the metropolis, for her father's town house was located in St. James's Square, amid all the hustle and bustle of city life. It would have been impossible not to be intrigued by the array of goods on display in the shops, and if the endless

amusements with which society entertained itself varied little from season to season, at least the days were
fraught with interesting sights and sounds. But she
did think it a sad pity to have become forever confronted with the possibility of impending marriage.
She never lacked for masculine attention, and if her
parents seldom entered their drawing room without
stumbling over some enthralled admirer of hers, they
were proud of their daughter's success. It had never
occurred to Lydia that she would not one day meet a
man she could love. The possibility had occurred to
her mother. At the beginning of this season Lady Lenora had vowed not to let Lydia's rejection of all suitors for her hand worry her unduly, as it had during
her daughter's first two seasons, but she was conscious at times of qualms, which she went to great
lengths to conceal.

At one of the final balls of the year Lydia's dance
program had been, as usual, filled to overflowing. But
on this occasion, as on all past occasions, she felt nothing but relief when the music came to an end and her
partner led her to a chair beside the dance floor. A
vision in a gown of turquoise crepe echoing the
unique color of her eyes, and her hair a rioting of au-
burn curls confined by velvet ribbon, she had grown
accustomed to hearing herself proclaimed a beauty.
While she might enjoy the flattering attentions of her
partners, the sight of gentlemen vying for her notice
failed to pique her interest. Since she had looked forward to this, her third season, in high expectation of
at last meeting men who were pleasant and charming,
who would be gay and handsome, debonair and witty,
her disappointment was perfectly understandable. No

one gentleman in particular had proven especially fascinating.

Nearby, a darkly handsome stranger stood in the doorway, his eyes resting on Lydia with a strange expression in their depths, impossible to fathom. No amount of tailoring could conceal the breadth of his shoulders beneath a scented coat of satin, nor the muscles of his thighs encased in matching knee-breeches. From his carefully brushed, curling black hair to the toes of his gleaming slippers, he was the epitome of the gentleman of fashion. A more elegant and virile exquisite would be difficult to imagine.

It still lacked five minutes to twelve before Lydia, moving through the throng en route to partake of a cold collation, turned her glance toward a group of gentlemen and found herself staring into a pair of steely eyes. Recalled to an awareness of her surroundings by the quiet voice of her escort, she assured him she did not feel faint, only warm, and, after a moment, inquired after the identity of the tall stranger.

Lord Hertford looked around blankly. "Oh, that's Carrington," he said grudgingly. "Earl of Torquay. Has a castle in the west of Scotland. Great pile on some crag, I understand."

"Really?" Lydia murmured, digesting this. "Then he is new to town?"

"Been campaigning in the Peninsula, ma'am. Sold out after being wounded." An honest person, he could not bring himself to withhold praise, and added: "Understand him a credit to his regiment."

By the time the evening's entertainment concluded, Lydia's impressions of the Earl were confirmed. An air of detached hauteur proclaimed his unutterable boredom; the smile that only occasionally curved his handsome mouth seemed to mock; his cynical gaze lazily surveyed the world around him and found it wanting. A compelling person, surely, and the most fascinating creature ever to appear on Lydia's horizon.

The following morning found her cantering through Hyde Park perched atop her favorite mare. Trailed at a discreet distance by her groom, she had been making her way along a path when she became aware the Earl was approaching astride a huge stallion. She regarded him with flustered interest as he drew near, and regretted the pink suffusing her cheeks. The short distance separating them accomplished, he inclined his head in a slight bow, and passed on. Lydia was torn between annoyance at the languor with which his cold glance swept over her, and satisfaction at feeling perfectly sure he was not as indifferent as he would have her believe.

She was next to see him when attending a ball in the company of her brother. Indeed, he was the first person she saw after curtsying to Lord and Lady Cranleigh greeting their guests at the top of the stairs. He was laughing down at the small, exquisite beauty clinging to his arm, an intensely feminine creature in an azure gown that dramatically set off her golden hair and stunning milk-white complexion. Lydia surveyed the pair with feigned indifference. The Earl was dashing in ruby satin, with rubies in the foaming lace at his throat and on the fingers of his large, tanned hands. One curling lock falling forward over his brow only emphasized his appeal.

Gerald, having remained by Lydia's side and following the direction of her regard, remarked: "Lady Longford is wasting her time if she thinks Torquay will come up to scratch."

Lydia cast her brother one icy glance. Her cheeks had reddened, and she said with unusual brevity: "Don't be vulgar."

Gerald turned his head and looked at her in surprise. "He's a wily fellow, Lydd. He has to be. Half the mamas in town will be casting out lures."

Lydia's voice became more frosty still. "For heaven's sake, do hush," she said shortly.

Gerald studied her averted face, a thoughtful expression in his eyes, before relinquishing his place at her side to one of her more tiresomely persistent suitors. For Lydia, the evening began slowly, with nothing to indicate it would prove the most important night of her life. The rooms were crowded, but not unduly so; the orchestra, though not brilliant, was adequate; the refreshments, which consisted of jellied meats, a variety of tiny sandwiches, and champagne, were tasty and plentiful. But as each dance ended and her partner returned her to her mother's side, she experienced nothing but the customary relief.

It only lacked a few minutes to eleven when Lydia perceived Gerald approaching across the crowded floor with the Earl in tow. From a sudden feeling of weakness in the knees, she looked about for a chair, in fear her legs would give way beneath her. It could not be a more cowardly reaction. Lifting her chin, she stood quietly awaiting their arrival. She must have been introduced, and surely she had replied in some suitable manner, she thought later, though she remembered little of it. The next thing she knew, the Earl had escorted her to the refreshment room, procured a glass of lemonade for her, and sat facing her. The effect of gray eyes turned on her at such close quarters proved devastating. Taking herself in hand, she remarked: "I understand you have been in the Peninsula, my lord."

"For some time," he replied without elaborating. The hint of a humorous glint in his eyes told her all too clearly he had not missed the implication—her remark had betrayed a prior knowledge of his affairs.

A flush crept up into her cheeks. "Your bravery has been discussed in so many quarters, it is not to be wondered I would hear of it," she said faintly.

He looked at her penetratingly. "Let me assure you, ma'am, my own poor contribution has been greatly exaggerated," he said, a slight frown between his brows.

A little coaxing smile curved her lips. "May I say without appearing impertinent that being wounded in the service of one's country deserves acclaim. Quips just will not serve, my lord."

The humorous glint returned to his eyes, vanquishing the frown. "Do you know, ma'am, you make me realize I only wish I had been wounded earlier," he said with one of his rare smiles. "When I was last here, London had not yet been graced by your presence."

Lydia's cheeks fairly flamed. "Oh!" she said foolishly.

"You may imagine the debt of gratitude I owe your brother. I'm afraid I inveigled an introduction from him."

"I shouldn't think it took much doing," she admitted, incurably candid. Smiling, she added: "At times Gerald lacks discrimination."

His brows shot up. "The kitten has claws," he remarked appreciatively. "Am I to learn whether the door will close in my face when I call?"

Lydia gave her tiny gurgle of laughter. "Perhaps I

should warn you my Mama is hanging out for a son-in-law," she told him mischievously. "You really should take care where you leave your cards."

He looked startled for a moment, and burst out laughing. "But you're entrancing," he exclaimed, delighted. "Perhaps I should warn you to escape while you have the chance. Tomorrow may be too late."

"I rather think I have no wish to run," she replied, eyes sparkling. "I daresay my head will become quite turned."

"Incorrigible," he remarked, chuckling. "I need have few scruples, I see."

"Well, as to that, I very much doubt you would recognize one if you met it face to face," she replied, taking the wind out of his sails.

"Do you indeed?" he returned, quite blowing them up again. "If this is a sample of the way you conduct yourself with your suitors, I daresay I won't encounter undue competition."

"The danger is that you might encounter too much," she told him, laughing. "I will inform you, sir, that I am an heiress."

"Are you now?" he countered, enjoying himself hugely. "I should think you would recognize in me a fortune hunter ready to pounce on unwary females."

"Well, if you aren't, there are those who are," she said before she thought. "I regret that remark," she admitted ruefully. "It—popped out."

"Been giving you a rough time of it, have they? I'm not at all surprised. You are so very lovely."

Startled, Lydia glanced away. "I cannot imagine," she began stiffly, "what I have done that you should speak to me in an ungentlemanly fashion."

"You cannot precisely blame me, ma'am," he replied

imperturbably. "Your whole aspect is entirely too enchanting."

She looked him full in the face. "You may deem it an honor to be the recipient of your compliments, sir, but I will inform you that you go too fast."

"Of course," he continued ruminatingly, "somewhat tall ladies are not precisely in the mode, but I'm tall myself. We fit together rather nicely."

"You, sir, are insolent," she breathed, eyes flashing.

"Wonderful," he said approvingly. "You are pretty when you frown. Not beautiful, no. I wouldn't go that far. But other ladies are downright ugly when they scowl."

Lydia sat very much erect. "How the conversation took this deplorable turn, I cannot imagine," she said with as much sternness in her voice as she could muster. "I had supposed . . ."

"Now, that will never do," he said, chuckling. "You aren't one of those namby-pamby misses who take fright at the first hint a man finds her attractive. That's coming it a bit strong."

"I very much resent . . ."

"No, you don't. If I had insulted you, which I haven't, I would have landed us in a rare mess. If there is one thing my time in the Peninsula taught me, it is to take life in my hands and mold it."

"If you will permit me to speak without interruption, I will suggest we can scarcely quarrel at a ball, or at least I daresay we shouldn't, even if we wish to. Must you provoke me?"

"Yes," he replied audaciously. "If I didn't, you would forget me the minute my back was turned. What a disadvantage that would be!"

"Oh, for goodness' sake! Must you be so—so . . ."

"Intriguing?" he suggested helpfully.

Lydia suddenly chuckled. "You have been pitch-forked back into the town with no notion of how to go on in a society devoid of soldiery, my lord. May I suggest you engage to observe the gentlemen you see around you?"

"I suppose they will be continually underfoot. What a confounded nuisance that will be! I will find myself put to the trouble of thinning out the crowd."

She favored him with a tiny smile. "I will tell you, my lord, I reserve for myself the privilege of showing suitors the door. You may decide for yourself where you fit into the picture."

"Exactly so," the Earl replied, taking the bait. "But I shouldn't be tempted to hazard any large sum on that supposition, if I were you. I'm a seasoned campaigner, remember."

She twinkled at him and said sweetly: "Since this conversation is leading nowhere, perhaps we should join the dance. You need have no fear I will trod on your feet. I am generally acclaimed proficient in the exercise."

He immediately stood. "If you will honor me, ma'am," he said, bowing formally.

"It was vastly kind of you to think of it," Lydia murmured, rising to sketch a curtsy while controlling her quivering lips. He proved a superb dancer, as she had known he would, leading her through the steps with consummate ease. The glances cast their way did not escape her notice. It was perfectly understandable. He was not only the handsomest gentleman in the room, but quite the most eligible as well. Not entirely to her surprise, she experienced a feeling of regret when the dance ended and he withdrew his arms.

"I prophesy we will be served up with the eggs at every breakfast table in town," he remarked, strolling with her from the dance floor. "I will do myself the honor of calling on you tomorrow. Shall we say two?"

Her eyes danced. "Did I grant you permission to do so?" she demanded with feigned reluctance.

"You did not," he replied audaciously, and raised the hand he still held to his lips. With that he restored her to her mother, bowed politely to Lady Lenora, and left them. Lydia would have sworn he favored her with a slight wink before moving away.

The tall case-clock in the blue salon of Weldon House was just striking the hour of two the following afternoon when he was ushered into the room. Lydia got up from the settee where she had been seated with Lord Hertford beside her and advanced, extending her hand. The Earl, taking it in his own, ran his eyes over the crowded room. "Accept my felicitations," he said. "Who, in God's name, is the furious puppy glowering at me from the sofa?"

"Arnold," said Lydia, restraining the tendency of her lips to twitch, "is a most devoted son. Only his constant support saw Lady Hertford through the recent loss of her husband. I must make you known to him."

"I have not the smallest desire to meet young Hertford. Why should I?"

"Because you are intending to comport yourself with propriety, I make no doubt. And now, sir, if you will give me back my hand?"

The Earl tried in vain to think of some suitable retort. When none occurred to him, he released her fingers and followed her across the room, where she performed the introduction. Lord Hertford muttered the briefest of acknowledgments, not in the least pleased. Besieged as he was by jealousy, the length of time the Earl had held Lydia's hand and the way his eyes rested on her had not escaped his notice. He would have liked nothing better than to utter some clever remark, thereby casting Torquay in the role of charlatan, but could only stammer out a trivial excuse to bow himself away. The Earl watched him go and directed one of his devilish looks at Lydia. "I wish you will tell me what you thought to gain by it," he remarked with an unholy twinkle in his eyes.

"Now what have I done to put you into a twit?" Lydia replied, not in the least chastised. "Only think what a bore it would be if you were forced to spend the afternoon talking only to me."

"Don't tell me you anticipated you would find me a bore, and so invited in the town to rescue you from tedium. I know better, so don't blow up that breeze."

"That is unworthy of you," she replied, but with a twinkle in her eye he could not miss. "What right have you, pray, to expect me to deny admittance to friends paying a call?"

"I'm afraid you coerced me, ma'am," he informed her outrageously. "It's high time you realized you have me on your hands, like it or not. And don't pitch up at me. It won't do you the least good."

Lydia proved equal to the challenge. "I will own I shan't come to cuffs with you in public," she remarked, adding: "However much I might deplore your behavior."

"As bad as that?" he asked impertinently. "What other treats have you in store for me? Don't tell me I am to entertain the dowager in the yellow turban.

Good God! It must touch the ceiling when she stands."

"Then you will be advised to see to it she remains seated," she replied with perfect composure. "I do appreciate your volunteering to entertain our callers. I'm sure it will be a credential for you with Mama."

"Oh?" he said, startled. "Have I incurred her ill will?"

"Not at all. But Lady Cornelia is Mama's cousin, turban or no."

"And is the timid blond in the unbecoming gown her daughter?"

"I will admit Cousin Cornelia has deplorable taste. Properly dressed, Emily Lou could be quite passable."

"She giggles," said the Earl unfeelingly. "Believe me, fair torment, I would endure the next moments for no one but you."

Lydia watched him cross to bow over Lady Cornelia's hand, and turned to greet a caller waiting patiently to engage her notice. Torquay, his initial assignment fulfilled, moved on about the room, and was next seen talking to Lady Lenora until a gentleman was announced. The General's call was of short duration, but he stayed long enough to infuriate the Earl. Torquay had been an officer under his command. Despite his efforts to the contrary, the story of Torquay's heroics in the Peninsula was brought forth and put on public display. The General, with his usual lack of perception, prosed on, holding center stage and reveling in the telling. The Earl undoubtedly heard the complimentary murmurs running over the room, but he gave no sign of it. Lydia rather fancied his carefully expressionless countenance concealed something more than mere annoyance. Had she but known it, he was seething.

The only child of elderly parents, he had been orphaned at the age of eight, much too young to come into a title and great wealth. No sooner had the funerals taken place than he had been spirited off to Edinburgh to live in semi-seclusion, attended by servants and taught by an unending procession of stern-faced tutors. Only on holidays had he been permitted to visit Castle Torquay. The results were predictable. Upon reaching his majority he had, if the tales told of him were true, embarked upon a career that embraced all the more outrageous forms of extravagant behavior. It would not be too much to say that the ladies fawned on him, that no door was closed to him, regardless of the talk, and that his relatives battened on him for their livelihood. For whatever reason, one thing was sure: He became firmly convinced that society in general, and all ladies in particular, were only interested in his title and in the comforts his wealth could buy. Disillusioned, and feeling like a puppet on a string, he had withdrawn to Castle Torquay, remaining there in virtual isolation until enlisting in the army.

Lydia, of course, had no way of knowing this. The unexpectedness of the coldness she read in his face when he very soon approached her sent a quiver down her spine. Moving forward to meet him, she said apologetically: "The General should have heeded your reluctance to have your exploits bruited about."

"It appears I have provided your guests with an afternoon's entertainment," he replied with a mocking little bow. "Accept my compliments."

Lydia looked startled, and pinked in spite of herself. The touch of sarcasm in his voice was marked, but she was not unduly perturbed by it. The Earl's anger, she concluded, sprang from embarrassment at being made to appear ridiculous in his own eyes. On more than one occasion her own brother had reacted in much the same way. Gentlemen, she had early discovered, suffered from an incurable sense of pride. It needed only the least assault on their dignity to set them off.

The Earl, who had erroneously concluded that Lydia was no different from the ladies he had known in the past, stood observing the potpourri of emotions flickering across her face. After a moment he said with controlled politeness that he had a pressing appointment elsewhere and would take his leave. Her eyes went swiftly to his face as a feeling somewhere between regret and dismay swept over her, but she quickly extended her hand, only hoping the color would not rise in her cheeks to betray her. Something of what she was feeling must have shown in her face, for he did raise her fingers to his lips before going out of the room without another word.

CHAPTER TWO

Lydia was to experience a great deal of frustration in the days ahead. The Earl was usually in attendance at social gatherings and acknowledged her presence with a most proper, and perfunctory, bow, but he did so unsmilingly, allotting her the barest civility demanded by social address. Never before had she been confronted with a state of affairs affecting her life for which she could find no solution, and it annoyed her almost beyond enduring to see him showering attention on an unending parade of simpering and, if he but had the wit to see it, vapid misses. The fact that the majority of them were endowed with at least some claim to beauty, and were of impeccable lineage, vastly overset her composure, making it difficult for her to view the situation with the calm reflection she had previously displayed when confronted with unnerving circumstances. When she recalled what had been his obvious sentiments on the occasions of their earlier acquaintance, she had no doubt at all in her own mind the direction of this thinking. She had quite taken him by storm. Admitting to herself that he had, in his turn, stirred in her emotions she had never before experienced, and which she found to be far from fleeting, only served further to tangle her already agitated thinking. No man had ever before affected her in quite the same way.

Her mother, of course, was shattered by it all. When Lady Lenora recalled the many offers of marriage that had been made to Lydia, and her subsequent refusals, her peace of mind became thoroughly cut up. The child could, at any time throughout the season, have become betrothed to the heir to a dukedom, or to one of any number of highly eligible gentlemen. But as matters now stood, her only daughter could very well end her days an old maid. This dismal prospect proved more than the state of Lady Lenora's nerves could withstand. A bottle of smelling salts joined the contents of her reticule, and the family, observing her reclining limply on a sofa with a solution of ammonia on the table beside her, could not miss the message. It was not to be supposed that she could longer bear with equanimity the vacillations of her offspring. Lydia did not in the least grudge her mother's lamentations. The prospect of a life bereft of the Earl by her side she found hard to face, for she had by this time owned to herself that she had, unaccountably, tumbled headlong into love. The admission brought her little comfort. The wisest thing for her to do, she concluded during one long and sleepless night, would be to bury herself in good works and strive to put him from her thoughts. After which, of course, she continued to have very little else at all on her mind.

It was at one of the final balls of the season, when

she was torn between a desire to leave rather than endure the sight of him partnering others in the dance, and the knowledge that she could not tear herself away, that she saw him approaching across the crowded floor. She dropped her eyes, the dark lashes fluttering against her cheeks, and waited, feeling strangely breathless. No one, observing her at that moment, would have suspected she felt slightly giddy and that her pulses had quickened alarmingly. The depth of his voice requesting the pleasure of the dance brought her to her feet, but try as she would she could not put words to her tongue. He seemed not to notice and, having drawn her hand within his arm, led her forward. She found she was not proof against the touch of his hand on her waist, and trembled, though she did contrive to keep her eyes averted. She knew he was gazing down at her, but she started nevertheless when he said: "Have I offended you to such a degree you will not look at me?"

Giving herself a mental shake, she raised her eyes, and replied in a somewhat uncertain voice: "Not at all. I am afraid my thoughts were wandering. Pray say no more about it."

"So I have hurt you. I won't say I meant to, but I'm sorry. My damnable pride was at fault. Forgive me?"

She looked away and strove for a lighter tone. "Why in the world should you apologize? I assure you I have not taken exception to your conduct. Why should I?"

"I suppose it will be more to the purpose for me to explain. May I call tomorrow?"

She raised her brows in apparent surprise and said: "But, of course, my lord. I am sure we will be happy to receive you."

"If you mean that for a set-down, ma'am, I may deserve it, but it won't put me off."

Silence fell between them then, and continued until the dance had drawn to a close. He appeared to be giving consideration to voicing some thought, and glanced down at her searchingly, but apparently changed his mind. Watching him move away, the thought that his moods were as mercurial and unpredictable as her own brought the hint of a smile to her lips. She could not help feeling glad of it, for the prospect of marriage to a paragon of exemplary behavior struck her as onerous in the extreme. And unless she was wholly mistaken, the Earl had every intention of patching up their differences. The road ahead, she knew, since she was too honest to deceive herself, showed no signs of running smoothly. A well-regulated courtship, with its extravagant compliments and flattering attentions, had become a question open to doubt. The idea no sooner occurred to her than she banished it from her mind; he would never utter flowery phrases, nor overly exert himself to please her. Thinking of him in this light, she gave an involuntary chuckle. A man more unlikely to do so than the Earl she could not imagine. Nor, she mused, as the thought darted through her mind, would he attract her half so much were he so inclined.

Early the following morning she slipped from the house and sought refuge in the gardens, thinking to occupy herself with the roses. She did indeed poke about in the soil with a trowel, and pinched off a faded bloom or two, but she made slow progress. The Earl's handsome face continually obtruded in her thoughts, and she would find herself gazing dreamily into space. After she had cultivated the same bush for the third time, and had looked ruefully down upon the ruin of her handiwork, she gave it up and went back into the house.

Eldridge, coming up to her as she prepared to mount the stairs, announced that the Earl had called and had been ushered into the small salon. "I informed his lordship the family was not at home to callers before the hour of eleven," the butler continued in disapproving accents, "but I'm afraid it went for naught. His lordship, if I may say so, my lady, deemed it wise to request I not—his lordship's exact words, my lady, were that I not keep him standing about kicking his heels when I should be informing your ladyship of his call." Eldridge paused, a slight tightening about the lips the only emotion disturbing the schooled impassivity of his bearing. "I felt it incumbent upon me to admit him, my lady."

"No doubt you were right in doing so, Eldridge," Lydia replied, a slight quiver twitching at her lips as she mounted the stairs to freshen up. "Pray tell him I will be with him shortly."

Entering the salon some fifteen minutes later, she went forward, holding out her hand. "I understand you have been standing the household on its heels," she said with an impish little smile. "Eldridge is quite done up, I assure you."

"I don't care a fig for that," he returned, carrying her fingers to his lips. "I didn't intend waiting an instant longer than necessary to see you. We've wasted too much time already."

She gave him a saucy glance. "Do you know you are the first person ever to succeed in ruffling Eldridge," she said impulsively. "I could hug you."

"Please do," he said with devastating promptness.

Lydia flushed and withdrew her hand. "Won't you be seated, my lord?" she said, crossing to a chair to cover her confusion.

He followed her across the room, but stood looking down at her with an expression in his eyes that set her pulses racing. She had wondered what his first words would be, but could never have anticipated them. For he said unexpectedly: "I'm far beneath your touch. You should show me the door."

It took her an instant to recover from surprise, but she quickly rose to the occasion. "That's a horrid thought," she said, and gave her tiny gurgle of laughter. "What have you been about, to deceive yourself into thinking yourself a knave? My curiosity is now thoroughly roused."

"I shan't sully your ears with the story of my past. A soldier's life isn't at all pretty," he told her frankly.

"No, I hadn't supposed it was. I do hope you aren't intending to speak in an exaggerated fashion."

His gray eyes studied her seriously for a moment before he said: "Hasn't your knowledge of me convinced you I'm the worst of all possible husbands for you?"

Lydia gasped, and put out her hand in a gesture of supplication, meeting his searching stare with pleading eyes. "Don't rush us," she said somewhat breathlessly. "We need time to become better acquainted."

"You must have seen I'm deep in love with you. So don't tell me we aren't well enough acquainted. Is it my past? I won't deny I have frequently had a highstepper under my protection, but you know very well that ceased the minute I clapped eyes on you. You are all I want."

Such an admission might well have shocked some

few of her contemporaries, but Lydia was not in the least shocked. She was, in fact, amused. "Be quiet, you wretch," she said sternly. "Have you no modesty?"

"None at all," he replied promptly. "I thought it my duty to tell you, since I intend having no secrets from you. At least there will be no dreadful disillusionments in store."

Lydia choked, and went off into a peal of laughter. "This will never do, sir," she gurgled. "You are trampling on my innocence."

The Earl's shoulders began to shake. "I see that doesn't trouble you in the least. We couldn't be better suited."

"You are forever attempting to astonish me," she told him, indicating a chair. "I do wish you would take a seat and tell me about Scotland. I understand your home is located there."

He did not seem at all offended by the change of subject; rather, he appeared pleased. The idea of a cool reception to any mention of marriage on his part was as refreshing as it would be thought to be unusual, and was in no way dampening. His eyes dwelled inscrutably on her face before he said: "Some may think Scotland remote, but to me it is home. My earliest memories center around my return from school for holiday. I'm afraid I ran wild. Nanny was forever scolding."

Lydia smiled, picturing the scene. "She undoubtedly had reason. Did you return with your kilt torn and your knees grubby?"

He threw back his head as his laugh rang out. "Don't tell me you were never banished to bed on warm milk and bread. I know better, my girl. You were never a proper little miss, busy with your embroidery. Pity both our nannies."

This drew a chuckle from her, and she said pertly: "I fear you are sadly mistaken, my lord. My nanny was snugly round my finger. I had cookies with the milk."

At this point he suddenly leaned forward and took her hands in his. "The earls of Torquay have always been named Iain. I trust you won't wait until we're married to use it."

She eyed him askance. "I haven't said I will marry you," she told him faintly.

"But of course you will," he replied imperturbably. "I'm not offering you carte blanche, you know."

"Good God!" Lydia gasped, appalled. "Is there anything you won't say?"

He looked thoughtfully down at her. "Now that you know the worst of me," he said, "have I your permission to pay a formal call on your father?"

She felt the color rushing into her cheeks, and asked tremulously: "You've known me such a brief time, how can you be sure you love me?"

"I would hazard a guess you are sure you love me," he replied outrageously. "It's all very well for you to want a courtship, and I intend giving you one. But that shouldn't preclude our becoming betrothed. If you imagine that I intend hanging about your skirts like a love-sick cawker, rid yourself of the notion. May I call on your father?"

Her hands moved in his, but only to return the clasp of his fingers. "We may have a future together, Iain, but it won't be an uneventful one, will it? I should think we would rip up at each other at times, for your temper is every bit as scraggly as my own, but neither of us would mean the things we say. Aren't you going to kiss me?"

"No," he said with so much regret in his voice she trembled. "Not until I receive your father's blessings."

Lydia gazed at him wonderingly. "I shouldn't have thought that would deter you," she admitted frankly.

"With you, it does," he replied, turning her hands over to press a kiss into each palm.

Laughter bubbled up in Lydia. "Do but recollect a little," she said mirthfully. "Of all the untrue things to say!"

He smiled and shook his head. "I may have very little regard for the proprieties, but I know when to toe the mark. That being so, I will now return home to pen a missive to your father."

"Will I see you at Lady Trestler's card party tonight?"

"No, but I should imagine you will be on hand tomorrow following my conference with your papa," he grinned, assisting her to her feet.

"Wretch!" she said with her infectious chuckle, going with him to the door. "Have you no control over your tongue?"

"Very little," he replied, nodding to a waiting footman, who immediately brought his hat and gloves. "Good morning, Lady Lydia. Do make my excuses to Lady Lenora, I beg you."

"Good morning, my lord," she replied demurely. Amusement at his formality before the servants danced in her eyes, and she turned away to hide a smile.

As the Earl had prophesied, she declared, next morning while the family waited in the drawing room, that she had no intention of sitting out developments in her room. Lady Lenora strenuously opposed this, but Lydia remained determined. "Why on earth should we pretend ignorance about Iain's impending call?" she demanded rather crossly. "Don't be gothic, Mama."

Inarticulate choking sounds from Lady Lenora caused the Marquis to lower his paper and fix his daughter with a stern eye. "You are speaking to your mother," he said in reproving tones. "Apologize."

"If I have upset you, Mama, I beg your pardon," Lydia said obediently. "But to be plain about it, Iain won't expect us to stand on ceremony."

"I must say, I think it most improper of you to use the Earl's given name," Lady Lenora said, heaving a sigh. "Everywhere one turns, one meets with ill-mannered young, but I had not thought to find my own daughter among their number."

"Mama, I don't mean to sound impertinent, but you mustn't fancy Torquay the soul of propriety. Far from it. Oh, he can behave most properly when he chooses, but, you see, he seldom does."

"Lydia!" exclaimed Lady Lenora with a pained look. "You cannot be completely devoid of sensibility!"

Gerald, who was standing at a window scanning the street, turned his head to say: "I haven't seen all that much of the Earl, but if he isn't a simpering dandy, I'm glad of it. For myself, I shouldn't fancy one in the family."

"Pray, do not be provoking," Lady Lenora adjured him. Transferring her attention to the Marquis, she continued reproachfully: "I cannot conceive where our children inherited their medieval way of speaking."

The Marquis glanced at her, and said in amusement: "From my side of the house, no doubt. Don't take me wrongly, my dear, but if Lydia has set her mind on Torquay, the matter is more or less decided."

Lady Lenora looked a little startled. "I'm sure I have no objection," she stated flatly, feeling aggrieved. "No one could deny him a desirable parti, and I'm sure, quite regardless of Lydia's statement to the contrary, that there is nothing in his manners to disgust the most exacting critic."

The Marquis turned his gaze on Lydia. "I take it you aren't loath to have the Earl pursue his suit?"

She could not suppress a smile, but said as soberly as she could manage: "I wouldn't precisely say he hasn't already pursued it, Papa."

"You don't mean to tell us," Lady Lenora interjected, "that you have discussed it between the two of you before the Earl applied to Papa for your hand!"

"Conventions have changed, Mama," Gerald broke in to explain. "Gentlemen no longer are prohibited from speaking their minds."

A moment later he regretted the impulse. For Lady Lenora, from having her attention focused on Lydia, now turned it on him. "Surely you scruple not to discuss indelicate subjects with your sister!" she said severely.

Gerald looked astonished. "What the deuce did I say?" he demanded of the room at large.

"I trust you will come away from that window in your own good time," the Marquis said in his most damping tones. "It is just conceivable the Earl might think it strange to find you quizzing his arrival."

"Well, if he does, he has," Gerald announced somewhat cryptically. "By Jupiter! Will you look at those matched grays. I wonder where he found them. Do but come and see, Lydd."

Torquay was indeed in the act of springing down from a high-perch phaeton. He was dressed in a coat of blue superfine that set off his shoulders to perfection; the points of his shirt collar stood up stiffly above an intricately arranged cravat; his waistcoat was in the best of taste, as were his biscuit-colored pantaloons. From his carefully placed beaver hat, to his gleaming Hessian boots, he was the personification of the notable Corinthian. As he perceived Lydia watching from the window, a smile lit his handsome face, and he bowed slightly to her before mounting the front steps, to knock upon the door.

The Marquis, withdrawing to receive the Earl in his study, left Lydia radiant and her mother in a flutter of anticipation. Lady Lenora, having launched her daughter into society with every hope of a brilliant match, had seen her hopes very nearly dashed by Lydia's faulting every suitor for her hand. Now that the Earl appeared on the point of offering for her, Lady Lenora scarcely dared to pronounce on the outcome, though his request for a private interview with the Marquis did assuage the worst of her fears.

Fortunately they had not long to wait before the Marquis reappeared upon the threshold. "The Earl is desirous of speaking with you, Lydia," he said with an indulgent smile.

"Then?" Lady Lenora breathed, casting a glance at his face.

"That is for your daughter to say," murmured his lordship, stepping aside as Lydia, now looking a trifle nervous, hurried through the door.

Thus it was that when she stood facing the biggest

and hitherto most unobtainable prize of the Marriage Mart, Lydia felt unaccountably shy. She took a deep breath and, eyes lowered, managed to say: "You wished to see me, my lord?"

There was a moment's silence. "The Earl of Torquay is obliged to Lady Lydia Tremayne for the privilege," he said impishly after the pause.

She raised her eyes rather timidly to his, and saw he was looking amused. Unable to sustain his regard, she lowered her gaze to the contemplation of her fingers tightly clasped before her. The little gold tassels on his Hessian boots bouncing jauntily with each step he took swam into her vision as he came to a halt before her. "Why so diffident?" he said teasingly, taking possession of her hands. "Your father has granted me permission to pay my addresses. Only fancy, my love. Whatever do you suppose has come over me?"

Laughter bubbled up in Lydia. "Wretch!" she said, raising twinkling eyes to his face. "Cannot you propose to me properly?"

"Will you do me the very great honor of becoming my wife?" he promptly said, pressing her fingers to his lips before sweeping her into his arms. "Now do you know why I have never in my life wanted anything more than to win your love?"

"Oh!" she murmured foolishly, subsiding weakly in his embrace, a responsive quiver running through her body.

He felt it, and his arms tightened about her. "My adorable girl," he uttered, and kissed her again. "How I wish I had you at Castle Torquay!"

"In Scotland?" she said, startled. "Whatever brought that to your mind?"

"We Scots know that when the mist rolls in over the

hills, and spirits stalk the land, lovers are enfolded in a yellow glow from which there can be no escape. He must belong to her, and she must belong to him, and neither of them would have it otherwise."

Lydia raised her hand to touch his cheek gently. "How very beautiful," she breathed softly, hesitant to break the spell.

He caught her hand in his and slipped a ring on the third finger. "It is the betrothal ring of the Carringtons," he said, carrying her fingers to his lips. "Brides of Torquay have always worn it."

Lydia gazed at the glowing emerald, the tears stinging her eyelids. "Shall you take me to Scotland?" she asked softly, blinking the tears away.

"Very soon, if your parents assent. The fishing is good, and I can offer a tolerable shoot. I know your father hunts. Does Gerald?"

"He has given it a try on occasion, though not as expertly as you, I'm sure."

"Good. It's settled, then. Shall we say next week?"

"Next week!" Lydia gasped, stunned. "Mama would never agree!"

"Then we will make it two. No more. And now, my girl, you have just received a proposal of marriage, and most properly, I might add. You haven't given me your answer."

"The answer is yes, as you very well know. But I will inform you, sir, I shan't submit to being bullied."

"Incorrigible!" said the Earl, pulling her back into his arms. "There is nothing for it. I must kiss you into submission."

Lydia, emerging breathless from the embrace some few minutes later, tucked a wayward curl in place. "I hadn't suspected it would be like this," she admitted, a good deal surprised.

"You hadn't expected to thrill to my kisses? Come, come. Well, I think it only fair to warn you that you will, most properly, very soon become accustomed to them."

"I will? Then I shan't set up any objections, for naturally you must know what is proper. I must just make the best of it and pray you won't do me violence. Shall you do me violence, my love?"

"The most glorious violence, my darling. I imagine you must know what that means, but I won't put you to the blush."

"For goodness' sake, Iain!"

"Shaken with outraged propriety, are you? Perhaps I should restore you to your mother before I sink myself beyond reproach."

"Really, Iain, this is too bad of you. You are attempting to shock me again. No such thing! I'm awake upon every suit!"

"Now you are the one who is talking nonsense. I'm convinced you are awake upon no suit at all, but we'll explore that at a future date. For the present, shall we go and relieve your mother's apprehensions?"

And so Lydia, controlling an errant tendency of her lips to twitch, showed him a face of sweet innocence, and allowed him to usher her from the room.

Lady Lenora, once she had grasped that she was to set forth on the tedious journey to Scotland with only two weeks' time allotted for preparation, and had brought forth every objection she could call to mind, found herself unable to resist the pleading in Lydia's eyes, and reluctantly allowed herself to be persuaded. It was not many days before she strongly regretted having permitted her heart to overcome her judgment. "I'd as lief not go," she mourned for the hundredth time. "I'm sure I haven't the least notion of what to pack! Your papa should exercise more control over you, Lydia, but, manlike, he leaves it all to me!"

"But Mama," Lydia protested, laughing. "Papa says . . ."

"I know exactly what he says," Lady Lenora interrupted somewhat waspishly. "I have known what he will say any time these many years. I daresay he will be in perfect accord until we arrive in Scotland and some part of his wardrobe comes up missing. I'm sure part of my own will."

"What a rapper that is, Mama!" Lydia remarked, chuckling. "I am persuaded you will arrive in Scotland with every stitch you own. Just ask Claxy. She is doing your packing."

"Lydia, I will ask you not to refer to Claxton in that revolting way. I know you have known her since childhood, but she is my personal maid and has her own position to uphold."

"Very well, Mama," Lydia replied obediently, then spoiled the effect by adding: "But it is Papa's man, Reevers, after all, who is doing his packing."

Lady Lenora seemed to consider her daughter dispassionately for a moment, and then said: "You might deploy your time to better advantage by overseeing your own abigail. In fact, I insist that you do so."

"I already have, Mama," Lydia replied in a tolerably steady voice. Unable to sustain her gravity, she went off on a peal of laughter. "I told Letty to pack everything I own."

Lady Lenora found herself at a loss. Her son she could deal with, for Gerald cared little for mundane matters and cheerfully donned any garments laid out for him. Lydia was of another bent entirely, from having decided ideas of her own, and would have it that all the frills and furbelows were necessary, albeit her taste was excellent. Lady Lenora sighed and went sedately from the room to order yet another coach available to carry still additional trunks and valises on the journey north.

Despite dire predictions to the contrary, and in spite of Gerald's putting in a tardy appearance at the breakfast table, to the consternation of his mother, the family did emerge from the house fairly well on time. If the Earl, standing beside his own coach waiting to hand Lydia up, was startled by the cavalcade, he concealed it well. For no less than six coaches bearing a quantity of luggage, plus the Marquis's own traveling coach, were drawn up before the door. Add to this the Earl's own two vehicles, servants from his own and the Tremayne household, and they presented quite an impressive entourage. At least those few early risers privileged to observe their progress through the nearly empty city streets seemed to find it so, and gaped from the sidewalks, awed. Lydia, surprised at being permitted to ride alone with the Earl, settled herself comfortably against the luxurious squabs, and leafed through the pages of a *Traveller's Guide*. "It says here it is the better part of four hundred miles from London to Glasgow," she remarked, startled. "I shouldn't have thought it nearly so far."

"Shouldn't you?" murmured the Earl, transferring his gaze from her hair, turned fiery by a shaft of sunlight striking it, to her face. "We will be a good week upon the road before we reach the Scottish border. I should like to explore the sights along the way with you, but it would take a month."

"Yes, I can see it would, but you mustn't think you can fob me off," she replied, smiling. "One day, sir, you shall."

The Earl looked at her seriously and said: "A lifetime together hardly seems enough time, there is so much I want to show you."

"Well, if it isn't too much trouble, you may begin by pointing out things of interest along the way when we pass by them. The *Traveller's Guide* speaks of Roman ruins and places where the Druids worshipped."

"You will see more intriguing sights than those in Scotland. For bleak majesty and desolate beauty, the country around Castle Torquay cannot be equaled. I want you to love my land."

"What I am wanting, Iain, is to see you on it," she replied, a twinkle in her eyes. "Not in it, for I understand Torquay is located amid the lochs?"

"And amid the hills," he remarked, smiling in return. "In places, the cliffs fall sheer above Loch Broom. One must take care when climbing about, for it can be treacherous."

"It sounds menacing."

"Only along the northern boundary of the estate, where the loch joins the sea. There is a cave that runs so far back into the rock it has never been fully explored. I have attempted it on numerous occasions, but the tide runs high, and I was forced to flee. Such places give rise to old wives' tales."

Lydia turned expectant eyes on his face. "Then there is a mystery?" she asked, enthralled.

"There is always a mystery," he chuckled, flicking her cheek with a finger. "Doubly so, when one adds a blow-hole that sounds in a storm as if all the demons in Hell were screeching."

"What is a blow-hole?" Lydia asked curiously.

"It is a narrow opening in the roof of a cave. During a storm, the tide fills the cavern until the pressure builds. The noise occurs as it escapes through the funnel. To the superstitious among our people, the sound is the tormented wailing of pirates trapped within and doomed to howl for eternity. The cave becomes, as you might guess, a veritable storehouse for hidden treasure."

A twinkle came into her eyes. "Shall we search for it?" she asked, warming to the subject. "We could take a picnic lunch, and . . ."

"You are not to go near it," he ordered with awful clarity. "More than one fool has drowned in the attempt."

Lydia blinked, and decided on a light approach. "Being betrothed to you would seem to have its drawbacks," she said pertly. "Has it some advantages as well?"

His stern expression relaxed into a grin. "One day you will not need to ask me that," he replied, the devil in his smiling eyes.

"You terrify me," she tossed back, pleased with her repartee. "On what grounds do you intend to prove your challenge?"

"Don't press me to answer that," he said after a pause.

"Bested, are you?" she said smugly. "Well, sir, you aren't to be let off so easily. I will again ask . . . " Lydia halted in mid-sentence, the meaning behind his words suddenly coming into her mind. Flushing, she fluttered her eyelids and dropped her eyes.

"You may ascribe the astonishing guard I have so far clamped over my tongue to the fact that your mama has entrusted you alone to my care. I shan't abuse her confidence, but neither will I act the prude." When there didn't seem to be anything Lydia intended saying in reply, he took her hands in his. "Look at me, my love," he said quietly.

Lydia realized her performance was out of character, and raised her eyes. "I wasn't shocked," she admitted candidly. "I don't know why I blushed."

"You did because we are truly alone together for the first time. I'm affected myself, but I don't intend doing anything so very terrible. Trust me, dearest."

"I do, but I was afraid you might kiss me."

"I don't intend doing so, however much I might want to. I don't trust either of us that far."

"Well, if it comes to that, neither do I."

"Never be embarrassed with me, Lydia," he said softly. "I couldn't bear it. And now, I think we will be on safer ground if you tell me what other interesting tidbits you picked up in your *Traveller's Guide*."

Lydia responded readily to this suggestion, and continued chatting in a cheerful way as their coach rolled on through the sunlit morning. The Earl did not seem to have much to say, preferring to watch her with a tender expression in his eyes that, when her glance met his, set her pulses racing. At the first post-stage she remained in the coach while the horses were changed, but by the time they had covered another twelve miles, she was ready to descend and enter the inn. The landlord came bustling forward, bowing, to suggest his good wife show my lady to a bedchamber where a can of hot water waited her comfort. Lydia, eyeing the landlady's agitated curtsying from just beyond her husband's shoulder, felt decidedly foolish. Unaccustomed to obsequious menials—for her father's servants, while always polite, were never required to act subservient—it took all the resolution she could muster not to speak sharply in rebuke. Such an action would, she knew, only result in humiliation to the pair before her. To her very great relief, her mother's arrival at that moment put a period to her discomfiture, and she very soon went upstairs in the wake of Lady Lenora and the landlady.

The chamber allotted to her was, she guessed, one of the best the inn had to offer, though not the one originally intended, for no can of water reposed upon the stand. Chuckling at the switch in accommodations in favor of her mother, she crossed to the dressing table and somewhat ruefully inspected her reflection in the mirror. Wrinkling her nose at her image, she brushed out her hair and dressed it again, finishing the task just as a serving maid entered with the errant brass can of hot water. She was still smiling over her usurpation after washing her face and hands and twitching her skirts in place.

The Earl was awaiting her return at the foot of the staircase to usher her into the private parlor, seeming oblivious of the landlord bowing in the background until his nose seemed in danger of colliding with his knees. That her affianced was a personage of importance upon the road to Scotland became even more pronounced immediately they entered the room. Covers were laid on the table before the fire, and the Earl's liveried servants stood waiting to serve them. That his lordship's own chef had taken charge of the kitchens with the ease of long acquaintance further underscored the Earl's standing, and did him no harm

at all in Lady Lenora's estimation. Not that he stood
in danger of falling from grace. Quite the contrary.
From the moment the jellied consommé was set before them, until luncheon concluded with strawberries
from the Earl's London greenhouses, it was obvious
that he was prepared to go to any lengths to ensure
Lydia's comfort. Nevertheless, or perhaps because of
it, Lady Lenora could not rid herself of the conviction
that it was foolhardy to allow her daughter to continue the journey alone in the Earl's company. The notion struck a chord of memory, calling to mind the
Marquis's conduct on the eve of their own marriage.
She started, and her eyes flew to the Earl's face in a
look of veiled interrogation. Needless to say, his coach
sheltered an additional occupant for the remainder of
the passage north. If amusement gleamed in his eyes at
times, he remained the considerate host, sending retainers ahead of every stop to bespeak the finest accommodations available, and to prepare meals as varied as
they were delicious.

Lydia found much of interest in the changing scen-
ery as they neared the Scottish border. Though it
seemed unlikely the beauty of the landscape could improve, she found the Earl had not exaggerated when
they crossed into Scotland and proceeded along the
road from Glasgow to Fort William, and on beside the
shores of Lochs Lochy and Ness, to the city of Inver-
ness. She had thought that no further superlatives
could be called up and, as they turned northeastward
toward Loch Broom, found it not within her power to
do so, and allowed the expression in her eyes to tell the
Earl all he could wish to hear.

The road snaked onward along Loch Glascarnoch,
past Beinn Dearg and the Falls of Measach, to Ard-

charnich and beyond. The view was spectacular, with every vista revealing mountains bare of vegetation on their peaks, but with sheep grazing on their slopes. Ancient stone fencing meandering off in all directions caught Lydia's interest, and the Earl explained they were centuries old, laid without mortar, and served to restrict the sheep from overgrazing the land. Sparsely populated, lonely, and wild, it was a setting to fire the imagination of those persons sufficiently sensitive to appreciate its charm.

Castle Torquay, located high atop a steep, rugged crag, amid hills piled tall with rock, loomed in aloof majesty above the point of joining between sea and loch. Lydia, gazing from a window as the horses labored up the final incline of the drive, felt awed by the sight of turreted towers and crenellated battlements looming gaunt against the sky. In her heightened sensitivity, she could almost hear the swirl of bagpipes urging kilted Scots onward into battle. To the clansmen, the castle stood as a symbol of Scotland itself, strong, steadfast, enduring. Majestic, invincible, it personified the indomitable spirit of a proud people, and Lydia, climbing the front steps by the Earl's side, sensed a feeling of kinship for this land that would soon become her own.

CHAPTER THREE

The great studded doors swung silently open on well-oiled hinges, to reveal the brilliantly lit hall beyond. Lydia walked across the threshold and had the sudden sensation of having stepped back into the past. Shields and claymores of long-gone days were attached to walls above the wainscot, and tattered banners hung suspended from beams high above her head. Medieval armor stood guard beside a huge stone fireplace, along with heavy oak furniture carved with thistle entwined with heather. More recently, sconces had been set into the walls and were now ablaze with candlelight. To the left of the broad staircase a door stood open, and it was to it the Earl led her.

Her hesitation was momentary. She had expected a repetition of the lofty hall; instead, the room was of reasonable size, and quite cozy. The first thing that struck her was the flowers; they filled bowls sitting about on tables, and splashed across the coverings of sofas and chairs. Lydia became aware a group of persons gathered before a roaring fire had turned as one to stare. The first of them to speak proved very hard-of-hearing and shortsighted as well. A lady of uncertain age, much in the habit of conversing in tones sufficiently loud to be audible to her own ears, people seldom paid her the least attention. Not that it mattered. Lady Flora customarily beguiled the tedium of her days with an unending stream of vacuous small talk, uninteresting to herself and ignored by those around her. Peering vaguely about, she uttered in what she fondly believed to be a whisper: "Have they arrived? I declare there is nothing so irritating to one's nerves as being obliged to greet visitors. And so many of them, too. We will rue this day, depend upon it."

Lydia, moving forward by the Earl's side, affected to appear quite deaf, and failed. Thus it was that she found herself acknowledging introductions with a blush suffusing her cheeks. In addition to Lady Flora, who turned out to be a cousin several times removed, Lydia shook hands with: Lord Douglas Cavanaugh, a maternal uncle of the Earl, and a jolly gentleman who held Lydia's hand in a comforting clasp; Lady Cavanaugh, his lordship's ill-matched mate, and a woman much given to abrupt speech; Miss Maria Wingate, a friend of Lady Cavanaugh who had become more or less a permanent guest in the castle; and Lord Jaimie Carrington, only son of the Earl's deceased paternal uncle, and heir to the earldom. By the time the Marquis and Lady Lenora had been introduced, and Gerald had found a kindred soul in Lord Jaimie, the tea tray was rolled in, and the conversation became general.

Lord Cavanaugh lost no time in taking a seat on a sofa beside Lydia. "I cannot bring myself to say that I had thought Torquay on the verge of marriage, but it is high time he took a wife," he said, a smile wreathing his face. "I had thought him a hopeless case."

Lydia gave him an answering smile, and wished herself otherwhere. "I see," she said finally, inanely.

"And such a desirable connection," Lady Flora suddenly remarked from her chair across the room. As sometimes happens, her hearing could, on occasion, become quite acute.

"No, no! I hadn't meant such a thing," Lord Cavanaugh protested, shocked. "I'm sure we welcome Lady Lydia for her own, sweet self."

"Why was she on the shelf?" Lady Flora demanded, her hearing again at fault. Turning to Miss Wingate she added, sotto voce: "She doesn't squint, that I can see. Has she spots?"

Lord Cavanaugh looked across at her with disfavor. "Cannot someone distract her with a cup of tea?" he asked, glancing at Lydia apologetically. "You mustn't mind, my dear," he added, patting her hand.

The humor of it struck Lydia. "At least we know what is in her mind," she said, chuckling. "I should think it difficult, living in a world partially devoid of sound."

"You are expending your sympathy needlessly," Lady Cavanaugh remarked acidly. "Flora had the effrontery to purchase a screen!"

Lydia's cup was halfway to her lips. Holding it suspended in mid-air, she looked across its rim at Lady Cavanaugh. "I should think one would be useful in keeping off the draft," she said in surprise.

Lady Cavanaugh's lips tightened. "She isn't entitled. Her family connection is on the distaff side."

This dour comment left Lydia completely at sea. For the third time since entering Castle Torquay, she felt foolish; twice, she thought somewhat wryly, at the hands of a Cavanaugh, and once through the offices of Lady Flora. It needed only Miss Wingate and Lord Jaimie to complete the chain. Feeling suddenly stifled, Lydia set her cup down carefully on a table and lowered her eyes to her hands, not so much clasping them as gripping them together.

The Earl, attune to her every expression, strolled across the room and took a chair beside her. "Are you embarrassed? You need not be. I have no doubt I should have prepared you, but I have been away a number of years and had forgotten. They seem rather ridiculous, don't they?"

"One is fortunate if one can take so light a view. Tell me, Iain. What on earth was Lady Cavanaugh talking about?"

"Only Carringtons are rightfully entitled to wear our tartan. For my part, Cousin Flora may wrap herself in it from head to toe if she so chooses."

"What is so particular about the tartan?"

"Tradition, mainly. In the beginning, it was either a rectangle of cloth gathered on a belt about the waist, or it was made into trews, or trousers. The kilt, as we know it, came later."

"I should think the kilt the more comfortable."

"Ah, but you see, the trews became a sign of rank. Soldiers afoot wore the kilt; mounted chieftains wore the trews. The ladies, I must tell you, were limited to a screen. And that, my darling, is a tartan shawl."

A dawning light came into her eyes. She choked

and went off into a peal of laughter. "I thought Lady Cavanaugh referred to a fire screen," she admitted mirthfully.

Amusement gleaming in his eyes, he said: "It is clearly midnight chimes with you, my love. I would never have suspected it."

"Lady Cavanaugh's is not the only scurrilous tongue in your family, I see," she returned appreciatively. "I need only remember it a trait common to the lineage, and I will no doubt contrive to rub along tolerably well with your relations."

"Your mama has apparently found the key. She, I will point out to you, has managed to converse amiably with Cousin Flora, an accomplishment in itself if one refuses to shout."

Lydia looked across the room, her mind relieved of its weightiest care. The initial effect of Iain's relatives on her mother had been almost ludicrous, so stunned had Lady Lenora been by their uninhibited remarks. But she had quickly decided that, notwithstanding the oddness of certain of his family, it was her duty to Lydia to take such steps as would enable her to brush along smoothly in future. Charming them individually seemed the answer, and although Lady Lenora chuckled obligingly at Lord Cavanaugh's excursion into wit, listened with sympathy to a recitation of Lady Cavanaugh's physical complaints, and appeared convinced that Miss Wingate enjoyed the marked attention of numerous overly eager gentlemen, her polite courtesy was only superficial. It hardly mattered. Lady Lenora's optimism would, in the days ahead, appear to have been misplaced.

It was not until luncheon the following day that Lady Flora let drop a chance remark that was to have serious repercussions. Marveling to Miss Wingate in a whispered aside, her voice carried the length of the table. "It's a long while since we have seen Myrna. She feels cheated, does Myrna."

In the prolonged silence that followed, they all turned to stare, some with disapproval, and others with curiosity. "And who is Myrna?" Lady Lenora inquired of the room at large.

Lydia had paid the conversation little heed until something in the Earl's attitude caught her attention. He sat as if turned to stone, his hands gripping the cutlery until his knuckles showed white. Lydia held her breath and waited for his answer, her eyes instinctively on her plate. Unreasonably, her hands shook; she felt uneasy, insecure. "She is a neighbor," he said finally.

"A McDougall from near Ardcharnich," Lady Cavanaugh added in amplification. "Himself has four sons, but only the one daughter. The light of his life is Myrna."

"Ardcharnich," mused the Marquis. "I seem to have heard of it."

"It's the grouse-shooting, Papa," Gerald said enthusiastically. "Jaimie tells me it is excellent around Meall Dubh."

"The peak rises to some twenty-one hundred feet, you know," agreed Lord Cavanaugh. "You must arrange a hunt, Torquay."

For Lydia, the subsequent discussion could not sweep away the last moments and the mention of a girl named Myrna. She found she was trembling. It was small wonder, when she considered Iain's unaccountable reaction. He had seemed so shaken. It wasn't any use trying to banish the thought; it had taken hold of her almost immediately Lady Flora uttered her inopportune remark. Though she might assume an air of interested attention to the conversation going on around her, she had little notion of its content.

Lady Lenora's thoughts, however, were far from tangled. Having noted the malicious enjoyment with which Lady Cavanaugh observed Cousin Flora's embarrassment over her untimely gaff, she waited only until after luncheon, and after the Marquis had entered their rooms, to vent her spleen. "Well!" she said in tones of extreme reprobation. "What a very strange household this is indeed! I have never before encountered a set of people who speak so improperly!"

"Now, my dear," he said soothingly. "I'm sure we cannot judge them on short acquaintance. Do not permit yourself to become distraught."

"You may make light of the matter, but I'm sure I don't!" Lady Lenora replied indignantly. "I feel it your duty to speak to Torquay. In fact, I am astonished that you have not."

"Speak to him about what? That he has an odd set of relatives? I have never heard of anything so foolish. He would no doubt retaliate in kind, and what a proper set-down that would be! No, my dear. Rid yourself of the notion. I shan't come to cuffs with him."

"There is more to this than meets the eye, and don't tell me there isn't, for I know there is. I saw the expression on their faces at mention of a girl named Myrna!"

"A neighbor only, Torquay explained."

"Well, if you were taken in by that, let me assure you, sir, I was not! Lady Flora distinctly said the girl felt cheated. Why should she, if she had not cause?"

"Surely you don't suspect Torquay of having designs on the girl's virtue? You are far and away off the mark if you do. He is engaged to Lydia, remember."

"Fiddle!" Lady Lenora shot back rudely. "I collect it is not unknown for gentlemen to bestow attention on females other than their wives, much less their betrothed. You must rescue Lydia before she contracts an alliance that might prove disastrous."

"Lydia is in scant danger of that, my dear. I have seldom seen a man more in love than Torquay."

"Well, if you won't speak to him, I will speak to Lydia!"

"Now that, I forbid you to do. Your daughter, ma'am, is perfectly capable of handling her own affairs. Should she find herself in a situation not to her liking, she will break it off in her own good time."

The Marquis, had he but known it, was far and away off the mark himself. For Lydia, having agonized throughout the day, withstood the temptation to question the Earl until, upon entering the drawing room some thirty minutes before dinner, she found him awaiting her arrayed in kilts. The breath catching in her throat, she thought he looked just as she expected he would, magnificent and impressive. His jacket of black velvet was adorned with silver buttons, and his chin rose square above a jabot of finest lace. A white sporran ornamented with silver hung over his kilt, a tartan predominantly of yellow and shot through with lines of blue and scarlet. A skean-dhu (which she later discovered to be a short knife) was tucked in the top of his diced hose, and a large cairngorm brooch secured the plaid to the shoulder of his jacket. Never had she seen him look more handsome nor more fully the proud Scot.

Sinking into a deep curtsy, she cast up twinkling eyes to his face. "Dazzling," she breathed, holding out her hand. "I am wholly spellbound."

"Very properly," he replied, carrying her fingers to his lips. "I have something for you. It's a small token, but it carries my love with it."

Lydia gazed at the tribute, an orchid nestled in a spray of fern, and smiled with becoming gratitude. "How thoughtful of you," she murmured, and with great nobility allowed him to pin the flower to the bodice of her gown. The brush of his fingers against the flesh around her breast caused her to tremble, nor was it lost on her that his own hands seemed not quite steady.

He regarded her fixedly, affording himself an opportunity to regain some measure of composure. "I think you will find tonight's recognition of the anniversary of Culloden out of the common way," he said, leading her to a sofa before the fire. "Each year at this time, we pay homage to the clansmen who gave their lives for Scotland."

"Were many of them from this vicinity?"

"The Carringtons and McDougalls suffered heavy losses."

Lydia took a deep breath and abandoned the unequal struggle to still her tongue. "There was mention of a McDougall woman," she began, trying for a steady tone. "Did she—mean something—well, special to you?"

The result was as quelling as it was unexpected. Torquay raised his quizzing glass and looked her up and down. "I should have thought your delicacy of principle would have come to the fore. Obviously I was mistaken," he remarked in sneering accents.

An involuntary exclamation rose to her tongue. She suppressed it and said: "You must have known I would wonder who she . . ."

"The name is Myrna. Why the devil can't you say it."

"Please don't use that tone with me," she replied frostily. "You put me forcibly in mind of a spoiled child who flares up over the least opposition to his wishes."

"Now you are the one who is mistaken, ma'am. I have no wishes at all where Myrna is concerned. I never did."

Lydia looked surprised. "Then why have you flown up into the boughs?" she asked rather stiffly. "I'm sure I never gave you cause. Perhaps you will be so good as to explain why you must keep me in the dark."

"Is that what I have been doing?" he said, a sardonic smile curving his lips. "I had not supposed it concerned you, nor had I thought to involve you in the mess. It was over and done with a long time ago."

"I am obliged to you for relieving my mind of a great weight," she shot back with ironic gratitude. "Since I now know you have no wishes at all where this Myrna is concerned, I now know all I need to know about what you know that you don't wish me to know."

A flash of amusement at this somewhat tangled utterance gleamed in his eyes for a moment before he said: "You won't rest until you drag the whole sorry story out into the open, will you? I set little store by what others think, but I had hoped to spare you knowledge of my perfidy."

Her eyes flew to his in concern, for it had suddenly

occurred to her she was stirring over coals better left to cool. "I beg your pardon," she said, flushing. "I have no right, of course, to pry into your affairs."

For a perilous moment she thought she might be shaken, and indeed his hands did reach for her, but he recollected himself and said with strong feeling: "You tempt me to give you the trimming of your life. I should, but you would find some way to turn my words against me."

"You are being grossly unfair," she said in a manner calculated to abash him. "Why should you wish to give me a set-down when I have already said I'm sorry?"

"Why should you expect anything else from me?" he retaliated in kind. "You've always known I'm rag-mannered."

"I should be glad to know why, since you seem to think me a confirmed ninnyhammer, you bothered to propose to me at all!"

"I happen to love you," he replied acidly.

"Well, you don't sound as if you do! I'm only surprised you didn't marry your Myrna!"

There came a deadly silence. Lydia would have given everything she possessed to be able to retract her words. But she couldn't. She could only gaze helplessly at him until he spoke. "I joined the army to avoid being forced into marriage by the chieftain of another clan," he said finally, biting off the words.

It was so unexpected that she gasped, a horrid thought coming into her mind. "Myrna," she breathed, stating a fact. "Was she . . . ?"

His nostrils flared, but he said calmly enough: "Pregnant? She was."

Another silence fell before she favored him with a speaking glance. "Do not suppose I think you capable of fathering a bastard, Iain. Casting yourself in the role of monster would be as mortifying for me as it would be for you."

It was just such remarks as this, uttered with perfect composure, that had first endeared her to him. He laughed and shook his head. "Take care when within earshot of your mama, sweet, or I'll lay odds you will be off for London first thing in the morning."

"I know that," she replied more cheerfully. "I promise you I will speak with the utmost restraint." Contradicting herself, she couldn't stop herself from adding: "Is Myrna a buck-toothed female with a figure of a frump?"

"Not at all," he replied, a smile tugging at the corners of his lips. "Shall I describe her attributes?"

"Wretch! I daresay you had noticed—whatever it is gentlemen do notice. I only wonder that you fled."

His lips twitched, but he succeeded in preserving a sober mien. "Will it re-establish my credit with you to describe her as a pudding-face and completely devoid of charm?"

"I gather," she said thoughtfully, "that she is a very ravishing female."

"But you see, my love, I much prefer a son who happens to be mine. Add to this the fact that I expect to be in love with his mother, and you will not wonder at my flight."

"I would be excessively sorry for Myrna, had she not tried to lodge the blame with you. She did tell her father . . . ?"

"And her brothers," he added bitterly. "I found that persuading them to believe anything they did not choose to believe when it came to Myrna was a task beyond my powers. Aunt Mary will tell you that all females should keep a proper distance, lest they fall afoul of my own particular brand of lechery."

"What rubbish!" Lydia exclaimed indignantly. "Lady Cavanaugh must have a good deal more bone than sense!"

"Papa extracted a promise from me on his deathbed that I provide a home for them," he explained in a voice at variance with the appreciation in his eyes. "Uncle Douglas is improvident, I'm afraid."

"Well, I promise you they shan't trouble me. I've seen very little of them, in any event."

"As a rule, they keep to the west wing of the castle. Aunt Mary may be eccentric, but not enough so she doesn't enjoy queening it in her own quarters." He paused, his eyes hardening. "Jaimie tells me Myrna runs tame in their rooms."

The absurdity of the situation struck Lydia, bringing a gleam of enjoyment to her eyes. "What a plot for a Shakespearean tragedy," she said, chuckling. "You must be covered with mortification."

Encouraged by the merriment brimming in her voice, he said, relieved: "I see you haven't flown into a pucker over it. You deserve a treat."

But what this was to be, she was not to learn, for the entrance of the others put a period to their privacy. "Upon my word!" Lady Lenora ejaculated, eyeing the intimate way in which the Earl was leaning toward Lydia.

He rose and crossed to bow over her hand. "We call them kilts, ma'am," he said, deliberately misinterpreting her meaning. "I imagine you must have heard of our national dress?"

"Well, yes, but . . ."

"It comes as a surprise to everyone at first," he continued with perfect aplomb. "I trust you will wish a glass of wine before dinner?"

Lady Cavanaugh refused the offer, a look of revulsion on her face, but Lady Lenora gratefully accepted a glass of Madeira. "Well," she said, seating herself beside Lydia. "What have you children planned for tomorrow?"

"I thought I would visit Ardcharnich, Mama. Jaimie tells me the draper carries velvet ribbon."

Lady Lenora's brows shot up. "Alone?" she said in a voice tight with disapproval.

"Iain has an appointment with a crofter, so Letty will accompany me. Don't make a coil of a simple matter, Mama."

Lady Lenora's intent of calling upon the Marquis for conjugal support was forestalled by the shrill sound of bagpipes issuing from the hall. The Earl offered Lydia his arm and led her between double rows of tartan-clad clansmen to the dining room. The sight of the table laden with gold was so unexpected it surprised a gasp from her. The room seemed to shimmer with candlelight glittering on golden plate and sparkling on shining crystal. Three times around the table marched the clansmen, kilts swinging merrily to the skirl of pipes, before they came to attention, one of them behind each chair.

"To the heroes of Culloden," said the Earl into the sudden silence, wine glass in hand.

"To the heroes of Culloden," echoed the others, drinking the toast.

The many courses of dinner consisted of foods to be found in Scotland. The salmon was followed by grouse, the grouse by roast leg of lamb. It seemed to

Lydia she could scarcely put down a glass but that it was instantly replenished by the kilted groom stationed at her elbow. She was torn between awe of the spectacle unfolding before her eyes and satisfaction at being part of it. And when, at the conclusion of the meal, they were escorted from the room by the marching clansmen, she thrilled again to the music of the pipes and felt very much as if she did indeed belong.

Not so Lady Cavanaugh. At last succeeding in buttonholing the Earl in private, her remarks on the impropriety of strangers sharing in the celebration of Culloden were caustic and pointed. "I cannot but think it a mistake," she finished in denunciatory tones. "You should be fearful of angering the clans."

"Indeed?" he said, a faint sneer twisting his lips. "Then perhaps you will wish to keep to your rooms until the danger passes."

"You do not seem to comprehend the delicacy of the situation. The McDougalls . . ."

The Earl's expression hardened. "I have no wish to speak of them," he gritted through his teeth.

"You need not take umbrage," Lady Cavanaugh replied stiffly. "I'm sure I intended no offense. But as I was telling Myrna . . ."

"Been in the west wing again, has she?"

"Don't take that tone with me, Torquay! When I think of how it could have been between you, and how Himself must feel . . . "

The Earl stared at her a moment, a thunderous look upon his face, before turning on his heel and walking away, banishing the McDougalls, or so he thought, from his mind.

Lydia awakened to sunlight early the following morning, and lay for a few moments recalling events of the evening before, a feeling of well-being flooding her senses. Somewhere in one of the bedchambers a housemaid was singing, and from the floor below the murmur of servants putting the rooms in order drifted dimly up the stairs. She was content for some minutes to lie listening to the awakening house until the promise of the dawning day lured her from her bed. Crossing to a window, she pulled back the curtain and gazed out across the brightening lawns. The yellow mist Iain had described so surely hung hazy over the land, dew sparkled on the grass, and the leaves of trees in the park fluttered on a soft breeze. It proved impossible not to be in tune with nature on such a glorious day. She was no sluggish lay-about, content to laze around her room, but she was surprised nevertheless to find the Earl present when she came into the breakfast room at such an early hour. He was in the act of conveying a cup to his mouth, but he immediately set it down and rose to his feet. "You are up early," he remarked, pushing in her chair. "Quite starving, are you?"

"Not really," she replied, unfolding her napkin. "I am not sharp-set, at least. Tea and toast will do."

"Order bacon and eggs for her ladyship, McTavish," he said firmly to the butler, and waited in silence until McTavish left the room. He then tilted up her chin and bent his head to kiss her, his lips lingering sensuously on hers.

Lydia watched him resume his seat, and felt warmed by the glow in his eyes when he turned his head to look at her. "Wretch!" she said, laughter bubbling from her throat. "Do you always kiss the ladies before breakfast?"

"When the opportunity arises," he replied brazenly.

"You may have heard the adage that man does not live by bread alone?"

"If this is the way you mean to conduct yourself after we are married, sir, you will continually put me to the blush."

"After we are married, my sweet, I will not need to await your appearance at the breakfast table to demonstrate my love. Your bed will do quite nicely."

Whereupon Lydia surprised herself by blushing. "How odious you are!" she exclaimed, her voice ending on a caressing note.

"My darling girl, do but recollect before you become confused. I behaved most properly before McTavish. I observe the proprieties, I will have you know."

"Yes, you do, don't you," she said, and went into a peal of laughter. "You can't take me by surprise with the shocking things you say, Iain. The thing is, I've lately spent a great deal of time in your company. It has left its mark, believe me."

He smiled at her, saying softly: "How soon will you marry me?"

An arrested look came upon her face. "Why, I—I hadn't thought . . ."

"Please do. I have no wish to press you—no, that isn't true. I have every intention of rushing you down the aisle at the earliest opportunity," he amended, his hand going out to hers across the table.

"I'm persuaded you and Mama would be in complete agreement," she replied, putting her hand in his. "She lives in hourly dread I will let you slip through my fingers."

"Shall we prove her fears groundless?" he murmured, pressing a kiss into her palm.

"If you wish it," she said, smiling. "But I will need time to buy my trousseau."

"You can acquire it while on your wedding trip."

"That is all very well, Iain, but Papa would never permit such a shocking breach of etiquette. Nor would I wish him to."

"Then you will need to see to it without delay. Perhaps the ribbon you purchase in Ardcharnich today will suffice?"

"Silly," she said, turning the word into a caress.

"We will discuss it further when I return this evening. In the meantime, oblige me by giving thought to setting the date."

"I will try to, sir," she said demurely as McTavish ushered a groom bearing her breakfast on a silver tray into the room.

Shortly before eleven o'clock, Lydia entered the open barouche with Letty for the drive to Ardcharnich, arriving before the draper's shop shortly before time for tea. Lydia, acquiescing to the maid's breathless request for permission to stroll about on her own, descended to the ground and instructed the coachman to have the barouche before the tea shop by the hour of three. After gazing into the window in admiration of the woolens on display, she went within to spend an entrancing half hour among the spools of ribbon while carrying on a lively conversation with the draper. Her selection made, she went on down the street to the tea shop, unaware she was being trailed at a discreet distance by three Scotsmen. Their unprepossessing appearance made it unlikely they would attract undue attention to themselves. Nor did they. The Earl's coachman and his groom failed to notice them waiting patiently beside their horses for Lydia to emerge from the shop. It happened too quickly for them to do anything about it in any event. With a kind of bemused horror, they gasped as Lydia, in one swift movement, was seized from behind and tossed up into the waiting arms of a mounted Scot. She struggled with all her strength, to no avail, and was carried off in full view of a goodly number of the residents of Ardcharnich.

CHAPTER FOUR

The house stood on a rise of ground and had the advantage of mountains spread out behind it to break the winds sweeping down from the north. Lydia and her captor led the way into the cobbled carriage-yard and were met by the surprised expression on the face of the head groom. "I wouldna hae expected ye tae coom 'oam with a gurl across ye saddle, indeed I wouldna," he remarked in disapproving accents.

"Mind your tongue, old man," Lydia's captor growled, sliding to the ground still holding her in his arms.

"Ye ken full weel what I mean, laddie," the elderly retainer replied laconically. "'Isself willna be best plaesed, I nae doot."

"It is not your concern. See to the horses." He spoke in a curt tone meant to convey that the limit of his patience had been reached, but since the groom merely spat upon the ground before turning away to lead the horses to the stables, the message fell decidedly flat. Lydia, hustled somewhat precipitately into the house, took heart. The very boldness of the groom augured well for her own predicament.

The room in which she found herself, a large apartment dominated by an immense fireplace stretching across one entire wall, was decorated somberly with furnishings in a masculine style. Standing with his back to the room was a grizzled Scot who, at hearing the disturbance, glanced over his shoulder "What does this mean?" he asked in surprise.

"I daresay you will agree, Papa, that Myrna's embarrassment must be avenged. We have brought you Torquay's doxy."

Himself regarded his stalwart offspring with a smoldering eye. "Are you so drunk you would disgrace your Clan?" he demanded furiously. "Well? Have you lost your tongue?"

Lydia realized at once that she had been abducted by the McDougalls' sons. The tallest of them took a deep breath and said: "You have wanted revenge on Torquay since Myrna bore his bastard. Well, so have we!"

"On Torquay, you fool! I've told you before I do not make war on women!"

"We think you are making a mistake, Papa. This is the one who thinks to supplant Myrna . . ."

"How dare you question me!" Himself roared, fairly spitting out the words. "I'll have your hide!"

"Send for Myrna," Angus stubbornly insisted, his lower lip stuck out defiantly. "It is for her to say."

It proved unnecessary to do so, for the door opened at that moment, and the most beautiful creature Lydia had ever beheld walked into the room. She was rather above the average height, and her golden hair had undoubtedly come down to her from some long-dead Viking raider, as had the startling blue of her eyes. Any sweetness that might have been expected to curve her mouth, however, had long before become replaced by a habitual expression of discontent. Myrna, the apple of her father's eye, was very much in the habit of ordering Himself precisely as she chose. "So this is the baggage Torquay thought to wed," she remarked, looking Lydia up and down in an insolent fashion. "Quite the innocent, isn't she?"

Lydia drew herself up to the full extent of her own not inconsiderable height. "As a guest of the Earl of Torquay, I must demand that you release me at once!" she said with a courage Himself could not help but admire.

"You demand?" Myrna said before he had opportunity for speech. "Why, you little hussy . . . "

"That will do!" he interrupted with unusual sternness. "The girl goes back."

"I won't permit it!" Myrna said sharply. "Torquay will never come here of his own accord. How can he be made to marry me if he has already wed another?"

The reason behind her abduction became very plain to Lydia. "He will never marry you," she said wearily. "Why should he? He is not the father of your child."

Myrna glared. "So he convinced you he is blameless," she said, laughing jarringly. "Lady Mary thought he would."

"So you have discussed me with Lady Cavanaugh."

"How else do you think we knew you would visit Ardcharnich unprotected? When we are through with you . . ."

And then a voice interposed from the doorway, its

soft tones echoing around the chamber. "Now that you are through with Lydia," the Earl said, advancing into the room with Gerald by his side, "we will escort her home."

"Iain!" Lydia cried, starting up from her chair.

His eyes came to rest on her for a brief moment before his attention became riveted on Myrna. "I had been from home on business, but when I returned earlier than anticipated, I met with the intelligence that Lady Lydia had been brought here—on a visit?"

"You might call it that," Myrna smirked, a satisfied little smile curving her lips.

"I know we both thank you for your hospitality," he replied, bowing formally. "May I present my brother-in-law, Lord Gerald Tremayne?"

"You aren't to consider yourself a visitor in this house, Torquay," she answered rudely, ignoring the implication of the introduction. "A son-in-law seldom is."

The Earl smiled, and his attention seemed to become fixed on Lydia. She raised her gaze to his face, and found that he was staring at her intently. "We haven't announced it yet," he said, "but we are married. Lydia is my wife. She is the Countess of Torquay."

A collective gasp ran around the room. "Is this true?" Himself asked Lydia, his tone grim.

Lydia read the message in the Earl's eyes and said simply: "Yes."

"What do you mean, yes? Are you Torquay's wife?"

"Yes, I am his wife," she repeated, not comprehending the sudden gleam of understanding that came darting into his eyes. Glancing at the others, she saw that they stood staring with a mixture of surprise and fury on their faces.

The Earl crossed to her side. "Come, my dear," he said and, drawing her hand within his arm, led her from the room.

His coach was waiting before the house. Lydia climbed into it and sank back against the padded squabs, feeling strangely weak now the danger had passed. "You may safely leave everything to Torquay," Gerald grinned, poking his head in the open door. "Won't Mama be surprised!"

"Please, Gerald, no riddles," she replied, looking at him doubtfully. "I don't feel up to it."

"Oh, very well. I will go. But not before I name you Countess. I'm the first to do so, remember."

"Gerald, for heavens' sake!" Lydia exclaimed under her breath.

He cast her a devilish glance. "You don't understand Scottish law, do you?" he remarked somewhat enigmatically, and withdrew his head. "Congratulations," he said to the Earl, holding out his hand.

Torquay returned the clasp of his fingers, and said: "You are sure you are able to find your way back?"

Gerald assured him he was, and accepted his horse's reins from the hands of the Earl's groom. Grinning, he swung into the saddle, said he would relate events to his parents, and rode off, whistling a tune that sounded very much like the strains of the Wedding March.

The Earl chuckled, gave his coachman the office to proceed, and entered the coach. "Are you comfortable?" he asked Lydia, settling down beside her. "Poor darling. You had a rough time of it, didn't you?"

"You were clever to convince them we are married. Myrna had plans for you."

His arms went around her, and she found herself being ruthlessly kissed. "We are married, dearest," he murmured against her lips.

Lydia pulled away. "You may have hoaxed the McDougalls, but . . ."

"I didn't hoax them, darling. We both declared our marriage before witnesses. By the laws of Scotland, we are now man and wife."

"I wish you will turn your thoughts to a solution for my predicament," she said with some asperity. "We cannot go racketing about the countryside together without occasioning talk. I know you rescued me, but . . ."

"Marriage by Scottish law is as legal and binding as marriage by English law, my dear. You may have noticed that Gerald understood this. He would never have left you alone with me otherwise."

The stresses of the day took their toll. Lydia buried her face in her hands and burst into tears. "Here, now," the Earl admonished, gathering her close. "Finding yourself married to me is nothing to cry about."

Lydia gulped. "It is only that I am so confused," she murmured, laying her cheek against his chest.

"Do not be frightened, my love," he said quietly, and enfolded her trembling body within his coat.

She gave a watery chuckle. "I'm not shivering from fright," she said mischievously. "I'm cold."

"You must forgive me for not having provided better weather. It has started to rain, sweet."

Lydia turned her head and gazed through the window upon an increasingly sodden landscape. Rivulets trickling from the hills mingled with other rivulets to become rushing torrents. The coach was making slower and slower progress on roads becoming mired in mud. The rain, driven on the north wind, intensified, beating against the windows and pouring off the flanks of the straining horses. When it became apparent they would not reach Castle Torquay, the coachman climbed down from the box and pulled open the door. "I nae see as 'ow we micht gae on, me lord. 'Tis richt fearsoom oot, dinna ye see."

"Then you had better pull in at the first place of habitation. I trust that is possible?"

"Aye, my lord. I hae nac doot o' it."

It seemed at times the coachman's confidence was misplaced before The Clansman loomed out of the gathering dark. The innkeeper, perceiving the crest upon the door of the coach, sent servants forward with umbrellas, while waiting himself snug and dry within the doorway to welcome them. In a very short while, a private parlor had been bespoken, a maid had carried their cloaks to the kitchens to dry them, and Lydia had been escorted upstairs to remove the stains of travel. When she presently came back downstairs and entered the parlor, she found the Earl warming himself before a roaring fire. He had ordered a substantial meal, and engaged a single chamber for an indeterminate stay on the advice of the landlord. The storm, he was told, might last for days, turning the roads into a quagmire and rendering them impassable. He felt it inadvisable to communicate his sleeping arrangements immediately to Lydia, considering it wiser to wait until the perfect opportunity presented itself.

They sat down to an unexpectedly good meal, which progressed from chicken basted in cherry cordial, pigeon pie with a flaky crust, and apple fritters, to egg custard floating in brandy sauce. It was while they were enjoying after-dinner coffee that she said she was longing for her bed. "That sounds agreeable," the Earl remarked, his eyes studying her face with a guarded look. "I will be up presently."

"I have no idea which bedchamber has been assigned to me. If you will summon the landlord . . ."

"That won't be necessary," he said with a great deal more assurance than he felt. "We will occupy the room at the head of the stairs."

"We?" she breathed, stunned. "Surely you cannot think . . ." Unable to continue the thought, she gasped to a halt.

"According to the landlord, we should be quite comfortable," he continued, undaunted.

"But we can't. It—it wouldn't be proper."

"Why not?" he said calmly. "It is perfectly fashionable for married couples to share a room."

She looked him full in the face. "You are not being fair. Whatever you may say, I have no assurance—no, that is not fair of me. I want to believe you, Iain, really I do. But . . ." She gave a sad, negative motion of her head and fell silent.

He regarded her with a sinking heart. "Lydia, I wouldn't dream of lying to you any more than I would dream of seducing you. I know it sounds incredible, but . . ."

"Iain, please," she begged, eyes lowered.

A prolonged silence fell until, finally, he sighed and rose to his feet. "I will bespeak a further chamber," he said heavily, and went from the room.

The rain was pouring in torrents when she awakened the following morning. Being without a valise, she had slept in her chemise, and now turned her head to survey ruefully her somewhat crumpled dress laid across the back of a chair. Climbing out of bed, she made a necessarily hasty toilet, lacking even a comb, and struggled into the gown, smoothing it over her hips as well as she could. After briefly considering knocking on the Earl's door and deeming this unwise, she went downstairs to order breakfast. His entrance into the parlor some few minutes later coincided with that of the landlord bearing a number of dishes on a tray. "I trust you will approve my selection," she remarked, lifting the cover of a bowl.

His brows shot up. "Jellied trout?" he said. "Thank you. I believe not."

"I daresay you think it a horrid choice . . ."

"I haven't said so." A distinctly skeptical expression covered his face, but he accepted the plate she passed across to him. "I suppose I will survive it," he remarked, unfolding his napkin.

"Iain, the landlord tells me the bridge to Mourgerry—wherever that might be—is washed out. If his information is correct, and I have no reason to think it isn't, we will need to detour around it."

The Earl made a noise in his throat indicative of assent, and continued chewing.

"The rain shows no sign of abating," she ventured, casting him a glance from under her lashes. "If we are to be detained in this place, we will need to—consider what is best to do." She paused once more, but since he refrained from comment, she added in her most matter-of-fact voice: "It seems to me we should claim I'm your sister."

A cynical expression came upon his face. "I see," he said briefly.

"No one here would be the wiser," she added reasonably.

"I would," he muttered, a wry twist to his mouth. "So you have thought it all out, have you?"

"I think it best for you to continue to call me Lydia. When one plays about with names, one can become horribly confused. It shouldn't be any time at all until you think of me as your sister."

The Earl hit his stride at last. "My thoughts of you are not at all brotherly," he said succinctly.

Lydia pinked. "Well, you could try," she said with determination. "The proprietor must think the situation odd."

"It is odd."

"Do not provoke me, pray. I do think you should consider it, Iain. It is really quite a good notion, and should solve our problem admirably."

"You refer, I collect, to your extraordinary reluctance to welcome me to your bed."

Lydia's cheeks fairly flamed. "We should not argue in public," she murmured, lowering her eyes. "It will be remarked."

"One of a husband's privileges, and they are few, believe me, is to be seen arguing with his wife without occasioning remark. If you would trust my integrity, it would be a good thing."

His tone was so far removed from being loverly she found herself at a loss. Fortunately, since no reply rose to her tongue, the landlord entered the room at this moment to remove the covers. She permitted him to refill her cup, quizzing him on the possibility of having her clothing freshened, and turned surprised eyes on the Earl when he said that perhaps the maid could oblige his sister in this request. Arrangements made, the landlord withdrew.

"I thought I might as well," the Earl remarked immediately they were alone. "I would only receive a put-off if I were to suggest I join you. I presume you will need to take to your bed while the maid launders—whatever it is you have on under your gown?"

"For goodness' sake, Iain!"

"On the other hand," he continued coolly, "since I am faced with the same problem, perhaps we should join forces?"

Flushing slightly, she raised her gaze to his face, and saw he was watching her with a longing expression deep within his eyes. "I wish you won't look at me like that," she said contritely. "It makes me feel so—selfishly circumstanced."

"You were accustomed in the past to being sought after every time you set up a flirt, but I am not one of your rejected suitors, my dear. Depend upon it, I won't take fright so easily."

There was no vestige of emotion in his level voice, but she was amused nevertheless. "You needn't take that attitude with me," she said playfully. "I make no doubt that when it comes to boasting of one's flirts, my consequence can't hold a candle to yours."

She received, after a moment, an answering smile. "I won't allow that to be true, but rather than stay and cross swords with you, I will seek out our host for my own arrangements." Rising, he stood looking down at her. "God, what a waste!" he said half under his breath, and went from the room.

Altogether to Lydia's surprise, only a matter of an hour elapsed from the time the maid gathered together her garments until she returned with them hanging fresh and crisp over her arm. Smiling shyly, she put a comb and toothbrush down upon a table, curtsied, and beat a somewhat hasty retreat through the door. Would the Earl notice her improved appearance? Lydia wondered as she slipped from beneath the quilts. It was a melancholy thought and sent her scurrying to contrive a toilet that would ensure he did so.

Coming down the stairs some thirty minutes later, and with plans for dazzling him whirling through her head, she had just reached the bottom step when the inn door opened to admit an elegant gentleman shepherding before him a downy-cheeked youth and a damsel clad in the raiment of a schoolgirl. The expression of boredom on his face could not be more pronounced. Lydia, immediately intrigued by their arrival in this of all imaginable places, listened with interest to the landlord's vacillations between injunctions to the servants bringing in the valises and his harried explanations of a shortage in accommodations. The availability of a further private parlor was soon seen to be his prime concern. "Do not suppose we will be so odiously selfish as not to share ours," she said, coming forward. "I know just how vexed it makes one feel to be inconvenienced when one travels."

The landlord, much relieved, bowed and said obsequiously that if they would all repair to the parlor, he would have tea sent in while bedchambers were made ready. The elegant gentleman, looking somewhat surprised, bowed and said they would hesitate to intrude themselves upon her privacy, but Lydia brushed aside his expostulations, saying it was her pleasure to rescue them from their horrid predicament, and led the ill-assorted trio down the passageway, wondering what kind of contretemps she had stumbled on.

"Iain, the most diverting thing," she said immediately upon entering the room. "We have company."

"We are indebted to—your wife?" the gentleman began in tones of inquiry.

"His sister," Lydia interposed.

"We are indebted to your sister for granting us asylum. The common room appears the only alternative to sharing your parlor."

It could not be claimed that the Earl's countenance bore any indication of delight, but he said politely, holding out his hand: "You are most welcome. I am Torquay, by the way."

"Sir Charles Brodie, sir, at your service," the gentleman replied, clasping the Earl's hand in a firm grip.

A few civilities were exchanged, and the young people introduced. They were cousins of Sir Charles, Frederick and Helene by name, and it would have been too much to say they returned their older relative's pleasure at developments. What Sir Charles had seen of Lydia he liked. He turned a rather quizzical gaze on her face and said: "Do you reside at the castle, ma'am?"

Lydia glanced at the Earl. His expression had altered at the hint of admiration in Sir Charles's voice, and a slight flush came into his cheeks. "I have been long in London," she temporized. "I take it that you, sir, are a Scot?"

"My home is less than two miles from here. Had we not been forced to shelter from the storm, I might have missed the pleasure of meeting you."

Fortunately for Lydia, for she had no idea what to reply, Miss Brodie intervened. "If you will excuse me,

Cousin Charles," she said, casting a speculative glance at the Earl, "I will go upstairs to change."

"Certainly," he replied, crossing to the bellpull. "I will instruct the landlady to direct you to your room."

"I vow I never could abide your sending me off to Miss Winthrop's school in the first place," she remarked, casting the Earl an arch look. "His lordship must think me the veriest chit."

Whereupon the Earl, who strongly suspected there was little of the blushing schoolgirl in her makeup, uttered the expected disclaimer, his manner a subtle blend of civility and indifference. Miss Brodie, piqued, dropped him a curtsy and, raising her gaze to his face, favored him with a look she fondly believed to be worldly. Assuring him she would not be above a minute, she disappeared up the stairs, followed by the landlady, whose state of agitation, the Earl noted, had given way to one of expectation. Never in her memory had so many persons of rank arrived at once to enliven the monotony of her days.

Miss Brodie's notions of time, it developed, were hardly nice. A full hour was to elapse before she came tripping back into the parlor. The alteration in her appearance was, to say the least, startling. Gone were the plain palisse and unbecoming bonnet. Gone, too, was any influence the redoubtable Miss Winthrop and her school might have had in directing the wayward steps of her former charge. The velvet ribbons that adorned Miss Brodie's gown echoed the brilliant green of her eyes and confined the curls cascading from atop her head. No one of her audience could have thought the décolleté of her dress decorous in the least. The Earl was not at all dazzled by her smile, nor was he gratified to find himself the recipient of her wiles. He was, in fact, as appalled by the coming necessity to put a period to her pretentions as he was miffed at the amusement he read in Lydia's eyes.

Frederick, his attention fixed upon his tea, was not immediately struck by the entrance of his sister. "Good God!" he ejaculated upon glancing up. "Surely you are not proposing to deck yourself out like that in this place!"

"Fiddle!" said Miss Brodie scornfully. "The Earl appreciates my appearance," she added with the supreme confidence of the very young.

"Ha!" snorted Frederick. "Of all the distempered freaks!"

To a gentleman of the Earl's experience, her resentment was to be expected. "Actually," he said, thinking to soothe ruffled feathers, "you look quite nice."

Lydia, who had not failed to catch the reassured expression flickering across her face, broke in to say: "Very nice, Helene."

"I daresay she thinks she's beautiful," asserted Frederick, his eyes dwelling maliciously on her darkening countenance.

Sir Charles rose to his feet. "Oblige me this once," he said in peremptory tones, "by abandoning this childish bickering. You are becoming dead bores, and I will not tolerate it. Unless you want to be sent to your rooms, you will create no further ill-bred scenes. Permit me to tender their apologies, Lady Lydia."

"They are really quite charming," she replied composedly. "Pray don't give the matter another thought."

He regarded her quizzically. "I have a notion, ma'am, that you would despise me if I did. I shouldn't wish that."

She colored faintly. "Would you care for another

cup of tea, Sir Charles," she said, glancing at the Earl.

"Turning the subject, I collect," he replied, unaware of Torquay's seething reception of his brazen flirting.

Lydia stared at him, wondering at a further ploy to alter the trend of the conversation. "Do stop talking nonsense, sir," she said, looking at him imploringly.

"Am I? I believed I had said something to establish my credit with you. If I accept the cup of tea and promise not to say anything distasteful to you, will you sit and chat with me?"

"It would be shabby of me to refuse," she responded, pouring out a cup.

CHAPTER FIVE

I ought to draw his claret, the Earl thought wrathfully, watching Sir Charles tête-à-tête with Lydia, and knew he could not yield to the impulse. He had little thought when he agreed to her preposterous scheme that, once the wheels were set in motion, he would be powerless to retract. Her doubts, her refusal to believe in their marriage, he laid at his own door. By his very reluctance to force the issue, he had relinquished whatever advantage he had had. He should have overcome her resistance, rather than allowing her to seek her lonely bed. The Earl grimaced. Sister! he thought disgustedly and, turning on his heel, stalked from the room.

It would have been wiser, Lydia mused in her own turn while gazing after his retreating back, to have told Sir Charles she had the headache. Iain was furious, not because she had given him cause to doubt her love, but because he was jealous of the attention showered on her by another man. In response to Sir

Charles's remark concerning the conduct of Helene, she smiled somewhat faintly and said: "I doubt it will do her any harm to receive a set-down. Most girls do, in the process of growing up."

"That's coming it a bit thick," he replied. "You didn't, unless I miss my guess."

She flushed, but he assumed an unawareness of it. "I imagine I lacked the opportunity," she remarked in an offhand way. "Under certain circumstances, I might have done. The thing is, you see, if Helene tries her wiles on Iain, he just might rebuff her in a way that could prove disastrous to her confidence."

"In that case, I daresay I should warn her off. Knowing her as I do, I can assure you that the least encouragement, however reluctantly tendered, is enough to set her off. The mildest of flirtations would become, to her way of thinking, romantic in the extreme. The Earl would be, after all, a grand prize for her to win."

Lydia turned her head in surprise, but found herself unable to read the expression in his eyes. "You may well tease," she said somewhat tartly, "but it is a serious thing with her. She is at an impressionable age, you know."

"The one thing that would impress Helene would be to marry a title. That of Countess would suit her very well."

"Marry a—which Countess?" Lydia demanded, thunderstruck.

"Why, the Countess of Torquay. Who else?"

"Of all the ridiculous—this is foolish beyond permission. For her to think to form a connection with Iain . . ."

"Why is the notion so foolish, Lady Lydia? A pretty

chit, once she sets her mind to it, has been known to snare the wiliest male. Wouldn't you welcome the match? Helene is young, but her lineage is impeccable. The Earl could do worse. Far worse."

"Good God! Iain isn't—he wouldn't . . ."

"Since you find the idea objectionable, I will do all within my power to scotch her hopes before you are subjected to embarrassment. In the meantime, ma'am, will it offend you for me to say I trust you will become reconciled to me for my assistance?"

She wrinkled her brow and said faintly: "I should inform you—I fear—I expect to remain quite—quite unattached." Having delivered herself of this somewhat incoherent speech, she rose and excused herself, giving as her reason the ever useful headache.

She was still thinking of this interchange when she returned to the parlor to partake of luncheon. Helene, the only person present, fixed her with a frigid eye, and said: "You may have brought Cousin Charles around your thumb, but you shan't gainsay me. The Earl knows I am not that many years his junior, so you needn't think to put him on his guard."

Lydia came close to smiling, but she controled her features with an effort. "You should know, since you seem to think he might succumb to your wiles, that he is accustomed to the consequences of quite the most elevated ladies of the ton. His taste runs to females of a complexion beyond your years."

"You think me a child."

"I should rather think I do. You are a charming girl, Helene, and one day you will meet the man who will win your love. In the meantime, don't wish your girlhood away. It will pass all too soon, believe me."

"I'm not surprised you are an old maid," Helene said spitefully. "You must be all of twenty-five."

"Not quite, but we will pass over that for the present. I feel it only fair to warn you that you are courting a horrid set-down if you persist in pursuing the Earl. I should hate to see you hurt."

"What makes you think you can speak for him?" Helene shot back.

"We are—close."

"You are only his sister. That's a very different matter from being his wife."

"I am well aware of that," Lydia replied, the smile she was now unable to control curving her lips. "It is the most sensible thing you have yet said."

"You think to make me avoid his company, but I shan't," Helene said, quivering with fury. "He will develop a tendre for me. You will see. Not that it is any of your concern. You are only jealous because you haven't succeeded in snaring a man for yourself. For my part, I think you odious, and I don't mind telling you so."

"I wish you will come down off your high ropes and consider that I am rather more up to snuff than you. Should you continue to puff yourself off as a Nonpareil of the first stare, you will only give people a disgust of you. And you needn't glare at me. I have nothing further to say, other than that you might do well to control your unbridled tongue."

Helene, white with fury, whirled on her heel and flounced out of the room. Her exit was followed immediately by the entrance of Sir Charles. "What has that tiresome child been about?" he inquired, helping himself to a seat on the settle beside Lydia. "You need not scruple to speak frankly."

"I am very much afraid I am the one at fault. She appears in danger of forming an infatuation for Iain. I thought to spare her heartache, but it seems I only succeeded in miffing her."

He chuckled. "I rather fancy you might have. Helene detests guidance, however well intentioned. It is quite uncivil of her to reject you, ma'am, but her taste was ever execrable."

Lydia's face darkened. "I have been little in her company, Sir Charles, but it would have been wonderful indeed should she not suffer from ennui upon being stranded in this place."

"I will need to exert myself to see you do not become bored."

The expression on her face became a frown. "My spirits are seldom jaded, sir," she said, staring at him puzzled.

"Let me assure you, ma'am, you inject enthusiasm in me for your company. I desire to know more of you. Much more."

Frederick's voice spoke from the doorway behind them. "I wouldn't advise it unless you want to land yourself in the suds," he remarked, strolling forward. "There was never such a one for putting one in the wrong."

Lydia glanced over her shoulder. "You have your own ends to serve, sir, while I have none at all," she said with perfect truth.

Frederick shrugged. "Well, it's on your own head, ma'am. Where is Torquay?"

Sir Charles surveyed him from under drooping lids. "Perhaps you could go and see. In fact, I insist that you do so. Ask the landlord."

Frederick shot him a speculative look. "Is it worth

my while?" he asked somewhat enigmatically and, upon receiving Sir Charles's nod, went into the tap-room.

"What was that about?" Lydia demanded the moment he was out of earshot.

"Frederick considers me far too dangerous to trust you in my company," he replied with disarming frankness.

A chuckle escaped Lydia. "No one has warned me of your wicked ways," she told him, eyes twinkling.

"You are far too desirable for me to permit it."

The laughter fled from her eyes. "I fail to see why you should say such a thing to me," she said indignantly.

He studied her for a moment before replying. "You mustn't pay the least heed to Frederick, my dear. I admit to a shocking reputation in some quarters, but I assure you my thoughts of you are of a different bent entirely."

It was on the tip of her tongue to tell him she did not at all care what his thoughts were, but Frederick returned at this moment with the intelligence that the Earl was in the stables and sent his regrets. One of his wheelers, it seemed, had sustained a badly strained hock in the mire of the evening before, and his lordship was with the coachman tending to the horse's leg. Lydia saw little for it but to partake of luncheon in the company of Sir Charles and Frederick.

It was past five o'clock when the maid scratched on her bedroom door. The Earl sent word he was detained and would see her in the morning. Lydia sighed and instructed the maid to serve her dinner in her room. She had spent a trying afternoon avoiding the company of Sir Charles, alternately dozing and reading somewhat desultorily from a tattered volume unearthed in a drawer of the chest. Glancing around her chamber, she thought she surely must have memorized every board. The room was of a respectable size, and some effort had been made to decorate it, but it remained commonplace nevertheless. Gloomy was a better word, Lydia thought, eyeing the rickety table and chair that, along with the chest and bed, comprised the furnishings. By the time she had partaken of her solitary meal and had crawled fully dressed beneath the quilts in an effort to keep warm, she felt much inclined to think there was a good deal to be said for well-run households in which coal was to be found in the scuttle beside a dying fire.

She awoke with a start, wondering what had roused her, and lay listening intently. Not a sound disturbed the night, but there was something in the very stillness that brought her instantly alert. The conviction that someone was in her room took such strong possession of her senses that she felt stifled, and lay holding her breath, straining her ears and eyes to detect the tiniest indication that she was not alone. At last she heard it, the merest creak of a loose floorboard, as if someone had stealthily shifted his weight from one foot to the other. It seemed to come from right beside her bed. She lay perfectly still, rigid and terrified, until she could bear it no longer. "Who is it?" she said breathlessly. "Iain?"

A hand instantly clamped over her mouth, she was rolled in the bedcovers and snatched from the bed. Held immobile, unable to see or cry out or even to detect sounds in the profound silence of the smothering quilts, she was carried from the inn, and unceremoniously dumped inside a waiting coach. Freeing herself of the bedclothes in the jolting vehicle was no easy task, but she accomplished it and took stock. She had no idea where she was being taken, or the direction. Stretching out her hand, she groped for the door handle, only to find it had been removed. Ever sensible, she leaned back in a corner to await developments.

It seemed they traveled but a short while before the coach drew up with a lurch. The door was jerked open, and she was staring into the face of Sir Charles. "What does this mean?" she gasped, appalled.

"Welcome to Brodie Hall, Lady Lydia," he replied with perfect aplomb. "Won't you step down?"

"I certainly will not! Explain yourself, sir!"

"Such a little spitfire," he said approvingly, and made her a gallant bow. "You could not be so unkind as to refuse my hospitality?"

"I do not understand your intent, but it cannot concern me. Please say no more."

He reached in and lifted her out, holding her so tightly she was unable to move. She could only glare while he carried her inside and set her on her feet. Standing perfectly still, she was aware of the silent lackeys emulating marble statues, and flushed painfully. "I have a pleasant surprise for you, my dear," he said lightly. "Shall I tell you what it is, or would you prefer a bite to eat first?"

"This is the greatest piece of impertinence I have ever heard of!" she said wrathfully. "You will do well to return me to the inn at once."

He laughed. "My coachman has endured quite enough for one night. The rain may have ceased, but handling a team in the mire is no easy thing. You can appreciate that, I believe."

"It is what Iain will appreciate that should concern you. When he hears of this . . ."

"When he hears of this, he will extend his congratulations. By then, you see, you will be my wife."

"You must be mad! You don't know much of him if you think—what do you mean, your wife!"

"Marriage by declaration is not unknown. In fact, it is quite common." Upon perceiving the dumbfounded look on her face, he chuckled. "I can supply an ample number of witnesses, I assure you. Do, I beg you, smile."

Lydia found her voice. "You are out of your senses," she said hotly. "If you won't send for your coach, I will walk back to the inn."

"You will not leave this house," came his hateful voice in reply. "Whether you marry me tonight or wait until morning is for you to choose. I need hardly remind you that you have no other choice. You would be ruined to spend the night here with me and not marry me."

Her brows contracted. "We will get back to that in a moment, but for the present, I will ask you why you are doing this."

"That is an aspect of the situation you would do better not to know." He paused, studying her pensively. "Though the matter is rather delicate," he continued, smiling faintly, "I will admit to being a trifle out of pocket."

"Gambling debts?" she shot at him acidly.

"Among other things. I have expensive tastes. To put it bluntly, I have need of your wealth."

"Which, naturally, as the sister of the Earl of Torquay I have in abundance," she said ironically.

"Which, naturally, you have in abundance."

"I hesitate to upset your plans, Sir Charles," she began with a great deal of satisfaction, "but I am in no position to oblige you. I am already married."

To her surprise, he laughed. "Very handsomely said, my dear. But you need have no fear. To be plain about it, I have no plans to make demands on you, however much I might admire your spirit."

"I can be just as honest as you, Sir Charles. To tell you the truth, I had not realized until this moment that I really am married, so I imagine I owe you a debt of gratitude."

"Your revelations quite unman me," he replied mockingly. "What further enlightenments have you in store?"

"You have made a quite understandable mistake. To make short telling of it, I went through a marriage by declaration with Iain. So you see, what you propose is out of the question."

His eyes narrowed. "You will need to do better than that, Lady Lydia. You could never have married your brother, whatever the circumstances."

"I am not his sister. I am, or was, his fiancée."

He burst out laughing. "You adorable liar," he said complacently. "We should deal extremely together. I might even fall in love with you."

Her eyes traveled to his face. "You have heard of Myrna McDougall? Yes, I see you have. Her brothers abducted me. You can imagine why. To rescue me, Iain told them we were married. I didn't realize the implications when I agreed that we were, but I did. So you see, sir, to put things bluntly myself, your scheming has come to naught."

He regarded her from under slightly raised brows.

"Gullibility was never a weakness of mine," he said briefly.

"You don't want for sense, Sir Charles. Have you ever heard of Iain having a sister? How could you, since he hasn't. We were pretending at the inn; why we saw fit to do so is none of your concern."

"I am inclined to believe you," he said thoughtfully after a moment. "Even your imagination could hardly be so fertile. This becomes a trifle delicate."

"I fail to see why," Lydia said with a great deal of resolution. "You need only return me to the inn, and no one will be the wiser. I would strongly recommend it. Iain will kill you if he learns of this."

"He could try. He might even succeed. I imagine neither of us will be foolhardy enough to relate to-night's events to anyone."

"What of your cousins?"

"They are safely asleep at the inn, I should think. Well, come along before my coachman retires for the night. And don't expect any apologies, for I shan't give them."

The coach splashed through large puddles in the road, and clouds obscured the moon, but the rain held off until they reached the inn. Lydia, relieved to see that no light shone from the windows to indicate her absence had been noted, slipped within and went quietly to her room.

She would have preferred not to set eyes on Sir Charles again, but he was seated at the table with Frederick and Helene when she entered the parlor the following morning in company with the Earl. It was fortunate that in the business of ordering breakfast conversation was not possible, and by the time it was, his manner was so far removed from flirtatious that

Lydia relaxed. "I should imagine you will be able to continue your journey," he was saying to the Earl. "The roads are treacherous but passable."

"One of my wheelers has a strained hock," the Earl replied more pleasantly than Lydia had any reason to expect. "We will remain here until a fresh team can be brought from Torquay."

"I will gladly lend my own horses," Sir Charles said generously.

"Thank you, but I would not consider subjecting another man's cattle to present road conditions."

Helene raised her eyes and smiled prettily at the Earl. "In that case, sir, perhaps you will oblige me?" she said sweetly. "I have a favor to ask of you."

He looked surprised. "Indeed, Miss Brodie?" he said politely. "If it is within my power . . ."

"I only want you to teach me to handle the ribbons. I understand you are a notable whip. It would be such fun to boast of it."

He surveyed her with some amusement. "Absolutely not, Miss Brodie," he said.

"I wish you might," she begged cajolingly. "Would you consider it if I say please?"

Frederick, who had been listening incredulously, ejaculated: "Good God!" in lively dismay. "What can you be thinking of? The Earl would never waste his time on a scrubby schoolgirl."

Sir Charles's gaze swung from Lydia's face to Helene's. "Finish your breakfast," he said curtly. "We leave for home this morning."

Helene's lip trembled, but within a brief span of time she was seated in Sir Charles's coach, furiously drawing on her gloves and laying plans to ensure that Torquay would very soon again come her way.

Lydia, meanwhile, refilled the Earl's cup and passed it across to him. "What do you plan to do today, now that you won't be teaching Miss Brodie to drive?" she asked, laughing.

"Since you have apparently taken a vow of celibacy, I haven't made plans," he replied, and smiled when she pinked.

"You must think me a—no, I shan't say it."

"A singularly stubborn female?" he finished for her. "Would it bother you if I did?"

Lydia prepared to do battle. "No, because I have no idea what you are thinking half the time," she said archly. "I daresay it is the same with every man, for I seem to remember Gerald would take some odd notion into his head and then refuse to divulge it."

"I'm not secretive. If you would care to step up to your room, I will gladly divulge the odd notion I have taken into my own head."

She regarded him with a twinkling eye. "I see how it is," she remarked. "You spent yesterday in the stables and became chilled. You think to find a roaring fire in my chamber, but you won't. The scuttle has been empty since last evening."

"Perhaps it is just as well you did not instruct the maid to refill it. You may decide to spend the day in bed."

"Do you think so? I hope not, for nothing could be more dull."

"It needn't be."

An arrested look came on her face. "Oh, dear," she said foolishly.

"I am not perfectly sure what you mean by that. I hope it's another way of saying, 'Oh, love.' It is, isn't it?"

Lydia laughed somewhat uncertainly. "What an abominable creature you are. You think to bullock me . . ."

"No, I don't. I mean to make very sure you are perfectly willing. Eager, in fact. Oh, lord, now what!"

It was the landlord with a message from the stables. His lordship's groom awaited orders before departing for Torquay. The Earl looked impatient, but he told Lydia he would be back presently, and went from the room. There was nothing for her to do but drink another cup of coffee and wait. Tiring of this, she rose to wander around the parlor, coming at last to the open window.

The Earl, meanwhile, having instructed the groom to return with his favorite stallion and a mare for Lydia, along with a fresh team for the coach, left the stables. A demurely delivered exclamation caused him to glance up. "Good day," Miss Brodie trilled, favoring him with a saucy smile. "I can't tell you how glad I am to have come across you again so soon."

He regarded her disinterestedly. "You didn't expect to, I apprehend," he remarked in sardonic tones.

A hint of uncertainty gleamed for a moment in her eyes. "Would it flatter you to know I did?" she said, recovering from the snub.

"Not in the least. Does Sir Charles know that you are here?"

"Don't be stuffy," she said, shrugging. "Do you think my new habit becomes me?"

He ran his eyes over her slender form perched atop her horse. "There is little likelihood you will gain approbation with such tactics," he remarked coolly, affording her not the least encouragement.

She needed none. "Is there no chance you will pay me a compliment?" she asked, pouting prettily.

His brows rose. "Until I see cause to do so, none at all, Miss Brodie."

She gave a trill of laughter. "Then I will need to give you cause. I have had my share of suitors, sir, so you need not think me green."

A mirthless smile curved his lips. "In general I would hesitate to speak rudely to a lady, but since you seem to delight in uttering shocking statements, I feel no compunction. Your conduct may have served you very well in a school for young ladies, but it is a rather different matter here."

She paled, and sat gazing down at him, stung. "I had not the remotest guess . . ."

"You are a lovely girl, but I am not the man for you," he said gently. "Run along home now before we both say things we will regret."

She fought for breath. "I am not a child, to be dismissed at your whim!" she said furiously. "I'm quite grown up."

He stood staring at her, seeming to turn some thought over in his mind. Coming to a decision, he said: "I am married, Miss Brodie. It is not something I care to boast about, but Lydia and I have been— teasing."

"If that is so, you have scant reason to censure my conduct," she said in a strangled voice. "Your own, sir, is disgraceful."

Lydia, watching from the window and perfectly able to overhear their every word, could only agree. Until this humilating moment, the effect of their pretense on other people had not been borne in upon her. The result was predictable. The Earl, coming back into the parlor, found her disconsolate. A few careful remarks did little to bolster her ego, and much to destroy his own. He sighed, and prepared to abandon for the time being (he ruefully admitted to himself) his avowed intent to storm her defenses. When he had at last induced a smile from her and had proposed they stroll about out-of-doors, a suggestion to which she readily agreed, there was little of the melancholy left in her demeanor. The Earl, taking heart, chatted pleasantly until she suggested a call at the stables. "Certainly not," he said.

"Papa permitted it," she argued persuasively. "I shouldn't tease, I know, but I should so like to visit the horses."

He found himself unable to withstand the pleading in her eyes, and reluctantly agreed. "Just don't go in the stalls," he added. "Animals can take exception to strangers in their midst."

She gave her promise, and contented herself with patting silken noses while the Earl sought the stall of his injured wheeler. Some ten minutes later, he looked around for her, finally locating her in the stable office. "Good God!" he ejaculated, eyeing the bit of fluff she held in her arms. "What is that?"

"It's a kitten, silly," she replied, cuddling the tiny creature under her chin. "The stable cat had a litter, and the coachman gave me one."

"I should rather think he might. Surely you don't intend keeping it?"

"It's a he," she replied, blithely expecting her remark to override any objections he might put forth. "I will keep him in my room."

"See that you do," he warned her grimly, and escorted her back to the inn to wash up before luncheon.

Unfortunately, through no fault of her own, she was not to comply with his behest. The chambermaid, upon perceiving Lydia descending the stairs, entered her room to tidy it and left the door ajar. The kitten, unhappy at finding himself in strange surroundings, made his bid for freedom and dashed down the stairs. Lydia, nearing the bottom step, made a grab for him, lost her footing, and tumbled to the floor below. The Earl, drawn into the hall by the maid's scream, hurried across to her and dropped to one knee. "Don't attempt to move," he begged urgently.

"I may have turned my ankle," she said, groping for his hand. "Just let me rest a moment before you help me up."

His fingers clasped hers reassuringly. "You mustn't place weight on it until we determine the extent of the injury. Put your arm around my neck, and I will carry you to the parlor."

"I feel so foolish," she admitted childishly. "It was shockingly careless of me, but I do not believe I am seriously hurt."

"We will decide that after we remove your slipper," he replied, laying her gently down upon the settle. "How came you to do such a thing?"

"The kitten was escaping. I'm afraid I grabbed for him and lost my footing. Where is he, by the way?"

"I'm sure I don't know," he said with strong feeling. "I will try not to hurt you," he added, removing the shoe and gently examining the injured member.

The ankle was swelling fast, causing her to grimace with pain. She found to her dismay that she could not swallow a gasp, and averted her face to hide the tears. "Please," she said chokingly. "No more."

"The landlady is bringing fresh linen. I will need to bind it. Fortunately, no bones are broken. You will very soon feel much better." He paused, and remarked: "Crying won't help, my dear."

"I'm not crying," she asserted, while surreptitiously drying her eyes. "It is just that I am such a bother. Gentlemen never can abide troublesome females."

"Repentant, my dear? Now you have given me cause for alarm. To own the truth, I'm glad to hear it. I had thought never to see you contrite."

She gave him a wan smile and shook her head. "I'm not feeling so spry as to rise to your bait, sir, provoke me how you will."

"I won't provoke you," he assured her, and rose. "I want you to lie here quietly while I procure a measure of brandy."

She watched him walk toward the taproom, made an attempt to rise, and fainted peacefully away. Regaining consciousness some few minutes later, she opened her eyes, to look up into his frowning ones. "Let me tell you," he said severely, "you will, for perhaps the first time in your life, do as you are told."

"Are you vexed with me?" she asked weakly, and gave a shuddering sob. "I don't know how I came to swoon."

"You fainted because you refused to heed me." Slipping an arm beneath her shoulders, he raised her and placed a wine glass to her lips. "Drink," he said, and tilted the brandy down her throat.

Lydia gulped, choked, and pushed the glass away. "You needn't drown me," she said tartly.

"Reviving, are you? Then I suggest you lie still while I bind the ankle."

She was perfectly ready to follow this advice, however brusquely given, for her head still swam unpleasantly. The wrapping tried her fortitude, but as the Earl, with surprising dexterity, accomplished the task in record time, she was able to endure the experience and even to summon a smile, albeit a weak one. She said with difficulty: "You should have been a doctor."

"I have, through necessity, assisted with far worse wounds on the battlefield. As soon as you have sufficiently recovered, we will carry you to your room."

"We?" she said glancing around. Surprised at finding herself the center of an interested audience, she looked embarrassed. "I am sorry to have put everyone to so much trouble, but I am quite recovered now," she told them with assurance.

The landlady beamed. "Now you just lie right there all nice and comfy, my lady, and I will fetch a bolster for your head. The rest of you," she added to the maids, shooing them before her, "get about your business. Shame on you, crowding about her ladyship like this."

The rest did much to restore Lydia's spirits. She refused to be carried to her room, saying she was feeling quite the thing, and demonstrated this by partaking of an excellent luncheon served on a table set up beside the settle. The Earl sent the waiter in search of her kitten and, when the lackey returned with it, lifted it by the scruff of its neck, placing it in her arms himself. "I am inclined to hazard the opinion that that animal will become the bane of my existence," he remarked, resuming the chair he had drawn up beside her sofa.

Lydia gave a choke of laughter. "He will do me credit, surely, by being on his best behavior when you are around."

"I trust," he remarked with the glimmer of a smile, "that he will absent himself on those occasions. My plans do not permit even a kitten as witness."

At this moment a disturbance was heard in the hall, and Lady Lenora walked into the room. "What have you two been about?" she demanded, eyeing Lydia's crimson cheeks questioningly. "Is it possible you have no consideration for anyone but yourselves? We have spent a wretched time of it, believe me."

"Now, Mama," Lydia began in conciliating accents.

"You, sir," Lady Lenora said, ignoring Lydia and fixing the Earl with a jaundiced eye. "This is surely a new come-out for you, to place your future wife in the position of coquette. Is it possible you are so completely lost to the proprieties that you would bring about her ruin?"

"Such was not my intention, Lady Lenora, believe me. Did not Gerald explain . . ."

"He arrived with some folderol of a marriage, but I'm not prepared to embark upon that at present. Explain yourself, sir!"

"Do, pray, Lady Lenora, take a seat, for I am sure you are exhausted from your journey. There is not the least cause for alarm, I assure you. Have you had your luncheon? I will gladly see to it . . ."

An expression of acute dislike crossed her face, but before she could muster her tongue for some further vituperous utterance, the Marquis came upon the scene. After bestowing one brief glance on her, he addressed himself to the Earl. "You must allow me to apologize for my wife's remarks," he said, holding out his hand. "I imagine you must know the strain she has been under."

"I do know it, sir," the Earl replied, shaking the hand held out to him. "Lady Lenora very properly wishes to discover the extent of my villainy. A poor sort of mother she would be if she didn't."

This caused Lady Lenora to swallow the remark she was about to make, and to blink at him, taken aback. "Well, but I merely want an explanation," she said somewhat less forcefully.

"Which you shall have, ma'am, the moment you have had some tea. You are quite fagged to death, and upset into the bargain. I wouldn't have had such a thing happen for the world."

"Mama, dear, pray do sit down," Lydia added coaxingly. "Do not let's discuss it further until we may do so sensibly. Of course you are right to be concerned, but it will all straighten itself out in your mind."

Lady Lenora did not look very much convinced of this, but just as she was about to take a seat, the landlady came bustling into the room, clasping a quilt in her arms. "Perhaps your sister could use this to place about her ankle, my lord," she said to the Earl. "I'm sure we shouldn't wish her to take a chill."

"Sister!" gasped Lady Lenora, stunned.

"Thank you," the Earl said hastily. "If you will be so kind as to bring a pot of tea?"

"And some trifle, my lord?" the landlady suggested. "It is fresh made just this morning. I will go fetch it." With these promising words, she dropped a curtsy and disappeared through the door to the kitchens.

"Well!" Lady Lenora exclaimed. "So I have no cause for concern, have I? We should have expected no less from a rake . . ."

"Lenora, be silent!" the Marquis snapped. "I don't know what the devil has been going forward here, but we will permit Torquay an explanation."

The Earl, only too well aware of the impression they must present, and of the difficulty in oversetting it, sighed, and embarked upon a rendition of events that sounded as improbable to his own ears as he thought it must surely do to Lydia's parents.

The Marquis, upon the recital's drawing to its conclusion, found himself so much in sympathy with the Earl that he shot his wife a silencing look and said: "The ladies will return to the castle in my coach, while we proceed to the McDougalls' in yours. My secretary accompanies me. He will prepare an affidavit concerning this marriage of yours. Then, and only then, my boy, will I entrust my daughter to your care."

"I think it my duty . . ." Lady Lenora began.

"If they were married by declaration, my dear, you have no cause for complaint. Whether the Earl has himself, in light of your daughter's conduct, is for him to determine."

CHAPTER SIX

It was considerably after midnight before the Marquis's coach drew up before the castle. The Earl, strolling into the hall with his father-in-law by his side, politely offered a cold collation, but the Marquis just as politely declined. "I'm not going to offer you advice, my boy," he said cheerfully. "Every man must discover the pitfalls of married life for himself."

"Baptism under fire, eh?" the Earl remarked, chuckling. "You think the terrors of the battlefield may well prove tame by comparison."

"Think it? I know it. If it's all the same with you, I will help myself to your best brandy before I retire."

The Earl, amused by the Marquis's notions of a tactful exit, watched him enter the blue salon, and took the stairs two at a time. At the door to Lydia's bedroom he paused. A low laugh escaped him, and he went back downstairs. "A bottle of champagne and two glasses," he told the night porter, and waited impatiently while his servant procured them. Returning upstairs he went quietly into her room and stood gazing down at her, a softened expression in his eyes. She was lying on her back in the center of the bed, sound asleep, her breasts glowing softly under the thin gauze of her nightgown. He stood devouring the sight until, a muscle twitching in his cheek, he turned to set the champagne down upon a table.

Lydia, moving restlessly to ease her aching ankle, opened her eyes and gasped in surprise. Jerking the covers to her chin, she said, suddenly shy: "What time is it?"

Having picked up the decanter, he was just in the act of pouring out two glasses when she spoke. "You will make me think you aren't happy to see me if the hour disturbs you," he replied, looking at her in a way that was hard to read.

She colored faintly and began smoothing the sheet with her fingers. "Perhaps you won't wish to hear what I have to say, but I must say it."

"I have little doubt I will be unable to prevent it," he commented, setting the decanter down again.

"I want to thank you for being so understanding with Mama."

He glanced at her with the suggestion of a smile, and picked up the glasses. "I wasn't being understanding," he said, handing her one. "She had my entire sympathy."

"I should have known better than try to be polite to you," she remarked, leaning back against the pillows.

"You are making me out a sad character," he grinned, pulling up a chair beside the bed and sitting down. "Am I to be absolved?"

She sipped the champagne. "I don't know why you

shouldn't," she said, twinkling at him over the rim of her glass. "The wine is delicious."

He smiled faintly. "I felt we should toast our marriage. God knows we can do little else at present."

"I'm sorry to have created such a coil, Iain. Is it so very hard on you?"

"Damnably hard. How is the ankle?"

"It aches." She drew a deep breath and launched upon the speech she had prepared during the return to the castle. "I am not insensible of the distress I must have caused you when I refused to believe we were married, but I know it must have been great. You were patient with me under the circumstances, and I want to take this opportunity to tell you how much I appreciate your forbearance."

His eyes gleamed. "Such a pretty little speech," he remarked. "It must have cost you much to deliver it."

"Common decency compelled me to say it, but civility has its limits. I take back every word."

"Common decency being your Mama."

"She seems to have swung over to your side. Among other things, she said I used you abominably."

"It is very true. You did use me abominably." He smiled and refilled her glass. "I console myself with thoughts of retribution."

"Oh?" she said archly. "You think to unnerve me, but you really should cure yourself of the notion."

The Earl laughed and put his glass down upon the table. "I can appreciate your anxiety," he said, rising. "You need to be taught a lesson, but you may comfort yourself with the thought that I shan't conduct it until your ankle heals. Is there some service I may perform for you before I retire?"

"There is something, Iain. Will you leave orders for

a groom to carry me downstairs in the morning? I have no intention of hopping about on one foot."

He bent over and lifted her face with a hand under her chin. "I will carry you," he said, and kissed her.

A good night's rest did much to restore Lydia's sense of well-being. The Earl, who was relieved to find her dressed and smiling when he entered her room, pronounced the ankle on the mend. A glance at the clock on her mantel showed him it was a few minutes past nine o'clock. "Perhaps we shouldn't go down," he said. "Cousin Flora has heard of your mishap and is waiting in the hall below to inquire after your welfare."

"What of Lady Cavanaugh?" she said in tones hopeful of a negative reply.

"No such luck," he replied ruefully. "My man tells me the entire Clan put in an appearance at the breakfast table. Shall we face them, or would you prefer to have yours here?"

"We must eventually satisfy their curiosity," she said, shrugging. "It may as well be now."

"Had you refrained from acquiring that loathsome animal, we would at this moment—well, never mind. It can't signify thinking of it."

"I should be obliged," she said with some asperity, "if you would refrain from putting the blame entirely on me. Do not imagine that I am not well aware you are merely miffed at having your desires set aside."

A devilish gleam came into his eyes. "I could say the same of you, but I should hesitate to offend your sensibilities." He scooped her up in his arms as he spoke, and carried her from the room.

She felt the red suffusing her cheeks, and glared. "Your conceit passes all bounds," she shot at him, annoyed all out of proportion to the provocation. "Do you think I care I sprained my ankle? Well, I shall take leave to tell you that I don't."

"Yes, you do," he replied, laughing down at her. "Next you will be telling me only maidenly reserve prompts you to mention desires that you should as yet know nothing about. Do, I beg you, smile. It might be wasted on me, but the family expects a glowing bride."

She opened her mouth to retort, perceived several pairs of eyes staring up at them from the foot of the stairs, and closed it.

"Lydia, dear!" Lady Flora exclaimed, moving forward amid the fluttering of her hands. "Cousin Mary has gone off on the oddest start, but I told her a basket of flowers from Brodie Hall shouldn't necessarily cause undue alarm. I will say that Sir Charles is the soul of kindness—at one time he called quite regularly here—but it won't do. It won't do at all. The thing is, Lydia dear, we once thought that he and dearest Miss Wingate might make a match of it. Cousin Douglas said all along they wouldn't—he fancied the notion hadn't occurred to Sir Charles—but you know yourself how troublesome Cousin Mary can be when things don't fall out as she thinks they ought."

Lydia, thinking Cousin Flora's agitation stemmed more from concern for the evenness of Lady Cavanaugh's temper than from any interest in her own injury, and unable to make the least sense of her tangled words, nevertheless smiled and said: "I shan't invite him here. Pray do not give it another thought."

Encouraged by this assurance, Lady Flora glanced hopefully at the Earl. "Cousin Douglas is persuaded you will not make a fuss about the flowers, or I would not have ventured to mention them. I am sure Sir Charles thought to be obliging—he is quite generous, you know—but the thing is, it is such a large bouquet. Really, it is too bad of him. Cousin Mary is quite distraught."

The Earl eyed her with disfavor. "What the deuce are you talking about?" he said shortly.

"The flowers from Brodie Hall!" Lady Flora declared in scathing accents, enjoying the drama to the full. "There must be all of four dozen blossoms. Don't ask me their names, for I can't tell you. I am not acquainted with exotic blooms."

"Oh, for God's sake!" he exclaimed, exasperated. "Can't you make sense! Has Miss Wingate received a floral tribute from Sir Charles?"

"Miss Wingate?" repeated Lady Flora, loath to abandon the most important role she had yet been called upon to play. "Were that it were she! They are for Lydia—at least the note is addressed to her. No one has dared to open the envelope, for her name is ascribed across its front."

A thunderous look came upon the Earl's face. "I have sometimes thought the lot of you meddlesome, but not until now have I thought any of you capable of harm."

Lady Flora colored and wrung her hands. "Don't, pray, let us quarrel, Cousin Torquay!" she begged, fairly running down the hall to keep pace with his long stride. "We didn't mean to set up censure of dearest Lydia. I'm sure you know we hold her in esteem."

Her apology fell sadly flat. The expression of anger on his face became more pronounced. "Perhaps you will oblige me by leaving the subject," he said shortly, and crossed the threshold of the breakfast room.

Lydia stared in disbelief at the ostentatious floral display occupying the place of honor in the center of the table, unable to make up her mind what to say. If she ordered it removed, Iain might ask her questions she would find difficult to answer; if she allowed it to remain, memories she would as lief banish could well rise up to haunt her. Weighing the possibility that he might think it odd of her not have told him of her encounter with Sir Charles against the certainty of her own shameful recollections, she decided to keep her counsel, and answered questions of her mishap without mention of either Sir Charles or his cousins.

When Lady Lenora put queries to the Earl on the subject of the flowers, she was heartily glad of it, for he related details of their meeting with the Brodies quite casually, saying that though they were near neighbors, he had been in the Peninsula when Sir Charles came into the title, and so had never before met them. Lydia, relieved to have him carry the conversation, put Sir Charles from her mind.

It was not until two o'clock the following afternoon that he came back into it. His coach pulled up before the castle to disgorge not only Sir Charles but Frederick and Helene as well. The object of the visit, it soon transpired, was not so much to pursue any villainous intent as to make the acquaintance of the occupants of Torquay. He conversed comfortably with the gentlemen, was perfectly amiable to the ladies, and ended by staying for tea. After this, Lydia was not at all surprised when, the following morning, Helene was ushered into the blue salon. "Dearest Lady Lydia, are you better?" she said with her sweetest smile. "I have brought you sugar plums."

"That was kind of you," Lydia murmured, accepting

the box. "Yes, I am much better. A few more days should see me set to rights." If she thought Helene's sudden interest in her welfare was an excuse for visiting the castle, she concealed it, and put herself out to entertain the child very agreeably, but Helene, upon discovering that the Earl was from home, did not tarry long.

The Marquis's feelings, when he learned of the visit, were not at all complacent. Alone among the family, he had not been at all pleased by Sir Charles's forwardness, and lost no time in telling Lydia so. "The man's a profligate," he told her severely. "I should have no compunction in speaking to Torquay, were he to offer you the least affront. I daresay he won't call here alone, but if he does, it will be best for you to remain in your rooms."

"I will own I was not pleased to renew his acquaintance, Papa, but I fancy we will see little of him," she replied soothingly. "Iain could not be more uninterested in pursuing the friendship."

"They could not be more different," the Marquis agreed. "One thing is sure; Sir Charles did not come by his insinuating ways through his father. Sir Edward was a proud man, and, while the Brodies are a respected family, I saw none of his son's manner in him."

"If Sir Charles comes of an old family, how can it be he is unacquainted in the neighborhood?" she asked curiously.

"I believe he resided in London with his mother. Sir Edward's marriage created quite a scandal at the time. I don't know how much truth there was in it, but rumor had her the daughter of a wealthy cit, quite pretty, but not at all up to snuff. Her airs of self-consequence seem to have alienated Sir Edward's father; at any rate, he refused to have her at Brodie Hall."

"Very shabbily done," Lydia remarked. "I could almost feel sorry for Sir Charles."

"Then you will abandon the thought. The man may play off the airs of an exquisite, but he has lived by his wits for years. He was used to play at the tables, as I recall, until he gambled away his fortune. I daresay he is by now reduced to penury."

"I should not doubt it," Lydia admitted, pinking slightly.

The Marquis regarded her thoughtfully for a moment, then said: "I would advise you, Lydia, not to offer encouragement to Miss Brodie. It would be the most natural thing in the world for you to do so, since there are few ladies near your own age in the neighborhood. But that is not to the point. She would not scruple to seduce your husband, my dear, given the opportunity."

Lydia choked and went into a peal of laughter. "Seduce Iain?" she said. "He would never make such a cake of himself."

"Probably not," he said, rising. "You will, however, I trust, give the matter some thought."

Lydia could not have told whether she preferred giving Helene an opportunity to flirt with Iain, thereby receiving her comeuppance, or whether she wished to keep her from his sight. The situation was out of her hands in any event, she ruefully reflected from the confinement of her rooms. Until her ankle healed, there was little she could do in ordering the comings and goings of the household.

It was to prove unfortunate for her peace of mind

that Sir Charles had by no means despaired of marrying her, irrespective of Torquay, and had for some days been busily devising plans for freeing her from her marriage. Bringing her to acceptance of divorce seemed to him the best solution. Calling at the castle, he lost no time in setting the wheels in motion. "Are you sure you should receive me?" he asked, taking a chair facing her and giving a little laugh. "The Earl doesn't wish you to have me for a friend, and I would hesitate to cross him. I should hate to place either of us in danger."

"Danger!" she ejaculated, staring at him in lively astonishment. "This is beyond everything, Sir Charles. You cannot, I am persuaded, have given consideration to your words."

"It is not my intention to alarm you," he returned blandly, "but you are not looking quite the thing. I only wondered at it. However little I might relish the necessity, you must be put on your guard."

She was silent for a moment, thinking him the strangest man she had ever met. "You are mistaken, of course," she said finally. "We will say no more about it."

"If you wish," he replied, looking at her intently. "I will only advise you to have a care."

She returned his look, the anger rising in her eyes. "Your words are very fine, but I have no reason to trust them, in the circumstance of our earlier meeting. I do not mean to appear rude, Sir Charles, but I must ask you to quell your tongue."

He immediately stood, bowed, and crossed to engage Lady Lenora in conversation. Lydia watched him go, and leaned back in her chair, oddly fatigued. Lately, it seemed to her, the strangest lassitude would come over her, sapping her strength and leaving her feeling tired. At times she seemed incapable of ordering her thoughts, and when this happened she covered her lapse by busying herself with her embroidery.

During the coming days her condition perceptibly worsened. She developed a tendency toward headaches, her throat became inflamed, and she spent much of her time resting in her bed. The Earl became concerned, but she refused to see a doctor. "I'm only tired," she told him, yawning. "Tomorrow I will feel refreshed, believe me."

"In the meantime, you aren't eating. I daresay you scarcely touched your luncheon."

"I wasn't hungry, Iain. I did eat a sugar plum," she assured him hastily. "Pray don't fuss at me."

"A sugar plum!" he ejaculated, stunned. "You cannot subsist on that! Where did you get it, by the way."

"Helene brought me a box some time ago. I thought it considerate of her, and they are quite good. Would you care for one?"

"No, and neither do you. I'm sending to the kitchens for a decent meal. When it comes, you will eat it if I must force it down your throat."

"Surely you are jesting," she began, and broke off, racked by a fit of coughing. "Just give me a moment," she said pleadingly when she was able.

"This is nonsensical," he replied, sitting down beside her on the bed. "You cannot go on like this, Lydia."

"I'm sorry to have put you in a horrid situation."

"You have put me in an impossible situation."

She frowned and said crossly: "I'm aware of that."

"I should think you would be, but do you know the extent of it? I have waited patiently for your ankle to heal, and the moment it does, you succumb to a cold."

She regarded him with a smoldering eye. "I shouldn't be at all surprised," she said, "to learn that I'm shamming it."

"I don't think that," he said. "It has been an interminable time, my dear, and I don't intend delaying longer. Get dressed. I will take you to the doctor."

"He would only say I have taken a chill and prescribe some vile concoction."

"In that case, you will be advised to swallow it." He rose and walked toward the door. Reaching it, he looked back over his shoulder and said: "I will order the coach brought around in half an hour. Be ready."

Two hours later the doctor, his examination complete, stood conversing in low tones with the Earl when Lydia emerged from the dressing room. "What is it?" she said. "Why are you looking at me so oddly?"

The Earl walked across to her and took her hands in his. "I know it will sound nonsensical, Lydia, but the doctor says you are being poisoned."

"Poisoned!" she gasped, clinging to his fingers. "Do not say so!"

"I think, my dear, we will say no more of it for the moment." He was looking so stern the words rising on her tongue died stillborn. She found to her dismay that the tears were stinging her eyelids, and she allowed him to draw her hand through his arm, to escort her to their coach. "Don't cry," he said gently, handing her in. "You need not worry."

"But why, Iain? Why would anyone wish to poison me?"

"I don't know," he said settling down beside her. "You may be sure I will find out. In the meantime, dearest, it is as well we know."

"When this is over . . ."

"Yes, dear heart?" he murmured, pulling her into his arms. "When this is over?"

She put her arms around his neck and clasped him close. "Silly," she said, and raised her face for his kiss.

"You have one week to recover," he murmured against her lips. "Nothing you can say after that will do you the least good. My waiting will be over."

CHAPTER SEVEN

It was some days before Lydia was restored to her usual composure, so much so, in fact, that she was able to sustain with an air of calm cheerfulness the arrival in her rooms of Lady Flora. It was immediately evident from the look on her face that she was conscious of having endangered her position in the household, and had come to make amends. Lydia had seen very little of her since the tiff over the flowers, and could well imagine what had been passing through her mind. Quickly taking in Lady Flora's frightened, pleading eyes, her heart turned over, and she set about putting the poor creature at ease. It proved no easy task.

"I do hope, dearest Lydia, that you will overlook my impertinence," she said tremulously. "I can't imagine what came over me. Sir Charles seems a civil person—a very civil person, I must say—but my first duty is toward the family. I quite expected you must have given me a heavy set-down, and am astonished that you have not."

Lydia smiled encouragingly and said in rallying tones: "Don't be a goose. I have no intention of doing so. Refine no more upon it. Pray, I implore you, do smile and set your mop-cap straight."

Lady Flora, desperately anxious to please, meekly complied. "You are very good about it, I make no secret of that. I do wish we had never met the Brodies—any of them!" she added, drawing a shaky breath. "Darling Jaimie tells me he has done all within his power to put an end to the friendship, but he is perfectly certain Lord Gerald is smitten."

"Gerald smitten!" Lydia gasped, appalled. "Good God! Not Miss Brodie!"

"You can't know how relieved I am to unburden my mind, dearest Lydia. I have been so worried. Not that I think we need fear Lord Gerald will act imprudently," she hastened to say.

"Are you certain you have not read a misconstruction into Miss Brodie's call? You may have noticed Papa took the Brodies in the greatest dislike. He could be expected to utter severe strictures against such an undesirable connection."

"He would certainly have put a stop to it, had he but known of it. Miss Brodie is not a proper young lady for Lord Gerald to know. Jaimie says they have been meeting secretly."

"Well, you may be assured that excessively forward chit will not be allowed to promote her precious schemes. Say no more about it."

"I declare I do not know what Torquay will have to say," Lady Flora avowed, tears starting into her eyes. "I don't think I could bear another quarrel."

"Now you are talking foolish beyond permission, you silly girl," Lydia said, smiling. "I shan't let him bully you."

At this moment the Earl walked into the room. He came forward to inquire how Lydia was feeling, taking little notice of Lady Flora. How much of their conversation he had overheard she could not tell, and only hoped they had not set his bristles up. "The most naggy thing, Iain," she said. "Cousin Flora tells me Gerald has set up a flirt with Miss Brodie. Papa, I fancy, will be in a taking."

"Indeed?" he said impatiently, glancing in his cousin's direction.

Lady Flora, flustered at finding herself witness to the invasion of a masculine presence into a female's bedchamber, however much they were married, was so overwhelmed that she uttered a faint shriek and clapped her hands to her mouth. She stood in horrified silence while Lydia assured him she had but related the truth, and seemed to derive little consolation from the words spoken in her behalf. Her modesty was so much shocked that she waited only until he took his eyes from her face to take to her heels.

"What in thunder has gotten into her?" the Earl demanded, directing an admonitory frown at Lydia.

She cast him a look of unholy glee. "You, I expect," she told him smugly. "Surely you cannot blame her for taking maidenly exception to your presence in my chamber."

"Of all the bibble-babble I have ever heard!" he snorted in derision. "If she thinks I shan't stop here when I choose, she will do well to accustom herself to the notion. As for you, ma'am, I beg you will refrain from inviting her here. I have no need of chaperonage."

Lydia opened innocent eyes at him. "Such a repelling thought," she said.

"Since it seems unlikely, it need not trouble you," he returned dryly. "I would suggest instead that you devote your energies to the question of your health."

"Certainly I shall make every effort to do so," she responded readily. "Being burnt to the socket would only bring down retribution upon my head. I will admit to having qualms on that score."

A reluctant smile was forced to his lips. "As a matter of fact, you should," he said. "To tell the truth, I was vexed at not finding you alone."

"Well, it was very bad of you to frighten poor Cousin Flora half out of her wits. I'm terrified of you myself when you turn your frown on me."

"You can't expect me to believe that, my girl, so you needn't turn yourself up sweet. Did you eat the tea I sent up?"

"Yes, I did. What an abominable person you are! A soft-boiled egg and broth indeed! You may as well tell me I'm hagged half to death."

"I make you my compliments on your appearance," he said, sitting down beside her and taking her in his arms. "Dinner will be up shortly. I hope you're hungry."

"Yes, I am," she said, subsiding thankfully against his shoulder. "I can't think what became of my box of sweets."

He gazed down at her, a closed expression coming on his face. "I took it away," he blandly explained.

"Whatever induced you to do such a thing?" she asked, lifting her head to stare at him.

"Bonbons spoil your appetite. Dr. McTavers says another day will see you recovered. If you put your mind to it, my love, you will recall my plans for you. You shouldn't wish a relapse, I trust."

"Odious creature," she said. "You haven't the least notion of gentlemanly address. I dare swear it is foolish of me to expect you to conduct yourself with anything approaching propriety. You haven't a shred."

"Not a shred," he agreed, and kissed her. "You will no doubt demonstrate your own sense of decorum by sitting upright. Unless my ears deceive me, the servants are bringing in our dinner."

She was betrayed into an involuntary chuckle, and turned to watch the butler usher in a procession of grooms bearing heavily laden trays. A snowy cloth was spread on a table before the fire, the covers of the first course were removed, and the servants withdrew. "You must think me the worst sort of trencherman," she remarked, allowing him to hand her to her place on his right. "You shouldn't put me to the blush."

His lips twitched. "All in good time," he said. "Tonight we concentrate on food. I have ordered your favorite dishes."

"Iain, whatever are we to do about Gerald?"

"He is in no way our responsibility," he replied absently. "Pass your plate."

"Do, pray, pay attention. I wouldn't bet a groat on the chance that he will listen to one disparaging word against Miss Brodie."

He glanced at her inscrutably. "A useless exercise, surely," he remarked, serving the poached fish. "When did you arrive at the conclusion our fair charmer is something less than pure?"

Her reply startled him. "The sugar plums were poisoned," she said.

A tinge of color stole into his cheeks. "Why should you think that?" he asked with considerable restraint, and set her plate before her.

"Give me credit for some sense, Iain. I will admit the thought hadn't occurred to me until you confessed to having removed them. Then I knew it had to be the candy."

He did not answer immediately, and when he did it was to speak with authority. "I will ask you not to discuss this, Lydia. Miss Brodie is under the protection of a guardian."

She looked at him meditatively. "I am not the least interested in Sir Charles," she said.

"I trust not, but I have a great deal of interest in him."

"Why?"

"Eat your dinner."

Lydia fought for control. "Of all the insufferable— Oh! I could hit you!"

"I doubt it," he remarked in a tone of amusement. "Very well. I had the sugar plums analyzed. They contained poison, but not in sufficient amounts to prove fatal. You must know this bore out my suspicion that murder was not a motive. Had that been the case, a more certain method would have been employed."

Her hand sought his across the table. "I cannot think that much consolation," she said, looking anxiously into his eyes.

"You need not be afraid, my love," he said, his fingers closing over hers. "It is my belief you were meant to develop a fear of me."

"But who . . . ?" She gasped to a halt, an appalling

thought coming into her mind. "Sir Charles," she murmured.

His face hardened. "Why should you think of him?" he asked sharply.

She flushed and dropped her eyes. "He thought to marry me when he believed me your sister. It was foolish of me not to tell you; indeed, I do not know why I did not. It just seemed so—so unimportant."

"Is there more?" he asked gently after a moment.

"He warned me you might do me harm," she admitted in a very small voice.

"He must be mad. Look at me, my dear."

Meeting his eyes, she struggled to regain her composure. "You must think me ridiculous," she said uncertainly.

"I think you enchanting," he replied, and raised her fingers to his lips.

"Iain, I shouldn't wonder at it if Sir Charles thinks to promote his own welfare at your expense. We need only demonstrate the unlikelihood of my turning away from you for him to cast his glance elsewhere. I am strongly of the opinion that any heiress will serve."

"Undoubtedly, but I do not consider it advisable for you to continue to receive him. Should he call again, deny him admittance."

"What of Gerald?"

"I shouldn't dream of offering insult to your father," he replied, ruefully reflecting that he would probably be called upon to interfere. A swift glance at her face confirmed his fears.

The Marquis, when informed of developments late the following afternoon by the Earl, who did so reluctantly at Lydia's insistence, surprised him by remarking that Miss Brodie represented the first real threat he had yet encountered when dealing with his son. "She's a pretty minx, I'll give her that, but she is as heartless a chit as I've ever encountered. The boy's enthralled. I will own to you I'd like nothing better than to ring a peal over Gerald, but I am convinced the least hint of opposition could well make the flirtation seem more romantic."

"It no doubt would," the Earl agreed. "I regret this should have happened while you are under my roof. If there is anything I can do to scotch the affair, I will be honored if you will enlist my services."

"There is little I can do, other than to remove Gerald to London. Lingering here would only provide Miss Brodie with an opportunity to improve her image. No, Torquay. We will be advised not to tarry here."

But Lydia, having teased the Earl into relating the gist of their conversation, felt much inclined to disagree. "Helene is not a precocious child," she insisted, immediately they entered her rooms following his conference with her father. "She is a scheming hussy, and old beyond her years. And Gerald will be a Marquis one day, don't forget. Besides being able to provide her with entry into the ton, he is quite good-looking and has a most engaging manner. He would suit her purpose very well."

"Must we discuss the plaguey chit?" he asked sardonically. "I would much rather talk about us."

"You think to change the subject," she remarked, crossing to the settee beside the fire. "The thing is, we must determine what is to be done about Gerald until Papa succeeds in removing him to London. You will allow that keeping an eye on Helene is less dangerous than these clandestine meetings they have been indulging in. What would you think of an expedition to the blow-hole you once told me of?"

"I will think anything you wish me to," he said, sitting down beside her. "Did anyone ever tell you that you wrinkle your brow when you ponder?"

"We could go on horseback; I'm sure nothing would prevail upon Gerald to go by carriage."

"I like the way you dress your hair. It is called 'A la Aries,' I believe."

"Do be serious, Iain. The weather has turned up fine, and if the distance is so very great, I imagine we could pause to rest."

He gave a low chuckle and swept her into his arms. "There is only one way to silence you," he remarked, and fiercely kissed her.

"Must you manhandle me?" she inquired, and snuggled against his shoulder.

"I will do a great deal worse if you don't concentrate on me," he grinned, and kissed her again.

"Odious creature, I am concentrating," she said, wriggling closer still.

Drawing an audible breath, he uttered, shaken: "You will be advised to dress for dinner before mischief is done."

Lydia could not mistake the effort behind his words. "I will wear the pink chiffon," she said quietly. "I know it is a favorite of yours."

When she arrived downstairs an hour later, she was relieved to find only her parents and the Earl waiting in the blue salon. "Iain and I have settled it between us to go on an expedition to Loch Broom," she said, looking at him in a way calculated to still any denial. "Before you raise objections to Gerald and Miss Brodie being invited along, Papa, let me say we will do well to provide her with an opportunity to expose herself. Ler her but lose her temper at being forced to go climbing about, and she will shock Gerald with her unbridled tongue. I know. I have heard her."

The Marquis naturally objected but, upon having it pointed out that Miss Brodie was perfectly capable of pursuing Gerald on the road to London, was brought to see merit in the plan. To her mother's strictures against ladies clambering about over rocky shores and subjecting themselves to heaven knew what in murky caverns, Lydia said she expected to find it sadly flat herself, but had determined to make the effort. By the time dinner was announced, an alarming twinkle gleamed in the Earl's eyes. He said, murmuring in her ear when he pushed in her chair: "If you find the idea so sadly flat, my dear, it will be my pleasure to raise objections."

Lydia was not deceived. It was very pleasant to be addressed in caressing tones, but she knew the danger in providing him with an opening, her parents' presence notwithstanding. Subduing him with a glance, she unfolded her napkin and embarked upon a flow of small talk that lasted throughout the meal. The Earl, listening with his habitual languor, had the mirthful felicity of knowing full well the reason behind her idle chatter.

Lady Lenora, immediately they returned to the blue salon after dinner, picked up her embroidery and requested Lydia to play for them. "Now, Mama," she began, but the Earl crossed to the pianoforte and opened it for her. Seeing no help for it, she sat down upon the bench and spread her fingers, glancing at him in mute appeal before she began to play. He stood leaning against the instrument, a look of so much tenderness in his eyes that she faltered once in the rendition before going on to complete the piece. "You are full of surprises," he remarked when she rose. "It would please me if you would play again."

"Another time," she murmured, and moved away toward the fire.

He followed her and sat down in a chair facing hers. "Your playing did give me pleasure," he said gravely. "I thought your performance skilled."

She shook her head. "You are flattering me," she said, smiling.

"Alas, no," he grinned. "Only attempting to flatter you."

"Then I accept the compliment in the spirit it was given. I trust it wasn't much against your will?"

"On the contrary. But don't tease yourself into thinking I will greet your every accomplishment with flattering words." A gleam of pure mischief came into his eyes. "Some of them I will accept as my just due."

"Then you are doomed to disappointment," she remarked, inspired. "One glance at my sewing was enough to send Nanny into the dismals, and even Mama could find little in my watercolors worthy of mention."

"Don't be gooseish," he said with an affable smile. "I wasn't referring to your infantry." He was interrupted in his mischievous assault by Lady Lenora, who, having laid aside her embroidery, came up to them to announce her intent of going to bed. "You are only just recovered, Lydia," the Earl said with a faint smile. "My sense of compassion prompts me to request you do the same."

She seemed to consider him questioningly for a moment before rising to go upstairs in the wake of Lady

Lenora. Letty, unable to fathom the indecisive way in which she discarded one nightgown after another before selecting a demure concoction of filmy gauze, silently went about her duty of preparing her mistress for the night. Lydia, critically scrutinizing her image in the mirror, nodded in satisfaction and dismissed the maid. "No, wait," she said just as Letty reached the door. "Have a bottle of champagne sent up immediately."

"Will your ladyship wish any particular vintage?" Letty asked, dropping a curtsy.

"The best in the house," Lydia replied, a slight smile curving her lips. Turning away, she laid another log on the fire and went around the room blowing out the candles. She had not long to wait before a tap sounded on the door, and the housekeeper entered bearing the wine on a tray. "Put it down here, Mrs. Leyton," she said, indicating a table beside the fire.

Mrs. Leyton was immensely intrigued by the unprecedented situation but, as were all the Earl's servants, was well-trained. "Will that be all, my lady?" she said in a voice wholly devoid of interest, and, at Lydia's nod, withdrew.

Lydia, suddenly nervous, began to wander around the room, picking up objects and setting them down again in a manner that clearly revealed the uncertain state of her composure. The Earl had entered his rooms by this time, and in a few moments his voice was heard speaking to his valet. Lydia fairly flew across the room. Seating herself at one end of the settee beside the fire, she arranged the train of her dressing gown in graceful folds about her feet, lightly clasped her hands together in her lap, and leaned back against the cushions. It seemed to her an unconscionable time elapsed before the connecting door to his bedroom opened. She took one look at the ruffle of his night-robe brushing his chin above the collar of his dressing gown, and lowered her eyes. "The fire looks inviting," he remarked, and crossed to stand looking down at her. "I see you ordered champagne."

She raised her eyes to his and said, rather shyly: "I thought to return the gesture."

He sat down beside her and turned, taking her in his arms. "Lydia, my love," he said, holding her carefully. "You are so beautiful. I can hardly believe that you are mine."

"Oh, Iain," she breathed, gazing at him with a look in her eyes that made the breath catch in his throat.

Trailing his lips over her face, he murmured: "I will always love you," and gently kissed her.

Lydia subsided limply in his embrace. "Will you pour the wine?" she said, timidly reaching up a hand to touch his cheek.

"Later," he whispered, and pressed his mouth to hers, lightly at first, and then abruptly more passionate as one large hand moved over her shoulder and arm, to cup a breast. Lydia started at the touch, but before she could gasp he was kissing her in a way he had not done before, quickening her pulses and sending shivering trembles through her body with his sensuous lips and seeking hands. He stopped only to lift her in his arms and carry her to the bed. Cradling her close, he gazed into her softened face and bent to her, his own face radiant.

Lydia, slowly awakening the following morning, was aware first of a cool pressure on her lips, and then of a warm breath against her cheek. Her lashes fluttered, and she opened her eyes to find herself looking up into his face. She stared for a moment, and murmured foolishly: "Oh! Is it you?"

His smile flashed. "Whom else would you expect to find in your bed?" he said, chuckling softly.

She thrust out her lower lip. "You enjoy teasing me," she said, brushing back the hair streaming forward over her forehead.

The Earl cocked an eyebrow. "I would not describe my lovemaking as teasing," he remarked, chuckling again.

An answering light shone in her eyes. "Not being an authority on the subject," she said, "I am in no position to judge."

"It will be my pleasure to remedy the deficiency," he grinned, drawing back the covers.

Her eyes grew round in surprise. "But Iain. 'Tis morning," she ventured, flushing.

He laughed softly. "We can make love in the daytime, sweet," he breathed against her throat. In a single movement he pressed her into the pillows and fastened his lips on hers. Lydia caught her breath at the ardor mounting in him, and trembled to the touch of his hands caressing her quivering flesh. A small weight crawling over his leg brought his head around. "Good God!" he ejaculated, stunned. Grabbing her kitten by its scruff, he bounded from the bed. Lydia, treated to her first full sight of him in all his naked splendor, gaped, her mouth forming a silent "oh" as he strode to the door and tossed the kitten out.

"He's used to being cuddled in the morning," she explained hesitantly as he moved back to her bed.

"Then he'll grow unused to it," he muttered, reaching for her.

CHAPTER EIGHT

Gerald, when informed of the proposed excursion to Loch Broom, gave the idea his unqualified endorsement, and lost no time in riding over to Brodie Hall to secure Miss Brodie's acceptance. Helene, at the moment in the throes of boredom, signaled her willingness amid much fluttering of eyelashes and girlish blushes, and even went so far as to concede the necessity for including the Carringtons in the outing. For, as Helene blithely informed him, while the Earl and Lydia were quite old, they were not too terribly stuffy, and therefore could be relied upon not to spoil the fun. Even Gerald could not mistake the rancor behind her remarks. He returned to the castle with a slightly tarnished image of Miss Brodie lurking deep within the recesses of his brain.

Lydia was up early on the morning chosen for the trip. She had, in fact, been awake off and on throughout the night, toying with the possibility of tendering her regrets. That, she thought somewhat snidely, should teach the Earl a lesson he would not soon forget. But no sooner had she entertained the thought than she rejected it. She would neither inquire after his whereabouts the evening before, nor allow him to think she cared he elected not to seek her bed. With this determination uppermost in her mind, she donned her most becoming habit and sat down to await the hour of departure.

By the time she came downstairs, Gerald was already astride a chestnut, and the Earl was waiting to mount her on a prettily behaved gray mare. Glancing at the aloof expression on her face, he said, too quietly to be overheard: "Are you offended with me for not coming to you last night? You need not be."

She flushed and said rather coldly: "You must suppose I did expect it."

"I do suppose it. I wanted to, believe me, dearest, but by the time I returned to the castle, you were asleep."

"You needn't expect me to inquire where you were, for I shan't," she replied stiffly, and gathered up her bridle. She allowed him to take her foot between his hands and throw her up into her saddle. Casting him one blighting look, she settled herself and set the mare forward down the drive, following in Gerald's wake.

The Earl swore softly under his breath, and swung aboard his stallion. "You might afford me an opportunity to explain," he said, coming up beside her.

She glanced at Gerald some way ahead, and turned her face away from him. "You owe me no explanation," she muttered, stumbling over the words.

He studied the side of her head, which was all that was available to him. "I went to see Sir Charles," he told her then, in his direct fashion.

Turning her eyes to his, she asked, startled: "What did he say?"

"Among other things, that he didn't put poison in the sugar plums."

Considering the matter, a slight frown came between her brows. "Helene may be a tiresome child, but I cannot think her capable of murder—or even of attempting to sicken me. Are you sure . . . ?"

"Quite sure. When I had done with Sir Charles, I had the truth from him, believe me."

She hesitated, and after a moment, ventured to say: "What did you do? You had better tell me, you know, unless you mean to anger me."

That made him chuckle. "You will need to do better than that, my dear. I'm accustomed to seeing you out of temper. Will it flatter you to know I meant to cross swords with him? I see it does. You needn't smile."

"I'm not, and you didn't," she replied somewhat mirthfully. "I can just picture it, with you waving a point under his nose while he cowers behind a chair."

"One of the things I most admire in you, my love, is your penchant for carrying on ridiculous conversations."

A tiny smile curved her lips. "What did occur at Brodie Hall?" she said, electing to ignore the parry.

The Earl's lips twitched. "I was not particularly magnanimous, my dear. Sir Charles was drunk. He took no harm of me."

A gurgle of laughter escaped her. "I hardly dare to ask," she said. "Were you in the same condition?"

"That remark doesn't surprise me at all," he said. "No, I wasn't foxed. Cold sober, in fact. I hesitate to spoil the effect, but humanity on my part didn't enter into the picture. I merely asked him what I wished to know, and he told me. The humor of it should appeal to you, fair torment. You no longer head the list of ladies destined to bail Sir Charles out of his financial difficulties."

"Well, I must own I'm glad to learn that. I haven't a sou, you know. In light of what you have told me, Iain, I don't think we should calmly ride up to Brodie Hall to collect Helene. We will do better to wait at the gates while Gerald does so."

"On the contrary, Sir Charles and I parted quite amicably. He may have been guilty of coveting you, but I can't blame him for that. I do myself."

"Don't be absurd! I daresay you think it would be diverting, but I don't. I can't at the moment call to mind a more revolting denouement. It is enough we must countenance Helene."

He appeared to give this home truth consideration. "That is true in the ordinary way, but I must point out that we will need to stand in their good grace if we are to ferret out the truth."

She hesitated, giving his viewpoint thought, and then said: "I will probably rip up at him."

"No, you won't. You are far too well-bred for that."

"I'm not too sure that would weigh with me, Iain. I just could rattle off at him in prime style."

"You might prefer to reserve your spleen for me," he remarked, casting her a provocative smile.

"Yes, I might," she replied, eyes kindling. "Why didn't you tell me you intended to challenge Sir Charles?"

"I expected to return with his heart skewered on the tip of my sword. Thus does a knight in shining armor lay his trophy at m'lady's feet."

"That's no answer!" she snapped curtly.

"Ladies are not informed of brawls, my dear." When she did not answer him but looked away, he added, his eyes on the side of her face: "Don't be angry with me."

She flushed and said in an uncertain voice, "I see Gerald is waiting for us," and broke into a canter.

Lydia harbored scant expectation that Helene would be ready to set forth immediately they arrived. When they reached Brodie Hall, however, Helene came dancing down the front steps, saying she had feared they were not coming. Lydia, watching the artful way in which she set about enslaving Gerald, set her teeth and rode off behind them, her eyes on Helene's back in a speculative way.

"You needn't worry," the Earl remarked, reining in beside her. "Today's itinerary should put her in a passion. You may well find yourself the center of a storm."

Lydia did not pretend to misunderstand him, and said: "You make me sound odiously scheming."

"Not at all, my dear. A poor sort of sister you would be if you made no push to prevent Gerald falling victim to her wiles. Shall we hold to the road? For my part, I prefer cross-country, but I shouldn't wish you to risk a tumble."

A challenging gleam came into her eyes, and she put her horse at the nearest stone fencing, soaring over it with inches to spare. The Earl grinned and, motioning to Helene and Gerald, followed after her. "There is no end to your accomplishments," he remarked while waiting for the others to join them.

It was an hour later when Lydia first noticed that some of the sparkle had gone out of Helene's eyes. Watching her, she realized the novelty of showing off her equestrian skills had worn somewhat thin. There are, after all, only so many ways in which one may gracefully jump a fence, and the necessity of guiding one's horse over rough ground precludes the opportunity to converse with wit and charm. They followed single file along a goat-track, past stones piled high to form a cairn, and on toward the top of a cliff. By the time a gentle surf could be seen creeping in to whisper its death against a rocky shore, Helene's lips were firmly compressed together.

"Surely this cannot be our destination?" she demanded impatiently. "I should have thought you could have picked a more likely spot."

"There is a cavern that runs back into the rock," the Earl explained. "We will explore it."

"You can't mean you expect me to go down there!" Helene cried, turning furious eyes on Gerald.

He looked thunderstruck for an instant, but a moment later he shrugged. "If you don't care for it, I will wait here with you."

The frown cleared from her brow. "We needn't remain," she said imploringly. "I daresay we can find amusement elsewhere."

Gerald shook his head. "Of course we won't abandon Lydia and the Earl. I wonder you would suggest such a thing."

"Lydia wouldn't mind," she said confidently.

Lydia looked taken aback and said: "You must know you cannot ride off with Gerald unchaperoned! There is nothing for it, Helene. You must join us."

The Earl, who had been listening in amusement, swung down from his horse and strolled across to Helene. "I hate to see a frown mar a pretty countenance," he said with a perfectly straight face. "Come, now. Smile, and let me help you down."

Helene shot Lydia a triumphant look, and slid into his waiting arms. She would perhaps have felt less smug had she seen the slight wink he directed at Lydia after setting her on her feet.

They clambered down the rocks to the beach below, and walked along the water's edge to the mouth of the cavern. The Earl distributed four candles he fished from a pocket of his coat, but they shed little light on the interior of the cave when held just within the narrow entrance. They squeezed through the opening and entered a mammoth chamber whose roof became lost in shadow high above their heads. Following in the Earl's wake across a floor littered with moldering wrack from the sea, they came to a passageway winding deep within the rock. Moving cautiously along the upward sloping tunnel, they came at length to a low entrance. Stooping to enter, they found themselves within a smaller inner chamber. Rays of sunlight filtering through an opening in the funnel of its roof provided sufficient light to reveal the remains of a ledge hanging drunkenly some fifteen feet above their heads.

The Earl glanced around at chunks of stone tumbled aimlessly over the floor, and remarked: "Since I was last here, the area must had experienced an earthquake. A portion of the ledge has collapsed."

Lydia, looking around curiously, stooped down and picked up an object from the floor. "Do look what I have found, Iain," she said, holding out her hand. "Whatever can it be?"

"A clump of soil," he said, laughing.

"I wonder that it became so smooth. I shouldn't

have thought the tide could have rounded it so."

"The wonders of nature," he replied cheerfully.

Incensed by his lack of interest, she dropped her eyes and saw more clumps scattered about. Taking off her high-crowned bonnet, she quickly went around gathering up all of them that she could find. They ranged in diameter from around half an inch to the approximate size of a hen's egg, and existed in plentiful enough numbers to fill the crown of her hat.

The Earl remarked, amused: "You are an exceptional female, my dear. Not many of your sex would choose to carry home balls of mud."

Inured to his banter, she said: "I shall allow myself to be the judge of that. Let me inform you, sir, I have a reason."

"Then by all means," he murmured in maddening tones.

"I don't know why you should think me a . . ." She broke off in mid-sentence and smoothed the wrinkle from her brow. "Professor Huffman is a friend of Papa's. When next we go to London, I will take them to him. He, at least, will view my find with interest."

He smiled. "Don't tease yourself into a temper over it. I am sure he will. And now, I think it time we leave. The tide will roll in soon, and I might find it incumbent upon me to keep all our heads afloat."

She was obliged to laugh at this, but before she could reply, Gerald came up to them to second the Earl's suggestion. By riding along the shore in the direction from which they had come, they would arrive at an inn beside the sea, Helene had told him, and they could procure refreshment there.

"What, at a place frequented by rough characters?" the Earl said. "Certainly not!"

Gerald grinned. "I'm afraid there is nothing for it, sir. Helene assures me she will perish without sustenance."

Lydia cast the Earl a look brimful of laughter and said: "Thus does a fair maiden in distress appeal to the conscience of a knight. I should hate to see your armor tarnished."

An answering gleam shone in his eyes. "I take leave to tell you, ma'am, you are jousting on unfamiliar ground. Before this night is o'er, you will give way beneath my thrust."

The remark proved more than Lydia could withstand. She pinked, and moved off in Gerald's wake, the Earl's chuckle ringing in her ears.

The inn was sturdily constructed of stone to withstand the ravages of gale-force winds and biting cold. The door opened into a low-pitched taproom made nauseating with the aroma of stale beer and inferior wines. The Earl's brows shot up, but he held his peace and followed across the room in the wake of the others to a table against the wall. Half an hour later he was regretting his indulgence. Having been served a tankard of ale called Stewart's Pride in doubtful honor of Bonnie Prince Charlie, he now put up his quizzing glass and subjected the food placed before him to a minute inspection. "Take it away," he told the landlord.

Helene, who was doing justice to her own serving, looked up and said: "Aren't you hungry?"

"Let us say I am not partial to shepherd's pie."

"Then what's to be done?" she said blankly. "Oh, I know," she added. "You prefer sweets."

"Thank you, no. I never touch them," the Earl replied politely. "Might I inquire where you obtained the sugar plums you gave to Lydia?" he said in a voice completely devoid of curiosity.

"Myrna McDougall gave them to me. There was no place I could have purchased them."

The Earl smiled encouragingly. "Did she request you give them to Lydia?" he asked casually.

"Well, yes, she did," Helene admitted. "But why make such a fuss over nothing more important than a box of candy?"

Gerald glanced up in surprise. "You don't mean that, I know," he said. "I thought it a pretty gesture on your part."

Helene tossed her head. "I'm tired of hearing about the sweets," she said. "I would much rather talk about what we will do next. I am persuaded it will be fun to ride on along the shore."

Gerald looked slightly taken aback. "It is much too warm," he said. "Perhaps another day when it is cooler."

Helene, angered at having her wishes set aside, became insistent. "If Lydia and Torquay don't care to come along, they could wait here for us," she said imploringly.

Gerald gazed at her, dismayed. "I can't think they would relish spending the rest of the afternoon in this place," he said in reasoning tones. "No, Helene. I have no wish to disappoint you, but . . ."

"Yes, you do!" she cried, rounding on him. "You don't care a rush that I was obliged to spend the afternoon clambering about a nasty cave."

Gerald, who was beginning to look extremely troubled, colored slightly and said: "There is no need to look daggers at me, Helene. I should have thought you would have enjoyed the novelty of it."

"Well, I didn't!" she replied sharply. "And I'll tell you something else, Gerald. You are nothing but a— but a dumb boy!"

Gerald turned beet-red. "Am I?" he snorted. "Well, I will tell you this, Helene. You have a spiteful tongue."

Lydia intervened, scolding Gerald for speaking in such a fashion, but her efforts at conciliation were doomed to failure from the start. Helene retreated behind a fit of the sulks, while Gerald divorced himself from the scene, evincing little interest in her company. Needless to say, the return ride to Brodie Hall was accomplished in virtual silence.

Gerald turned from watching Helene flounce into the house, opened his mouth to speak, caught the quelling expression in the Earl's eyes, and closed it again. Flushing to the roots of his hair, he wheeled his horse and galloped away.

"I won't deny it has been an interesting day," the Earl remarked to Lydia, moving forward to ride by her side. "It seems to have worked out very much as we intended."

She looked at him in utter astonishment. "We?" she said.

"We," he confirmed. "You may have set the stage, but I gave the actors their cue. Your mouth is hanging open, dear."

"One would suppose you could have worked out a better script," she returned coolly.

"Ah, but you did admire the finesse with which I played my part."

Lydia gave a gurgle of laughter. "I should have guessed you would exercise your usual hesitancy to boast."

"My good girl, it is the final scene that counts—in

this case the curtain will ring down on a happy one. Your Papa will now spirit Gerald off to London, and I will have you to myself. You stare! Well, it stands to reason, doesn't it?"

"No, you are off the mark, Iain, if you entertain the thought that the Cavanaughs will leave. Where would they go?"

"Does their presence irk you so very much?"

"Beyond enduring, but don't give it another thought. It is useless hinting them away."

"I think the best service I can render you will be to cast about for a situation that will answer their purpose. So far as I am aware there are no dwellings on the estate that will serve, but I will see what can be done. In the meantime, I will restrict their movements to the west wing. Will that please you?"

She cast him a rueful smile. "Enormously," she said regretfully. "I have become progressively more depraved since the moment I first met you, but you know you cannot do it. What would they think?"

"To tell the truth," the Earl admitted, "I have very little interest in what they may think."

"Yes, but you cannot cast them off so lightly. Your promise to your father must be honored, however much it chafes you. Pray don't frown at me, Iain. If they are thought to have been treated shabbily, I should be the one people frowned upon."

"You must instruct me how to contrive the affair in a manner designed to put the blame entirely on you. I imagine that must be my purpose."

She chuckled and said: "Wretch, you know very well what I mean. If you got rid of them and anything happened—you said yourself that Uncle Douglas is incapable of caring for them—then I would hold myself dreadfully at fault and deserving of censure."

They were still arguing the matter when they reached the castle. The Earl strolled beside her up the steps and into the hall. "What are you planning to do with your treasure?" he asked, glancing at the hat full of mud balls clutched in her arms.

Lydia fixed her eyes anxiously on his face and said: "Why—why, the fact of the matter is—I do not know. It will sound foolish, perhaps, but I—I really feel I should take good care of them."

"Woman's intuition?" he said, grinning. "Come along to the library. We will put them in the safe."

It was a large compartment, with ceiling-high shelving holding leather-bound volumes extending the length of one entire wall. Sofas and chairs arranged in groupings provided comfort for reading, and a mammoth desk occupied the space before the windows at the far end of the room. It was an extremely fine piece in mahogany wood, with bronze gryphons forming the legs, and with all of the mounts in the same bronze. The Earl crossed to a section of wall to the right of the desk, and slid back the paneling, to reveal the safe. Inserting the key dangling at the end of his fob-chain, he opened it and removed a casket. "This should do nicely," he remarked, and spilled out its contents onto the floor of the safe.

Lydia, bemused by the sight of gems tumbled in glittering disarray, gasped. "That wasn't necessary, Iain," she said. "Any container would serve my purpose equally well."

"That," said the Earl, "depends mainly on their worth. At the moment, my dear, you place a large value on your—baubles."

"Mud!" she corrected, going off into a peal of laughter.

"I am glad you realize that it is mud," said the Earl. "I was beginning to think you didn't."

"Of course, I do," she assured him, then spoiled the effect by taking especial care over the placing of each ball within the box.

The Earl restored the casket to the safe, and turned to look at her in a way that made her heart turn over. "It is customary to pay the toll in the time-honored way," he remarked, taking her in his arms.

"Naturally I must pay my debts," she said.

"Naturally," agreed the Earl, and kissed her, only releasing her when a tap sounded on the door.

The butler entered, to set a tray bearing glasses and a decanter down upon the desk. McTavish arranged these to his satisfaction, then bowed and withdrew, closing the door behind him. The Earl picked up the decanter, pausing with it suspended in mid-air, his brows raised questioningly. Lydia shook her head and sank into a chair, her eyes on him while he poured himself a glass. "Do you know the address of this professor friend of your father's?" he asked, walking around the desk to his chair behind it. "I intend writing to obtain his opinion of your find. If they have significance, he may know of it."

"Papa could know his address. If he doesn't, he will see to it that the note gets into the Professor's hands."

"It's settled then," he said, twirling the stem of his wine glass in his fingers. "I will speak to your father after dinner."

"What significance could they have?" she said, puzzled. "If the surf formed them . . ."

He was idly studying the light glowing in the wine. "They appear to have been formed by human hands," he told her in an offhand way. "Possibly by children. They may have been used to play some game."

Lydia stared. "Oh!" she breathed, relieved. "For a moment, I thought you meant something—well, supernatural."

The Earl was in the act of sipping the wine. He choked on it and lowered the glass. "Druids?" he said, casting her one of his devilish looks.

She was obliged to smile, and said: "I might have known you would have an odious answer ready."

But the Earl was fast losing interest in the subject. "Come here," he ordered softly, and leaned back in his chair.

Lydia, in nowise reluctant, got up and went around the desk. "I can't doubt that you have utterly unscrupulous behavior on your mind," she said.

"I won't deny it," he replied, pulling her onto his lap. "You looked at me with so much longing in your eyes . . ."

"Oh, no!" Lydia protested, laughing. "Don't say so."

"With longing," he insisted firmly, and leisurely kissed her. "Was that unscrupulous enough for you?"

"It will do until something better happens along," she replied, but since she palliated this remark by instigating the next kiss, he found no fault with it, and continued kissing her until she gasped for breath.

"That should teach you not to fence with me," he told her remorselessly.

"You are guilty of unhandsome conduct, sir," she said, and slipped from his arms.

"Of deliberate provocation only," he replied, his eyes on her as she crossed the room.

She threw him a kiss with her fingers and said: "For a husband, you must be unique," then vanished through the door.

CHAPTER NINE

The letter arrived with the morning coffee, and its effect would have brought a look of strong indignation to its sender's face. The Earl read it through a second time and groaned softly under his breath. "Why now, of all possible times, must Prinny take such a maggot into his head! Depend upon it, it is all a hum!"

Lydia, guessing the missive heralded the arrival of visitors, and aware of the real reason behind his annoyance, said in tones of gentle reproof: "I am sure I do not think you should speak so of His Royal Highness."

"If he is above foisting his wishes on the rest of us, I have yet to learn of it. This latest is just the sort of thing he would do. He is sending Clarence to Edinburgh."

He was evidently much put out, but Lydia was more interested in his final statement. "His Royal Highness is not coming here?" she said, bewildered.

"Was there ever such a coil! We are more or less ordered to attend the reception at Holyroodhouse."

Lydia, anxiously watching his coffee cup teetering dangerously above the counterpane, took it from his hand and set it on a table beside the bed. "That sounds exciting," she murmured. "Pray continue: When is the Duke of Clarence coming, and why?"

"Scots have disliked the English since Cumberland butchered our people following the battle of Culloden. The old hatreds have eased through the years, but some distrust may always remain. Prinny evidently thinks a visit by Clarence will help. Well, it doesn't signify talking. We will be obliged to go to Edinburgh."

"But where will we stay?" Lydia asked, ever practical. "I should think accommodations will be in short supply."

"It appears I have been remiss, my dear. We own a town house there."

Lydia stared. "Don't think me vulgarly inquisitive, Iain, but if, in addition to Torquay, you own Carrington House in London . . ."

The Earl chuckled and took her in his arms. "Did you think yourself in dun territory, my sweet?" he said. "You aren't, you know. I'm afraid the whole of my fortune is rather large. Quite immodest, in fact. Do you mind?"

"No, but we—I hadn't thought about it. It will take some getting used to. Is there—No!"

His lips twitched, but he said calmly: "Is there more? There is. If you are interested, my man of business will tell you all about it."

She had turned rather grave. "It seems—unfair," she said reflectively.

"My secretary would disagree. He will tell you that I give away far too much to charity. Perhaps I do, but I was brought up from the cradle in the belief that the strong must help the weak. My father, and his father before him, were philanthropists, so I suppose it's in the blood. Don't look so startled, sweet. I can well afford it." He paused, and added wryly: "Aunt Mary prophesies I will end my days in the poorhouse."

"Worse and worse," she observed. "I'd as lief not live there, but if you do, I imagine I could."

"Would you join me in poverty?" he said, his arms tightening about her. "Well, dear heart?"

"I would, but you needn't be concerned," she said. "You haven't given my wealth a thought, I know, but I inherited my grandmother's pearls."

He kissed her and said no more, but left her to sort through her wardrobe while he went to dress. Lady Lenora soon scratched on the door, for the Marquis had received the same royal summons. Among the dresses they selected to accompany Lydia to Edinburgh was a gown of silver tulle spangled all over with tiny diamonds and worn over an underdress of turquoise satin. Lydia would have liked to own a diamond tiara to wear with it, but put it out of her mind.

She had looked forward to the trip with a great deal of expectation. She was not only anxious to see Holyroodhouse, which the Earl had described to her in detail, she was equally eager to explore the castle and to visit the shops in the Royal Mile and on Princes Street. To her great joy, the day for setting forth dawned bright and clear. With no crisis occurring to delay their departure, the entire party started out surprisingly well on time. They had covered very little distance, however, when Lydia suddenly realized she had left her kitten behind. They must return for him; nothing else would do. He had been with her from the start, would be lost without her, and she could not enjoy herself from worrying about his welfare. The Earl set his teeth, ordered his coachman to return to the castle, and, when they pulled up before the door, went in search of the truant pet.

Returning, he tossed the tiny creature in her lap and took his place beside her. Lydia, hardly daring to turn her eyes to his face, made a great fuss over the kitten. She was looking her best in jonquil muslin, and a high-crown bonnet tied beneath her chin with yellow ribands. Perhaps this accounted for the Earl's saying something civil to her; at any rate, she became emboldened enough to glance at him and to say: "Don't you like cats?"

"What a ridiculous question!" he replied, his tone one of indifferent cynicism. "No, I do not."

"I don't understand why you should take that tone," she said with spirit. "Kitty is such a defenseless creature."

"You might understand it if you gave it thought, but I shan't pander to your vanity by explaining it."

"Well!" she said, casting an indignant look at him. "When have you pandered to me, I'd like to know!"

"Every morning when that animal crawls into our bed. Now are you satisfied?"

Lydia looked away. "Why must you always put me in the wrong?" she said, biting her lip. "I didn't know you minded."

"Of course I mind, you foolish child. What man wouldn't?"

She had been woefully obtuse, she now knew, but didn't intend admitting it. "I had looked forward to this ride with you, but if you are going to be disagreeable, I wish I'd gone in Papa's coach."

"I am not being disagreeable," he said. "On the contrary, I am being very pleasant, considering that I must share your attention with that confounded cat. Of one thing I am sure. Your Papa wouldn't."

She was a little mollified and said: "No, nor neither would Mama." Incurably honest, she was forced to add: "I should have sent him ahead with Letty."

The Earl fished his snuffbox from a pocket. "My knowledge of you led me to suppose you foisted him off on me in a spirit of pure mischief," he remarked, taking a pinch between finger and thumb. "Was I wrong?"

"Yes, you were. If you felt that way, why did you turn about for him?"

"Partly to please you, and partly to show you I can be damnably hard to fool."

"I was not trying— Oh! You are being abominable!"

"Yes, I know," he said, putting an arm about her. "I humbly beg your forgiveness."

She smiled a triumphant little smile and snuggled against his side. "Since you put it so prettily, I will accept your apology," she said. "Where do you suppose the others are?"

"Some distance ahead of us by now, I should think. It would appear your kitten has his uses."

The coach had been making steady progress and was fast approaching a stretch of woods near Garbat Forest. If the coachman noticed a group of horsemen winding their way among the trees, he thought nothing of it, for highwaymen customarily did not ply their trade so early in the day. When they had come abreast of the woods and he had realized his mistake, it was too late. A shot whistling alarmingly close to his head startled the groom, who dropped the blunderbuss in terror. A second shot set the horses swerving toward a ditch beside the road, and by the time the coachman brought the team under control, two ruffians clad in moleskin waistcoats had ridden up to point their weapons menacingly at his head. A third masked man leaned from his saddle, wrenching open the door of the coach and growling "Out!" while motioning with the pistol in his hand.

Lydia opened her mouth to protest, but the Earl stepped down in his leisurely fashion and held out his hand, the message in his eyes very clear to her. "Torquay, at your service," he said without a trace of emotion in his level voice, but with an arm protectively around her shoulders.

A coarse laugh greeted this polite remark. "Ye can stand aside, me 'earty, and be quick about it," the highwayman said in a rough voice. "Ye too, me pretty," he added to Lydia, swinging down from his horse.

It seemed as though he was not interested in Lydia's reticule or even in the contents of the Earl's pockets. With schooled thoroughness, he methodically searched the coach, pulling out the cushions and looking under the seats in growing exasperation. Evidently not finding what he sought, he climbed to the coachman's box, to subject it to the same exacting investigation. "They ain't 'ere," he then shouted to a fourth horseman waiting at the edge of the woods. "Ye want us to lope off?"

This produced a nod from the ruffian queried, but complaints from the other two. "Ye ain't looked in 'er purse," one of them growled.

" 'Tain't big enough," their leader snapped, and swung himself into his saddle. Turning to the Earl he said: "Ye'd best not follow us, or I'll put a ball in ye," and galloped away, trailed by the other two.

"Whatever do you make of it?" Lydia demanded, gazing after their retreating forms in amazement.

"I don't make anything of it," said the Earl, summoning up the groom. "I trust, Johns, when you have recovered your composure, you will replace the cushions."

The groom approached with his cap clutched in trembling hands. "You may wonder why I didn't fire, my lord, but . . ."

"Not at all. I commend you for quick thinking. Her ladyship's safety was involved. The cushions, if you please."

Johns, much relieved, hastened to obey him. The Earl handed Lydia into the coach and entered behind her; the steps were let up, the door was shut, and the vehicle moved forward on the road to Edinburgh. "I was sure they would take our valuables," Lydia remarked, craning her neck to peer out of the window. "What do you suppose they expected to find?"

"Certainly not a victim who enjoyed the encounter."

She drew in her head and flashed him a smile. "It was fun," she said gaily. "I daresay no lady I know has been accosted by robbers."

"I should hope not," he replied dryly. "Edinburgh will seem tame by comparison."

In this he was wrong. Lydia was ready to enjoy one experience as equally as another. When the coach drew up before a tall stone house in one of Edinburgh's finest neighborhoods, and a footman held the door wide, she crossed the threshold with a great deal of anticipation glowing in her eyes. The butler bowed and delivered himself of a speech welcoming her to Edinburgh, most properly done, and with all the not inconsiderable dignity he deemed suitable for the occasion. Lydia had no affectations, and smiled upon McTavish with so much sweetness that, as he later told Mrs. Leyton, she fair took his breath away. Not one trace of his approval was allowed to show on the studied impassivity of his countenence, however, and he turned her over to the charge of a second groom, who led her across the vast, marble-floored hall to a salon where her parents waited.

It was a lovely room, decorated in gold and white and with windows that looked out onto the square. The walls were hung with a patterned paper, and the draperies, of matching silk, were tied back with tassled cords. An Aubusson rug covered the floor and supported Louis XVI settees and chairs and innumerable small tables in the same style. A secretary with a drop front and the upper shelves enclosed in beveled glass doors stood between two windows, while a console table with a mirror above it occupied the space beside a door. Paintings in ornate frames, many of them by well-known artists, covered the walls, and attested to the taste and knowledge of the Earl's forbears.

Lydia crossed the threshold, then stood rooted to the spot, a startled exclamation rising in her throat, and stared blankly at the gentleman conversing with her mother. Sir Charles rose and crossed to bow over her hand, giving no sign at all that he was aware of her astonishment. "Your dear mother thought your arrival imminent," he remarked urbanely. "I have tarried overlong and taxed her patience, I know, but I could not bring myself to leave without first welcoming you to Edinburg."

"Oh?" said Lydia, coming close to snatching away her hand. "That is kind of you, but my husband has already done so."

Sir Charles smiled slightly and said: "Then I must content myself with second place."

Lydia's glance swept his face. "You flatter yourself, sir," she said, withdrawing her hand. "After my husband, there is my father, and my brother."

His brows drew together but, since Lydia moved across to seat herself beside her mother, there was little he could do but put a chair forward for himself. "I have many friends in the metropolis, Lady Lydia. It will be my pleasure to acquaint you with them," he said, the smile again upon his face.

"The Earl has as yet to tell me of his plans," Lydia replied in her calm way.

He turned to Lady Lenora. "Will you be offended with me, ma'am, if I presume upon short acquaintance and include you in the offer? Nothing would give me greater pleasure."

Lady Lenora had not the least notion of the cause of her daughter's coolness toward Sir Charles. She reflected, however, that Lydia had never lacked for sense. Accordingly she said: "You really must not press me, sir. We have only just arrived, and have as yet to confer with Torquay. Ah, here he is now. Perhaps you will discuss it between the two of you."

The Earl had indeed entered the room. If there was a certain lack of warmth in the gaze he turned on Sir Charles, he was too well-bred to speak his thoughts aloud. "Your obedient servant," he said. "I trust my people have looked after you?"

"No, no. I need no refreshment," Sir Charles hastened to reply.

The Earl's glance swept over the decanter of Madeira and on to the pot of tea. "Whiskey?" he said, and crossed to pull the bell. (Sir Charles accepted, but the Marquis declined, saying it was too early in the day for him.) "Yes, McTavish, I rang," he told the butler. "A bottle of whiskey and, yes, lemonade for her ladyship, if you please."

"Lemonade?" Lydia asked, brows raised.

"Precisely, my dear," said the Earl. "Unless you would prefer coffee?"

"It doesn't signify, so long as it isn't tea. Lemonade will be fine."

Lady Lenora watched the butler's stately exit from the room, and remarked with a touch of envy: "I must say, Torquay, there is no one whose servants are as well-trained as yours."

He bowed and turned the subject, noting the absence of Gerald and Jaimie. The Marquis chuckled. "They are off to see the town. Were I but twenty years younger, I dareswear nothing would have suited me better than to have joined them."

An answering twinkle shone in the Earl's eyes. "Perhaps both of us would have, sir."

Lydia held her peace. At any other time she would have chided him for a graybeard, but the presence of Sir Charles stilled her tongue.

McTavish came back into the room with a tray and set it upon a table. Sir Charles rudely helped himself to a glass of whiskey, pouring it out neat. A crease came between Lydia's brows, but she accepted the lemonade from his hand, thinking as she did so that his veneer had slipped. Whatever his background, he lacked the nicety of manner inherent in the ton.

"The youth of today want strength," Sir Charles remarked, resuming his seat. "When I was enjoying my salad days, a man was a man, regardless of his age. Nothing suited me better than a good set-to with my fellows, but times have changed. Young men nowadays are more prone to run from a fight than to stay and face it."

"You cannot be serious!" Lady Lenora exclaimed. "The flower of our youth are distinguishing themselves in the Peninsula, fighting, yes, and dying for England in the war with Bonaparte. Why, the Earl himself was wounded there." She spoke with unusual vehemence, her eyes fixed upon his face in decided reproof.

Sir Charles caught himself up short and attempted to laugh it off, but it was evident in the slight reserve that came over the room that his expatiations fell somewhat flat. A silence, which no one made much effort to break, soon fell, and Sir Charles at last rose to take his leave. The bell was pulled, a footman came to usher him out, and in a few minutes he was gone.

The Earl smiled slightly and drew a snuffbox from his pocket, opening it with the flick of a finger. "Are your accommodations to your liking?" he asked Lady Lenora, taking a delicate pinch of snuff between thumb and forefinger.

"I cannot conceive of better," she replied.

He shut the snuffbox and put it back into his pocket. "Shall we go upstairs, Lydia? You have yet to see your own."

Her eyes danced. "I was waiting for you to suggest it," she said.

"I thought you were," he replied, and went out of the room with her.

The Marquis glanced at Lady Lenora and said he didn't much care for Sir Charles. "I fancy he spells trouble. Torquay will do well to keep an eye on him."

"I'm sure he will. If you don't mind, dear, I'd rather not discuss it now. Nothing is more destructive to one's looks than worry over one's children."

The Marquis proved worthy of her trust in him. "There is nothing wrong with your looks, my dear," he said. "They have not gone off in all the time I've known you."

Upstairs the Earl was saying much the same thing to Lydia. But with a difference. He had locked the door and taken her in his arms, and stood kissing her, one large hand stroking slowly up and down her spine. She felt his fingers in her hair removing the pins that bound it and shaking it loose, to let it come tumbling down around her shoulders. Burying his hands in the curling mass, he drew her face to his and continued kissing her, his thumbs moving lightly over her cheeks until she quivered at the touch. He undressed her slowly and feasted his eyes on her slender form, his gaze roaming over her breasts thrusting pertly upward, rosy and ripe, and over her waist to her thighs. His arms closed around her again, his passion at fever pitch. Lydia trembled beneath his burning kisses, half suffocated by his ardor until, finally, she held him off and helped him remove his clothing. She ran her fingers lightly over the faint scar running diagonally down from his shoulder to his waist, and on downward still. The Earl gasped, and in a moment had swept her off her feet and carried her to the bed.

He murmured softly in her ear, barely intelligible words of love, and trailed kisses over her face and throat and to her breasts, and stroked his hands lightly over her skin until she writhed and clasped him close. He entered her then, slowly at first, and gently, then faster and faster, until finally, their passion spent, he withdrew from her and cradled her in his arms.

"You never did tell me how you received your scar," she murmured idly, touching it with a finger.

A glint came into his eyes. "If you tell me when you first noticed the mole beneath your tummy, I'll tell you how I received my scar," he teased, his chuckle filling the room.

There came a moment of silence. "I suppose," said Lydia, "that your mortifying excesses of a moment ago have emboldened you."

"My mortifying excesses, ma'am," replied the Earl, "have brought you to think yourself immune. No such thing."

"This malingering of yours is more suited to a beardless youth than to a Tulip of the Ton," she remarked, fitting her finest arrow to the bow. "It's a pity, but I don't think any harm will come of it," she added, loosing the shaft.

The shout of laughter that greeted this brought the color to her cheeks. "If I were a beardless youth," he said, "then I should pity you."

Lydia gave it up, and rose, wrapping the sheet about her. "It's a pretty room," she said, looking around.

The Earl crossed his arms behind his head and stretched out full length upon the bed. "I enjoyed having it decorated for you," he said, crossing his legs at the ankles. "Make any changes you wish."

"No, it's perfect as it is."

An outraged gasp brought her head around just as the kitten landed on his chest. Lydia rushed forward to retrieve her pet, became hopelessly entangled in the sheet, and collapsed giggling upon the bed.

"Oh, good God!" the Earl ejaculated, and stalked naked from the room.

CHAPTER TEN

On the following afternoon Lydia drove out with her mother in an open carriage to view the town. There was so much to see, so many sights to exclaim over. When they turned into Princes Street and proceeded along the broad avenue, Lydia gazed across the valley separating it from the Royal Mile, her eyes on the castle brooding protectively on its rock high above the city. There was never anything so wonderful; she could almost picture kilted soldiers at duty on the battlements, and almost fancied she could hear the swirl of pipes echoing over the rooftops far below. They spent an entrancing time going into the shops, and purchased a shawl for Lydia in the Carrington plaid. Back in their carriage, they traversed the road across the valley and turned into the Royal Mile. There was the well-known Forsyth's displaying tartans in its double windows beside the door. Nothing would do but that they stop. Lydia went into the shop, and came out again with a muffler for the Earl tucked under her arm. Going on up the street, they came at last to the magnificent wrought-iron gates before Holyroodhouse, and passed on through, to the forecourt before the Palace. Twin towers flanked the entrance façade with its platform roof and continuous balustrade, and above the doorway the great arms of the King of Scots caught and held the eye. Lydia gazed, enchanted.

When they returned home, she found the Earl waiting for her. The impending visit of the Duke of Clarence had precipitated a succession of social events such as Edinburgh had not seen in years. At any hour of the day footmen were to be seen delivering invitations for every conceivable form of entertainment to the homes of the socially select. McTavish, an excellent butler, found himself at a loss. He would have been affronted had the family not been the recipient of the gilt-edged missives, but never before had the evenness of his days been so interrupted by the doorbell sounding, as he told Mrs. Leyton, with monotonous regularity. Lydia, when confronted with the pile of invitations reposing on the Earl's desk, felt only dismay, and was perfectly content for him to accept or regret at his pleasure, only requesting they attend a drum given by the Countess of Hopetoun. Hopetoun House was situated beside the Firth of Forth, its neoclassic façade flanked on either side by forward-set pavilions, each of them joined to the main structure by curving colonnades. Built from designs of Sir William Bruce and William Adams, it was one of the celebrated houses in the neighborhood, and one Lydia was desirous of visiting.

They came on time to the drum, and were followed shortly by the Marquis and Lady Lenora, Gerald, and Jaimie. The Countess inquired after Lord Douglas and Lady Cavanaugh and, when informed they had remained at Torquay, Lady Cavanaugh being indisposed, passed the Earl and his party on to a footman, who took their cloaks and ushered them into the drawing room. Almost the first person Lydia saw was Sir Charles. He stood with several gentlemen before the marble chimneypiece, and his eyes met Lydia's with a curiously speculative expression in them. The Earl, observing him, steered Lydia to a settee pushed back against the wall, where Lady Cameron was seated. To his surprise she said: "There is no need to introduce your bride to me, Torquay. I knew her when she was a child. Her Mama and I were girlhood friends. Well, my dear, I see you have lived up to expectations. You have grown into a beautiful woman. Where is Lenora, by the way?"

Avoiding the amusement in the Earl's eyes, Lydia spread her skirts in a curtsy, and assured the Countess that her mother was right behind them, a circumstance that was immediately borne out by Lady Lenora's appearance upon the scene. Escaping under the flurry of reunion between the bosom-bows, the Earl next led Lydia to Lady McCraigie, who, in company with her daughter, was conversing with Gerald and Jaimie. A widow of several years' standing, Lady McCraigie, with a daughter now of marriageable age, had come out of seclusion to accompany Louisa to social affairs. That young Lord Jaimie's interest bid fair to become fixed upon her offspring had not escaped her notice. Thinking it a pity that Torquay's marriage could well produce an heir to the earldom ahead of Lord Jaimie, she nevertheless acknowledged the introduction to Lydia in her pleasant way, and soon bore her off to show her the wonders of Hopetoun House.

Explaining that the coved cornice of the ceiling, with its rococo spandrels at each corner, was the work of Robert Adam, she led Lydia on to a larger drawing room, also by Adam and perhaps the most elaborate chamber in the house. French and Chinese influences could be seen in the decoration of the ceiling, and the carved marble chimneypiece, executed by Michael Rysbrack of Antwerp, had draped female figures nearly seven feet tall at its ends, with a panel of cupids playing in between. Lydia wandered around the room, admiring the furniture by James Cullen, and exclaiming over the paintings and decorative mirrors.

When Sir Charles appeared at her side, she curtsied with obvious reluctance, and flushed a little at his insistence that she sit and chat. Having no ambition to further his acquaintance, she looked around for the Earl. Not seeing him, she turned her attention to Sir Charles.

"Shall we forget your husband for the moment?" he said, smiling. "There is no love lost between us, you know."

"Forget the Earl?" she said, staring at him in lively astonishment. "You forgot yourself, sir. You will remember that I am barely acquainted with you. Say no more."

"Your husband," he continued with deliberation, "has scant regard for your well-being. I had not intended to discuss it with you, but recent tidings have come to my ears that give rise to concern. You must put your faith in me, however much I might not relish being the one to cause alarm. What Torquay intended by exposing your person to danger, I have no way of knowing, but to hear of it was something of a shock to me. It was enough to assure me he poses a menace to you."

"This is beyond everything!" she exclaimed. "Have you been drinking?" she added, frowning.

"I am not indulging in conjecture; I wish I were, but Torquay did lead you into danger. Do not deny it, pray. Helene has already told me of your trip to the blow-hole, and a most treacherous undertaking it was, I own. Whether you could have been swept out to sea by the tide, I leave to you to decide."

She stared at him a moment and then said: "But the tide was out. The Earl picked a time when it would be, so you see, sir, you have no cause to meddle in our affairs."

"By no means, ma'am. I only thought to serve you."

A voice spoke immediately in front of them, saving Lydia the necessity of answering. She glanced up to see Lord Jaimie standing there. "I have looked all about for you," he said a little shyly.

"I'm glad," she replied, relieved. "Sir Charles is just on the point of leaving."

Sir Charles, caught, immediately rose and very soon moved away. "Do sit down," Lydia said to Jaimie. "When I saw you last, you were conversing with Miss McCraigie."

"I expect I was," he replied, laughing. "I can't tell you, ma'am, how glad I am you married Iain. The thought of stepping into his shoes gives me nightmares."

"Most young men would covet an earldom," she remarked, surprised.

"Not I," he replied cheerfully. "You'll never know my relief when he returned from the Peninsula all of a piece."

"Have you told this to Iain?"

"I rather fancy I haven't," he admitted, glancing at her sheepishly. "I had hoped you would make a push to help me. You will, won't you?"

Lydia looked astonished. "In what way?" she said.

"I want a career in the diplomatic service. I knew there wasn't a chance before, but now I'll not likely become the Earl, I should think it could be arranged. If you would put in a good word for me with Iain, he might secure a post for me."

"I will do what I can, of course, but I should think you could speak to him yourself."

"I intend to, but if you could, well, smooth the way?"

Lydia laughed and told him he was shameless, but she would be happy to assist. Catching sight of the Earl approaching, she added: "Here comes Iain now. You had best run along, Jaimie. If I am to plead your cause, it will not do at all for you to be present." She watched him retreat, and turned to smile at the Earl sitting down beside her.

He listened closely to her disclosure and said mildly, when she had finished: "The life may do very well for him."

"I didn't think much of the idea myself at first, but now I consider it, it does strike me, Iain. He possesses a certain presence and has a great deal of common sense."

But he shook his head. "He is too young and needs to be steadied. I will send him away to school for training. When he is ready, I will pull the proper strings. Are you enjoying yourself, my dear?"

"I was, until Sir Charles happened along."

The Earl put up his quizzing glass. "Would you care to elaborate on that remark?" he said.

"He expressed concern that you led me into danger, and not for the first time, you will recall. He seemed to think the excursion to the cavern ill-advised."

The Earl lowered his quizzing glass. "And how came he to know of it? Ah, yes. Helene. I think, my dear, you will avoid his company when possible, even at social gatherings. I will see to it that he avoids yours," he added dryly.

"Why?" she said. "Oh, I hope never to set eyes on him again, but that isn't it, is it? What are you thinking, Iain?"

"At the moment," he said, "I would rather not say. Shall we join the whist table in the anteroom?"

Sir Charles stood against one wall, watching their departure with hard eyes. Myrna McDougall, seeing him, went forward. "You play your cards poorly," she said. "Be warned, I beg you. Torquay is no fool."

He turned his head to survey her cynically. "Are you telling me how to handle the affair?" he asked softly.

"Someone must, if we are to get what we want. Your plans will be best served by serving mine."

"I quite agree with that, my dear Myrna, but may I say that your brothers hardly distinguished themselves?"

"How can you say that!" she replied stiffly. "They cannot be held to blame if you picked the wrong coach. We would have done better with the luggage."

"The luggage, as you well know, was situated between the coach bearing the family and another bearing the servants. Would you have had us attempt to stop all three?"

"Keep your voice down!" she hissed. "You can't know who may overhear you."

"Remember this, my dear. I don't need your assistance. You need mine. I have had the foresight to bribe a servant in Torquay's employ. If they brought them with them to Edinburgh, we will find them."

"Well, you just remember this! Unless we succeed in breaking up their marriage, your precious Lydia will remain beyond your reach. Or had you not thought of that?"

"I'll lay you odds that Lydia is more likely to fall to me than the Earl is to you."

"All you care about is money," she replied scornfully.

"Better money than a title for a bastard. I doubt you know yourself who sired the brat."

"I imagine I'm in a position to know who fathered my son," she said furiously.

"Don't fence with me, my dear. I know it wasn't Torquay. He might despise you, but he would have married you, regardless. Now I, I never would."

"You wouldn't have had the chance," she spat and, whirling on her heel, left him.

Sir Charles chuckled and went in search of likelier game. Coming upon Gerald in the small salon he said with forced cheerfulness: "Here you are, my boy. I've been looking for you as a matter of fact. It's no great thing, but I will be honored if you will be my guest at my club tomorrow. The stakes are low, and you may enjoy it."

Gerald looked pleased. "You're sure it won't cost the earth? I'm not too plump in pocket at the moment."

"Not a bit of it. You may even come away with your pockets stuffed."

"You think so? Well, I'm much obliged to you. There is one thing, Sir Charles."

"I will say nothing to Torquay. You may leave it safely in my hands. Shall we say twelve?"

"Just as you wish, of course, but I don't want you thinking I meant Torquay. It's m'father. He doesn't approve of gaming."

"He shall not be told of it," Sir Charles replied. "Until tomorrow, then."

Gerald arrived at Sir Charles's lodgings the next day precise on the stroke of twelve, and went with him to his club, his head in the clouds. He took his place at the table selected by his host, and stared at the rouleaux of guineas in front of players whose faces were masks to conceal any betraying emotion. Instead of the stakes being low, they were extremely high. Gerald, inexperienced, had no notion how to escape the trap, and so stayed on, flustered and losing heavily on each hand. Sir Charles, who held the bank, gently prodded and encouraged until, by the time the game broke up in late afternoon, quite a pile of Gerald's IOUs lay on the table before him.

Jaimie, when told of it, was aghast. "You're mad!" he gasped, shaken. "Where will you lay your hands on six thousand!"

"Devil a bit, I don't know," Gerald groaned, his head in his hands. "Oh, God! What am I to do? Think of something, Jaimie!"

"What?" Jaimie demanded. "We haven't a hundred between the two of us. What possessed you?"

"Lord, I don't know. Sir Charles promised the stakes would be low, but if you ask me, he egged me on."

"There is only one thing you can do. Tell your father."

Gerald shuddered. "You must be three parts mad, for God's sake. He would ante up, and I'd feel like a worm."

"Your sister, then."

"Sir Charles suggested that," Gerald admitted, much struck. "If you ask me, there is something smoky about him. Why do you suppose he wanted to bring Lydia into it?"

"I don't know, but if you'll take my advice, you'll tell Iain. I have myself, on occasion. I will say he always found a solution, and he didn't go top-lofty on me, as he well might have. And besides, Lydia is his Countess. He will be mighty picky where she is concerned, take my word for it."

Gerald, casting Jaimie a piteous look, mutely nodded and rose. "It's the devil's own business," he muttered ruefully, and went in search of Torquay.

He found him in his study. The Earl, who was seated before his desk, gave Gerald a fleeting glance and went on writing. "I will be with you in a moment," he said. "Help yourself to the Madeira."

"Thank you, no," Gerald said miserably, and sat down to wait, looking rather uneasily at the Earl's face.

Torquay, sensing the tension, laid down his pen. "How may I serve you?" he said pleasantly.

Gerald moistened his lips and took the plunge. When he ceased speaking, the Earl's calm expression had turned to stone. "Leave it in my hands," he said.

Gerald stiffened. "You cannot pay my debts, sir," he said indignantly. "Why should you, I'd like to know."

"I haven't said I would. And neither will you, may I add. Debts of honor are one thing; the tricks of a charlatan are something else entirely. As I said, leave it to me."

"But, sir . . ."

"I am afraid it isn't any use to argue. But let this be a lesson to you, Gerald. Never lose more than you can easily afford. In fact, my advice to you is this: Stay away from the tables for the time being. When you are older, you will know better."

Gerald suddenly grinned. "If you will allow me to speak, sir, I didn't come about my debts. I came to acquaint you with Sir Charles's strange suggestion concerning Lydia."

"Yes, I know. I'm not dull-witted. Neither am I a slow-top. If you think to go to a money-lender rather than face your father, banish the thought from your mind. We will discuss this further after I have seen Sir Charles."

Gerald was by now feeling very foolish, but he squared his shoulders and took his leave with a commendable show of dignity. The Earl watched him go, and swung over to the window, to stand staring thoughtfully out, a humorless smile curving his lips. Turning, he strolled from the room and went in his leisurely way down the stairs. Having requested the carriage brought around, and placing his beaver hat carefully on his head, he scrutinized his appearance in the long mirror over a console and picked up his gloves from the table. "Inform her ladyship I am going out," he told the footman on duty in the hall, and passed from the house.

Sir Charles occupied lodgings in a part of town that, while perfectly genteel, could not be ranked among the best. This did not trouble him in the least. Since the rent was reasonable, he was content. The

Earl, on being informed that his lordship was indeed at home, followed the porter up the stairs and down the hall. Sir Charles had slept until noon, and was partaking of breakfast in his dressing gown when a rap sounded on the door. "Come in," he said without looking up from his plate.

"Good afternoon," said the Earl briefly, crossing the threshold. "I trust you will spare me a moment."

Sir Charles started and dropped his fork. "Torquay!" he said after a moment. "I wasn't expecting you."

"I should rather have thought you would," remarked the Earl.

Sir Charles glanced at him covertly and offered coffee, which the Earl politely refused. Sir Charles turned sideways in his chair, and looked straight into a pair of steely eyes. A constriction came in his throat. He cleared it. "How may I serve you?" he said unsteadily.

"In several ways," replied the Earl.

Sir Charles's cup rattled in its saucer. He set it down. "You have but to tell me," he managed to say.

The answer was prompt. "You will first restore the IOUs you hoodwinked Gerald into giving you. Next you will retain the thought that the performance will not be repeated."

"I haven't the least notion what you mean," Sir Charles asserted, but with his eyes unable to meet Torquay's.

"I think you do. However, in case you don't, I am perfectly willing to jog your memory on the field of honor."

"A duel!" Sir Charles gasped. "You wouldn't!"

"Ah, but I would. Make no mistake about it." The

Earl spoke softly, but with a coldness in his tone that chilled Sir Charles to the marrow,

"You have made a mistake. I . . ."

"Cease lying to me, and we will understand one another tolerably well." The Earl fished his snuffbox from a pocket and flicked it open. "The IOUs, if you please."

Sir Charles shot him a surly look. "I protest, sir. A debt of honor . . ."

"Dishonor, more like," the Earl replied, taking snuff.

"There are those who will bear me out."

"You are, of course, at liberty to try. It will be for society to decide who speaks the truth. I think I will be believed before you. I trust I shan't be put to the trouble of requesting the vowels again."

Sir Charles reached a hand into the pocket of his dressing gown and brought out the slips of paper. "I hadn't intended keeping them," he said, passing them across to the Earl.

"On the contrary. I take leave to differ. You did," said the Earl, carefully storing the IOUs in a pocket. "We now progress to my final request. You will find it in your own best interest to keep your distance from my wife. Not only will you not choose to call at our home in the future, you will refrain from engaging my Countess in conversation, regardless of the circumstances. Nor will you find her name rising on your tongue in any company at all. I trust I have made myself clear."

Sir Charles forced a laugh. "There is no need for you to be insulting. If you came here to taunt me, I may feel obliged to take exception to it."

"Please do. Send your seconds around at any time. I

am generally not difficult to find. Just take care that your actions do not prove fatal." The Earl rose and picked up his hat. "That is all I have to say."

Sir Charles licked his lips. "Perhaps when you have had time to know me better . . ."

"I would rather know any man in all the world than you," the Earl said with unmistakable finality, and strolled from the room.

Lydia entered the Earl's box at the theater that evening in company with the Marquis and Lady Lenora, and was chatting with friends crowding in to visit when the Earl came in with a tall gentleman whom he introduced as Captain Turbull. The Captain murmured all the phrases expected of him, audaciously brushed the Earl aside, and attached himself to Lydia with an open admiration in his eyes that brought an answering twinkle to her own. The Earl, amused, laughingly accepted the usurpation and turned away to entertain Lady Lenora very creditably until the curtain rose.

The Captain maneuvered Lydia to a chair and promptly sat down beside her. "There is no blinking it," he said, grinning. "Torquay has all the luck. A middling scratch, and he is furloughed home. Now take me, for instance. I heroically stay and fight, and when I do return, I find him before me. There is no getting away from it, ma'am. It's grossly unfair."

She could not help laughing, but she shook her head and turned her attention to the stage, taking care not to glance at him again until the curtain rang down on the first act. Immediately it did, he stood. "If you have the slightest regard for one giving his all in the service of his country, you will stroll with me in the hall," he said, offering her his arm.

"If you apply yourself so assiduously on the battle-field, England has little to fear," she remarked, rising. "Do you invariably contrive to get your way?"

"Most of the time. No, don't look around for Torquay. I see no necessity for his coming along. Just turn your head and walk right past him."

"If he would permit my doing that, you must be very good friends indeed."

"He saved my life in the Peninsula, ma'am. He is now obliged to protect his handiwork. We may rely on his cooperation."

"You may elect to do sir, but I am not so sanguine."

The Captain executed a beautiful leg. "A good soldier knows when to retreat. Well, so be it."

The Earl had strolled up, and stood listening. "It is thoughtful of you to include me, Robert," he said, standing aside at the door of the box for Lydia to precede them into the hall. "You have reformed your ways since last I saw you."

"Iain, you dog. You didn't tell me she was so utterly lovely."

"I didn't? It must have slipped my mind."

The Captain's laugh rang out. "Slain by Eros, by gad," he chuckled, going through the door. "Well, don't worry, old boy. I shan't rat on you."

The thought that the Earl's wound must have been incurred in saving his friend's life struck Lydia, but she could discover nothing of it. Both gentlemen were ready to converse on any other subject, and paid her flattering court, but when they returned to their place to view the second act, she could only suppose the Earl's act a gallant one that, manlike, he refused to discuss.

During the second interval Lady Lenora bore Lydia

off to visit the box of friends, while the Earl and Captain Turbull strolled down the stairs in search of refreshment. They entered a salon to the left of the entrance doors where flunkies were moving among the throng distributing wine. The Earl picked up two glasses from a tray and turned to hand one to the Captain, then paused, his brows raised in sudden surprise.

Myrna McDougall had made her way through the crush of people and was standing beside the Captain, the suggestion of a smile curving her lips. "I hadn't expected to see you running tame," she said maliciously. "Where is Lydia?"

"Upstairs," he answered briefly. "Miss McDougall, may I present Captain Turbull? Myrna is a neighbor from near Torquay, Robert."

The Captain took the hand she held out to him, and lightly kissed it. "Your obedient servant, ma'am," he said politely.

Her eyes assessed him briefly and swung back to the Earl. "You haven't come to call," she said. "Indeed, several of my friends have wondered at it, yes, and remarked about it too. I should think you would wish to preserve appearances, even if you don't set much store by them."

"I imagine," he said dryly, "that I do set store by them."

"And what am I to understand by that?" she demanded crisply.

"Why, only that I am apprehensive of bringing your name to public notice," he replied blandly.

"You must know I don't care a rush for what the gossips say. Nor did you used to."

"Ah, but in this instance," said the Earl, "my motives are more chaste by far."

"That is something new for you," she snapped, and was gone on the instant.

The Captain watched her go, and turned to gaze at the Earl with a look of total amazement in his eyes. "My dear fellow, tell me about her. I have yet to see a more beautiful woman."

"Don't, I beg you, sing her praises to me."

"Good God! This won't do at all. Marriage must have blinded you."

"Possibly so, but the fact remains she was feeding Lydia poisoned candy. Yes, you do well to stare. I daresay it may sound conceited, but Myrna's excessively fanciful imagination has led her to suppose that Lydia can be made to terminate our marriage."

"Well, upon my word! Lucrezia under a beautiful façade, eh?"

"Quite, but I trust you will see your way clear to cultivate her acquaintance. I have need of your not inconsiderable ability with the fairer sex."

"By all means, dear boy. What would you have me do?"

"Just keep your ear to the ground," replied the Earl. "There is one thing, Robert. The charmer has four brothers who would like nothing better than to acquire a name for her nameless son. You will do well to tread with care. Before you ask, no, I am not its sire," the Earl added, and led his laughing friend upstairs.

The Captain had no difficulty at all in attaching himself to Myrna in the days ahead. They naturally attended the same routs and balls that enlivened the week prior to the arrival of the Duke of Clarence on the scene, but if he was successful in gaining her notice, he learned nothing of interest to the Earl. If Lydia disapproved of what she could only think a budding romance, no one could have suspected it from her demeanor. Sorry only that no propitious moment arose to mention it to the Earl, she put it from her mind.

CHAPTER ELEVEN

To Lydia's astonishment, Clarence's entrance into the city was accomplished with a surprising lack of pompous display. His coach was escorted to the Palace by troops of the Scots Grays, his Grace stepped down, acknowledged the plaudits of spectators held at bay behind the gates, and vanished through the door. All of this she learned from Letty that evening when, dressed for the reception, she stood gazing at her reflection in the long mirror. She was wearing the silver and turquoise gown, and her hair had been arranged by a professional hairdresser brought to the house for the purpose. Lacking further jewelry, she fastened her grandmother's pearl choker around her throat and left her rooms.

The Earl, when she arrived downstairs, was discovered in his study with a casket in his hands. "Here you are, my dear," he said, smiling. "I was just on the point of going upstairs. I had the Torquay diamonds cleaned for you."

"Good heavens!" she said faintly. "I didn't know there were—do you mean there is a . . ."

"A tiara?" he said, amused. "There is. Were you feeling ill-used?"

She was staring at him as if she could not believe her ears. "It is nothing to laugh about," she said. "I am persuaded all the ladies will be wearing one. I will confess I was feeling positively naked."

He gave a shout of laughter. "Shall we forego the reception and remain at home? I'm not averse to pursuing the possibility in the privacy of your room."

"Don't be absurd, you abominable creature," she said, going forward. "Must you keep me in suspense?"

Chuckling, he settled the tiara firmly on her head and stationed her before a mirror. "Oh!" she breathed, gazing rapturously at the diamonds glittering and sparkling amid her curls.

"The family jewels have been at the bank since my mother's death," he remarked, sorting through the collection of gems in the box. Lydia could only stare while he fastened a bracelet about each arm and slipped a ring on her finger. "It is gratifying to know," he said, "that you will appear before the ton adequately clothed."

The inner court of Holyroodhouse was surrounded by an arcaded loggia, and had fluted pilasters with Doric capitals on the ground floor, Ionic on the first floor, and Corinthian on the second. The Earl's party moved along the open gallery to the main flight of stone steps leading to the state apartments on the first floor. The long gallery, where the reception was to be held, was thronged with ladies gowned in every conceivable hue, and gentlemen in the full dress of their respective Clans. Lydia, glancing around, thought the

Earl the most magnificent of them all. A great ruby gleamed in the lace at his throat, another flashed fire on a finger. In one hand he carried a scented handkerchief, in the other a gold snuffbox studded with tiny rubies.

At precisely nine o'clock the door to the King's guard hall opened, and the Duke of Clarence entered. When it came Lydia's turn to be presented, she sank into a deep curtsy, and rose in one exquisitely graceful movement, her eyes twinkling into his rather protuberant blue ones. "My dear Countess," he said, a smile wreathing his good-humored face. "I'm not skilled at pretty speeches, but I will say I envy Torquay. For my part, I don't wonder he chose to marry you. When next you visit London, we must engage to think of some entertainment for you."

Lydia murmured the proper civility in return, and surprised him by adding: "I was nervous at the thought of meeting you, your Grace, but there was no need to be. You are quite easy to talk to, you know."

He chuckled, delighted, and took her hand in his. "Bless my soul, you are a charmer," he said, and raised her fingers to his lips. "You may depend on it, Torquay will be ordered to bring you south. Yes, that is just what I shall do. It's a famous notion. You can have no objection, I trust?"

Lydia assured him she hadn't, and stood chatting with him until he drew her presentation to a close. Moving away, she realized that every eye was on her. To hold Clarence's attention a full ten minutes was unprecedented, and caused a sensation among the assembled company. Lydia thought little of it, but the effects of her success were to be felt in the days ahead. She could not have prevented society from describing her triumph, any more than she could have prevented its members discussing it among themselves. Everywhere she went, she met with flattering words and envious smiles. This circumstance provided her with a fair idea of what she would be forced to endure until they returned to Torquay, and made her look forward to the date of departure with a good deal of anticipation. On the morning following the reception, however, she had no way of knowing this.

Awakening late, she was aware of disappointment to find the Earl already risen, and rose herself to ring for coffee. Letty, arriving hard on the heels of Mrs. Leyton, appeared to be in a state of extreme agitation. Lydia instructed the housekeeper to put the tray on a table before her elegant French settee. She then sat down and poured out a cup. "Letty, cease wringing your hands, I beg you," she said. "You are making me nervous."

"'Tis well we all should be, my lady," Letty replied, thrusting her hands behind her back. "It's right worried I am."

"Oh, for goodness' sake! Pray, do sit down and tell me what this is all about."

"It's about—I don't rightly know what it's about, my lady," Letty gulped, perching gingerly on the edge of a chair. "Several times lately I've thought your ladyship's belongings had been disturbed—you know how careful I am, my lady—but I couldn't be sure. Perhaps I should have mentioned it before now," she hastened to add, "but nothing was missing; just more tumbled about, like."

"Tumbled about?" Lydia repeated in surprise.

"Mayhap I should say replaced. Your ladyship's

wardrobe has been gone through, and the drawers aren't quite as I left them."

"But you said nothing is missing," Lydia protested.

"It's my belief young Timothy had something to do with it, my lady. Last evening while your ladyship was out, I ran spank into him in the upstairs hall. I'm not one to accuse as where there isn't cause, but what is an underfootman about to be upstairs? He has no business coming here without someone has told him to. He knows that well enough."

"Thank you for telling me, Letty. I will mention it to his lordship. And now, if you will lay out the yellow muslin, I will dress."

The problem was, in fact, resolved the moment Lydia told the Earl of it. He cast her one penetrating look, and rang for McTavish. In answer to the butler's explanation that the underfootman was new to the household, having come highly recommended by Sir Charles Brodie, the Earl said, briefly: "Dismiss him."

McTavish's customary composure momentarily deserted him. "My lord?" he said, staring.

"Without a reference," the Earl amplified. "In future, you will refrain from hiring servants referred to you by either Sir Charles or the McDougalls."

Lydia glanced at him swiftly. Dismissal seemed unnecessarily harsh in view of the fact that the infraction was a minor one. Waiting only until McTavish withdrew, she said: "Why are you making a big thing of it?"

The Earl shot her a quizzical look and picked up the pen from his desk. "I have never tolerated laxity on the part of my staff," he said, mending the pen.

"That is not what I mean, as you very well know.

Why are you so particular about persons recommended by Sir Charles and the McDougalls?"

The Earl went on mending the pen. "It would appear their standards do not equal ours," he said, drawing a sheet of crested paper toward him.

A martial light came in her eye. "The McDougalls referred no servant to us. You haven't answered my question."

"I am sorry if my reply disobliged you," he remarked, dipping the pen in the standish. "It is better to avoid problems before they arise. I'm sure you will agree."

"Oh!" Lydia stormed, stamping her foot. "You are the most abominable—the most unfeeling . . ."

The Earl leaned back in his chair, the ink slowly drying on the pen while he studied her. "My dear," he began in his maddeningly imperturbable way, "we were accosted by highwaymen in what must surely be the strangest non-robbery in the annals of crime. Your brother became ensnared in a web of lies, and now your belongings have been searched. You have but to consider."

Her lips parted, and she gazed at him intently. "You think there is a connection?" she demanded after a moment.

"I am rather afraid I have forgotten whether I do or not."

Sir Charles, she thought, recalling the numerous instances in which he had made her the target of his attention. Precisely what his purpose was in encroaching on their privacy she could not know, but he would soon discover they could also play the game. "I'm sorry if you don't like it," she said in tones that left no doubt she did not regret it in the least, "but I'm sure I can get the truth from Sir Charles. I need only culti-vate his friendship, and in no time at all I will have him round my thumb."

His brows shot up. "Good God!" he ejaculated incredulously. "Have you lost your senses? You will stay away from him! He's a degenerate gamester, made desperate by his losses. He will cavil at nothing that will serve his ends—nothing, do you hear?"

"I should imagine everyone in the house does," she replied, controlling herself with a strong effort. "You needn't shout. I have no notion of doing anything in-discreet."

"If you think yourself a match for him, you are very green indeed," he shot at her, but in lowered tones. "You must know his reputation as well as I do. If he took it into his head to act in some gothic fashion, you would lack the strength to oppose him. I cannot always be conveniently at hand."

There came a pause. "I shouldn't seek to be alone in his company," she said.

"The matter is now perfectly clear," he replied with a touch of sarcasm. "Having encouraged his attentions in public and eluded them in private, he would have no reason to suppose your interest had settled impar-tially on him. Don't be a ninny, Lydia. He would im-mediately contrive to get you alone. Very much alone."

She gave a gasp. "Do you think me a fool!" she de-manded, the martial light back in her eyes.

"I can't account for it otherwise," he replied without a trace of emotion in his level voice.

She regarded him keenly. "You are changing the subject of our original discussion," she said.

"I am. If I can hoodwink you so easily, my dear, what chance have you against Sir Charles?"

"You flatter yourself. You are merely my husband."

A twinkle came into his eyes. "Now I come to think of it, that does have its advantages. At least there are times when being 'merely a husband' is worth the candle."

She drew a deep breath. "Perhaps I should snuff it out," she said with difficulty.

"I hardly think you would succeed, my dear. I promise you I would only rekindle the flame."

She looked a trifle flustered, and avoided the amusement in his eyes. "It isn't as though I desire Sir Charles's company," she said rather faintly. "It is only that—that . . ."

"That you relish being in at—shall we say?—the kill. I naturally understand your maidenly repugnance at the very thought of gore, but I hardly think it will come to that. So you see, my dear, you won't miss a thing. The ending will be quite tidy."

"Is that all you are going to say?" she demanded in militant accents.

"Alas, I fear it is."

"Well!" she said, goaded. "I shan't come to cuffs with you! Thank you for your time, sir!"

"My time is yours," he replied, coming around his desk. "Can't you find it in your heart to be civil to me?"

"But of course," she said stiffly. "I am civil to everyone."

He smiled and caught her hands in his. "Shall we consign tonight's ball to the devil, my love?" he asked softly, pulling her toward him.

"No," she said rudely, and pulled away from him.

"Thank you, but I am attending with my parents."

Lydia felt confident she would find enough partners to get through the ball without the mortification of sitting neglected while others danced the hours away. Coming away from the wretched verbal conflict already regretting her hasty words, she found her mother waiting for her in the drawing room. "Lydia, dear, you should know better than to argue with a man. Never give one the satisfaction of knowing he has succeeded in vexing you. I recall your great-aunt Lelia—she died before you were born, I think—and a sweeter creature you cannot imagine. I liked her excessively. Well, she let her husband get the upper hand, and it wasn't long before he dictated her every conscious thought. And some unconscious ones as well, I'm sure. Let me warn you, my dear, never bandy words with Torquay."

Lydia soon found it was only the first of many pieces of marital advice Lady Lenora seemed determined to impart. She discovered that a husband's feet must early be made to trod the path most advantageous to his spouse. She also learned that, to this end, no wife must allow any special date to pass without receiving a costly token of her husband's esteem; that every wife must be possessed of jewelry sufficiently in keeping with her rank and station; and that a wife need extend to her husband only those favors most pleasurable to herself. "It isn't that I mean to imply you should deny Torquay his rights, for I'm sure I never denied your father his. But some women . . ." Lady Lenora ground to a halt. Having backed herself into a corner, she had no idea how to extricate herself.

But Lydia only laughed. "You are such a baby, Mama," she said, and added, scandalizing her mother:

"You have got it put all about. If you will talk of conjugal rights, I will have to say Torquay would find himself in the suds if he thought to neglect mine."

Fortunately for Lady Lenora, who was displaying alarming signs of going into shock, McTavish entered to announce morning callers, and the next moment found her too much engaged in welcoming guests to pay further heed to her daughter.

That evening Lydia, for reasons best known to herself, seemed determined to sparkle brighter than the diamonds around her throat. There were prior acquaintances to be greeted, and new ones to be charmed. It was soon seen, from the circle of admirers crowding around her, that the evening would be termed successful. She moved gaily through the steps of the country dance, whirled over the floor in time to the waltz, and danced the quadrille with grace and skill. No one, unless watching very closely indeed, would have noted how often her eyes sought the door. Nor would it have occurred to the revelers, had any of them noticed, that she was unfashionably pining away for her own husband.

As it turned out, she was dancing with Lord Jersey when the Earl came strolling into the room, and so was unaware of his presence until he walked onto the floor and summarily pulled her from her partner's arms. She saw him laugh down at her, and in an instant his arm was about her waist and she was swept into the steps of the waltz. "Must you behave so reprehensibly?" she asked, smiling up into his face in the most fetching way imaginable. "I'm sure poor Lord Jersey feels ready to sink."

"How was he to know you prefer dancing with me? I am merely obliging you."

"There is no accounting for the very queer notions you take into your head. Before you became too puffed up with your own conceit, I should tell you my object in being here on the floor with you is to keep an eye on Captain Turbull. If Myrna McDougall behaved as charmingly as she looks, she would not have stood up with him no less than six times. What I think of your friend's opportunism, I prefer not to say."

Unexpectedly, his laugh rang out, drawing the curious stares of those dancers nearest them. "Do you mean to say I am to swallow that fling?" he said, unrepentant. "What a sad disappointment you have in store. Robert is making up to Myrna at my request. You should appreciate his sacrifice. I do, for I found myself incapable of snuggling up to her."

"Well, I should think you had better. And you needn't look so smug. You have much to answer for, you know. Why hadn't you told me of this?"

"There is no pleasing a female," he replied, grinning down at her. "After all, I could have forced myself. I am no less resourceful than Robert."

"Then you shouldn't deprive yourself of the pleasure, now, should you? If you are wondering how little you can get by with telling me, disabuse yourself of the thought. I have my own methods, sir, which you will find out soon enough."

A frown came upon his brow. "What cork-brained scheme are you hatching now? I promise you that, whatever it is, I won't permit it."

"Oh?" she said, lifting her chin. "You can hardly refuse hospitality to any guest I choose to invite into our home. I intend," she went on calmly, "to stick to Myrna like glue. I have only to behave toward her with exquisite contempt, and she will be forced to repay me in kind. Tongues tying themselves in knots have a way of flapping, you know. You need only tell me the direction of her babble and leave the rest to me."

"I haven't a clue," he replied, the merest hint of a smile coming into his eyes. "Robert and I are trusting to luck. About what, I haven't the foggiest."

Startled, she stumbled and trod on his foot. "Are you quite sure," she said, after a pause, "that you haven't taken another maggot into your head? I daresay you are correct in your assumptions about Sir Charles—from what I've seen of him, I would say he fills the bill right down to his shoes—but Myrna's propensity for speaking her mind would rule her out, I should think."

"Not at all," he said, fitting her steps to his. "She can be devilish clever when she stands to profit by it. Who would know that better than I?"

"Well, you needn't look so—so martyred."

"Why not? I feel a martyr. If you are determined to drape the mantle of sleuth around your shoulders, I daresay it will fall to me to lure your quarry within reach. Unfortunately, that means I must dance with Myrna. Smile, dear. You are only receiving your just deserts."

"I am smiling," she replied, while continuing to frown at him. "You are entitled to your pleasures, of course. It remains to be seen whether you will spend the rest of the evening in propping up a wall."

Why the Captain felt so much relief at turning his charge over to the Earl he could not have said, except that there was something about Myrna that made him instinctively want to run and hide. He didn't, of course. Instead, he sought out Lydia and promptly asked her to stand up with him. It was perhaps fortunate for her that he steered her around the opposite end of the floor from where the Earl was cavorting about with Myrna. Being left little opportunity for monitoring the progress of his heroic sacrifice, she was able to enjoy the pleasure of gliding about the floor in the arms of a skilled performer. By the time the waltz came to an end, the Captain had elicited from her the whole story behind the Earl's sudden and, to the Captain's mind, thoroughly incomprehensible desire for Myrna's company. That he intended to contribute his mite to the effort became clear to her only after she had returned home in the wee hours of the morning. The Earl was ascending the stairs by her side when she turned her head to look at him. "Did you enjoy your evening, sir?" she said, raising her brows archly.

"You would be disappointed if I said I hadn't," he replied with perfect truth.

A complacent little smile curved her lips. "Where you acquired your unamiable opinion of me, I cannot imagine. Well, never mind. I expect the shock will pass."

"I don't think you unamiable. I think you a temptress carelessly committing the folly of baiting me."

"Dear me. Threats, sir?"

"I cannot admit that to be true. I never threaten."

They had arrived before the portal to her rooms by now, so she allowed the remark to pass. She had expected him to proceed on to his own quarters, but he opened her door and followed her in. She looked at him in surprise. "Won't your man be expecting you?" she said.

"I took the liberty of telling him not to wait up for me." His chuckle filled the room. "You may have noticed by now that your maid hasn't waited up for you."

She was silent for a moment, and then said, crossing to her dressing table: "It is just as well. I wish to discuss the problem of Myrna. I think I will first invite her to tea. If that works out, we can host a dinner. Do you think the Captain will agree to assist us?"

He was watching her in amusement. "He assured me he would cooperate, but I can't say he was in raptures over it."

"Well, I can't blame him for that. Neither are we. I was wondering, Iain, if we shouldn't be wise to fill the house with people. Conversation is less inclined to lag when there are sufficient numbers to contribute to it. If Myrna is entertained, she will be less likely to be put on her guard."

"The devil fly away with Myrna," he said, coming up behind her. "I will tell you that, as your husband, I have heard enough talk for one night."

"But we need to finalize our plans."

"On the contrary, you need to start undressing before you find your gown in shreds."

"You wouldn't!" she purred, laughing up at him over her shoulder.

Cupping her face in his hands, he tilted her head back against his chest and bent down over her. "You don't really think I wouldn't," he murmured against her lips, and pressed his mouth to hers. Lydia reached up and put her hands on his, holding his lips to hers, and thrilling to the touch of his fingers moving lightly over her throat and chin. He lifted his head once and gazed at her, his eyes gone stormy gray, before he bent to her again, his hands moving downward to her breasts. Lydia gasped, and shivered, and went limp, as she always did when he touched her. And when finally he raised up and took her hands in his to pull her up into his arms, she went eagerly into them, and collapsed in some disorder against his chest.

CHAPTER TWELVE

The Earl entered Lydia's sitting room late the following afternoon, and surprised a curious expression on her face. She was seated before her desk with the chair pushed back, a crumpled sheet of paper in her hand. His step slowed only imperceptibly before he came on forward, and bent to kiss her cheek lightly. "Forgive my curiosity, but shall I go away again?" he inquired quite gently.

"I beg your pardon?" she said, gathering her scattered wits.

He put forward a chair and sat down facing her. "I had no notion of interrupting your thoughts, my dear. Are they so very vexing?"

"She is without a doubt the most hateful, ill-bred creature—just read this!"

The Earl accepted the paper she thrust forward, and smoothed the wrinkled sheet. "I fail to understand your problem," he remarked, scanning the few lines of writing scrawled untidily across the paper. "It seems perfectly clear to me."

"She could have shown me common courtesy and given me a reason!"

"Good manners are seldom palatable to those who choose to scorn them."

"But to say only that she declines my invitation—Oh! I think her conduct perfectly scandalous!"

"That should come as no surprise to you, my dear. Her conduct has never been anything but scandalous."

"And what is more, she is heartless. I am sure there can be nothing more revolting than the sight of a single woman casting out lures to a married man!" She paused and glanced at him, but since he showed no disposition to answer the remark, she continued: "It is unfortunate that the Captain has been thrown so much in her company. I wonder that you aren't aware of the danger. Myrna has been bred up from the cradle to think that any caprice she finds amusing is quite acceptable. She wouldn't hesitate to break the Captain's heart. I shudder merely to think of it."

"I find that extremely unlikely, my dear. Robert is capable of reading her character, believe me. I have no wish to enact the heavy husband, but I should hate to see you lash yourself into a frenzy over a matter beyond your control."

If Lydia didn't go to quite that extreme, she did remain irate. By the end of the day the keen edge of her temper had worn less sharp, but enough anger remained for the Earl to know, when he stood watching her descend the stairs, that his love was in a stormy mood. Not a propitious beginning, surely, for a night destined by fate to yield a bountiful harvest.

The fete that evening was given by Lord and Lady Calhoun. The Earl's carriage joined the long line moving slowly forward to set down their occupants one after another before the door. The anterooms were crowded, though a great many of the guests had already moved up the broad staircase to the ballroom running across the front of the house. Prejudiced as Lydia was in favor of its counterpart at the castle, she had to consider the large chamber stately and grand. Floor-to-ceiling windows ran down the long side of the room overlooking the street, while gilt-framed mirrors occupied corresponding embrasures along the opposite wall. Lydia, glancing around, had the felicitation of perceiving many acquaintances in attendance, and was soon observed shaking hands and chatting with them. The Earl, meanwhile, was making Captain Turbull known to those persons whom he had not previously met. His handsome appearance and soldierly bearing were sufficiently outstanding to hold the feminine eye, but it was the information he could impart on the progress of the war in the Peninsula that made him eagerly sought after by the gentlemen and ladies alike.

The sound of a fanfare brought a hush over the room, and the next moment the Duke of Clarence entered, escorted by various officials of the city and high-ranking officers of the Scots Grays. Moving around the ballroom, he paused to bow and shake hands, and to exchange a remark here and there. When he arrived before Lydia, she curtsied, expecting him to move on, but he took her hand in his and led her to the floor, remarking as they went that he had looked forward to opening the ball with her. Lydia didn't believe a word of it, of course, thinking it more likely the thought had only occurred to him on the spur of the moment, but she murmured something appropriate, and concentrated on following his steps as he steered her rather ponderously around the ballroom floor. She knew them to be under the scrutiny of every eye in the room, and felt many must be watching them in amusement. He was enjoying himself hugely, and his face was wreathed in smiles, but Lydia felt only relief when other couples joined them on the floor and they became less conspicuous. The dance ended, Clarence restored her to the Earl and lingered to pay her perfectly affable court. Unable to bring a period to the flow of his rather labored apostrophizings, she cast the Earl a look of such entreaty that he abandoned his air of disinterested abstraction and bestirred himself to send Royalty politely on its way.

It was much later in the evening when Lydia saw the Captain approaching with Myrna on his arm. A glance at his face was enough to warn her to conceal her annoyance. "My dear Lydia, nothing could be more wonderful!" he said, the message very plain in the glance he turned on her. "Myrna has agreed to go down to supper with us."

It took a strong effort, but Lydia swallowed the gorge rising in her throat and said: "We're glad to have her, I'm sure."

"Indeed?" said Myrna. "Why should you be? You hate me almost as much as I despise you."

Lydia gasped. A little color stole into her cheeks, but she managed to say in protesting accents: "How can you talk so?"

"How else should I talk?"

An uncomfortable silence fell; the Captain had glanced away from Myrna, and was staring unconcernedly across the room, to Myrna's obvious amusement. Lydia felt compelled to say something, anything, and searched her mind. "I understand Royalty plans to leave on the morrow," she produced finally. "I'm sure we will long remember the gaiety his visit has given rise to."

"You may be in raptures over it, but for my part I don't see what there was to make so much of it," Myrna replied. "But then, I was not the recipient of Clarence's partiality."

Lydia's hands became clenched at her sides. She turned her head away and said in some confusion: "You cannot be unaware that he doesn't stand on ceremony."

"I should imagine he doesn't," Myrna said, laughing harshly. "If you think to supplant Mrs. Jordan in the role of Royal mistress, you will need to consider his children. I hear he fairly dotes on them."

Lydia stood rooted to the spot, quite bereft of speech. She would have given all she possessed in the world to be able to deliver Myrna a ringing blow across the mouth. It was not possible, however. She could only clothe herself in the not inconsiderable dignity at her command and allow herself to say: "That is a great deal too bad, is it not? I will be forced to return to Torquay in the company of my husband."

"And society will then applaud?" Myrna remarked in biting accents.

Lydia looked straight into the most hate-filled pair of eyes she had ever encountered. "There is nothing more reassuring to a woman than knowing she is under the protection of a husband," she said with commendable composure.

Myrna made a contemptuous gesture. "There has

been enough of this posturing," she said. "Every word you utter only convinces me I'm better off without Torquay."

Lydia's lip curled. "I seem to have acquired the notion he found it necessary to put the Channel between himself and your charms," she said, the battle fairly joined.

That the barb struck home could be seen by the glint in Myrna's eyes. "You forget, I think, that I have brothers. They may choose to bring Torquay to book, should word of this reach their ears. You will do well not to sully my name with scandal."

"Why should I? You seem to have a knack for besmirching it yourself."

"I could say the same of you," Myrna replied, eyes flashing. "How dare you!"

This way of putting the matter did little to cool Lydia's heated brow. "This discussion is leading nowhere," she said, holding onto her temper with an effort. "If you will excuse me, I will terminate it."

Myrna abandoned all effort at self-control. "Running to hide behind Torquay, are you?" she spat, giving full rein to her passions. "Let me advise you to seek your protection elsewhere, Countess. He played the coward before your eyes," she added in heedless satisfaction. "A fat lot of protection you had on the way to town."

The breath caught in Lydia's throat. "You are referring to the highwaymen?" she said not quite steadily.

"I daresay you would like to deny it," Myrna answered smugly. "Torquay, at your service," she mimicked in dulcet tones.

Lydia looked at her for a moment, then turned away. She took the arm the Captain held out to her, and went out of the room without saying another word.

"Forgive me for not coming to your aid," he said, smiling ruefully down at her. "You were doing so well I hesitated to intrude. Talkative chit, isn't she."

"Very. For a minute there I feared I would be unable to goad her into saying something indiscreet. I had no way of knowing just how foolish she can be."

"Thank God she is," he replied, grinning irrepressibly. "I'm off the hook. If you ever need a favor, Lydia, you have but to whistle."

It was some time before they located the Earl in an anteroom, in conversation with a group of gentlemen. He caught sight of them and beckoned, but by the time they came up to him the Captain had given it as his opinion that she wait on privacy to divulge her news.

She had no opportunity of doing so, in any event. Except for a moment when the Marquis and Lady Lenora preceded them into the house upon their arrival home following the fete, she wasn't alone with the Earl an instant. Crossing to the stairs, she paused with one foot on the bottom step and glanced at the door into the drawing room, which he was on the point of passing through in the wake of the Marquis. The Earl, in a way he had, sensed the uncertainty in her posture, and strolled across the hall to take her hand in his. "What is it, my dear?" he said.

"Nothing that won't wait," she replied. "Run along and enjoy your nightly coze with Papa."

"I will be up shortly," he said, raising her fingers to his lips.

Lydia touched his cheek and went on up the stairs. Looking back over the past weeks, she could not have said whether she had enjoyed herself or not. Everyone agreed that never before had such a variety of entertainments taken place, and everyone was sure that the Duke of Clarence's presence had enlivened the scene. All Lydia knew was that she would much rather have been alone with the Earl. Some time later she heard him mounting the stairs, and turned expectantly toward the door, only to hear his step pass on by. Dismayed, she ran out into the passage. "I have been waiting this age," she informed his retreating back. "Where are you going?"

He paused before his bedroom door and smiled. "To change my clothing. The thought of coming to you in full evening dress is quite appalling, believe me."

"I have something to tell you, but that can't signify, of course. As always, you will do just as you please."

"I would never express it in quite the same way, my dear."

"You needn't set tongue in teeth on my account. I have no notion of throwing myself at your head."

"I perceive the night is going to surpass even my fondest expectations," he said, and chuckled to see her flounce back into her chamber for all the world like an infuriated kitten.

When he strolled in some fifteen minutes later, he found her room in darkness. Moonlight filtering through the curtains provided just enough light for him to discern her slender form hunched up in the very center of the bed. She had pulled the covers so high only the top of her head was visible, and was now pretending sleep. The Earl grinned in the dark and went around lighting the candles. "I wonder what I should do," he remarked, strolling up to stand looking down upon tumbled curls. "Mrs. Leyton, quite properly, felt it unnecessary to make up my bed. It is all very well for you, my dear, but it's curst awkward for me. It would be cold sleeping on the floor."

A muffled expletive that sounded to his lordship much like an oath greeted this sally, and Lydia jerked the covers higher still.

"It seems extraordinary that a gentleman who owns no less than three homes should find himself without a place to lay his weary head."

Her head shot out from under the quilts. "When that gentleman happens to be an odiously abominable creature, it isn't to be wondered at," she said, and dove back under the covers.

"Very handsomely put," he remarked, removing his dressing gown and tossing it across a chair. "The thing is, a notion occurred to me at the fete that I thought might interest you. If I am laboring under a false impression, I beg your indulgence. Come to think of it, I beg your pardon. Ladies should never become involved with crime."

The covers twitched. (He grinned and waited expectantly. He was not disappointed.) Her face emerged to view. "You know about the McDougalls?" she said, eyes round.

"I am beginning to wonder. Enlighten me."

"Myrna knew we were stopped by highwaymen. How could she, unless it was her brothers? We told no one, other than Robert."

"My guess appears to have come comfortably close. When I saw them together tonight, I knew."

She cast him a pert look. "I'm too well acquainted with you to let it go at that, sir. What else do you know?"

He chuckled and sat down on the edge of the bed. "To tell you the truth, my love, I am only guessing. I bow to superior ability. You had the foresight to loose the serpent's tongue with guile. Your own suffered a like fate, I presume?"

"True," she agreed, wrinkling her nose at him. "Back to the point, you wretch. What do you guess?"

"A fourth horseman remained in the woods. Sir Charles, perhaps? You will agree that one thought leads to another."

"Hmm," she murmured cocking her head. "From the McDougalls, to Sir Charles, to—Helene?"

"I felicitate you, my love. A brain under all that beauty."

Back went the quilts. "You are the most maddening creature I have ever known," she said. "Get under the covers before you catch your death. An explanation seems to be called for."

"I will gladly get under the covers, but you perceive the position it puts me in. You know my preference in bed hardly runs to talk."

Lydia ignored this. "The thing I don't understand is, where are we when we get there," she said perfectly seriously.

A devilish glint came into his eyes. "I will allow you have a charming way of expressing yourself," he said. "We are arrived at a motive, sweet."

"But of course," she mused, much struck. "Why didn't I think of that. I expect it hasn't anything to do with money. Whatever do you suppose it is?"

"Your balls of clay," he answered without batting an eye.

She stared at him in lively astonishment. "Surely you jest," she said.

"But, my dear, of course I do not jest. It is quite true that the notion seems preposterous. I wonder myself why anyone should evince the least interest in worthless bits of clay."

She smiled and shook her head. "I know you possess an excellent mind—oh, very well. A brilliant one, if you will—but if you think to confound me, I warn you, sir, you won't succeed."

"Then I will conserve my energy," he remarked, his fingers busily unfastening the ribbons of her nightgown. "Your father told me tonight he plans to leave for London on Monday next. I will dispatch a query by him to Professor Huffman. Until we receive his reply telling us the significance of the box of mud we seem to have so inadvisedly become burdened with, I will hear no more about it. I have better things to do than talk."

"I have always found it an agreeable way to pass the time," she remarked, cutting her eyes at him.

"There are better ways," he replied, tossing her gown over the end of the bed.

"Wretch," she said with mock indignation. "What odious notion have you taken into your head now?"

For answer, he pulled her quite ruthlessly into his arms. "The grandest ever devised by God and man," he said.

Since she found nothing to say against it, he naturally concluded that his performance that followed proved it entirely to her satisfaction.

CHAPTER THIRTEEN

Four days later the omens were seen to be propitious. Two coaches stood before the door, one of them with trunks strapped securely in place, the other awaiting the Marquis's pleasure. By ten o'clock Lady Lenora's last tearful farewells had been spoken, Gerald had climbed to the coachman's box and been ordered down again, and they were off, to the accompaniment of much fluttering of handkerchiefs and waving of hands. Lydia went back into the house feeling quite sad, and it was several minutes before she could recollect her composure enough to summon up a smile. The Earl cast her one sharp glance and ordered the carriage brought around. By the time they had spent an hour in driving about the countryside, and had paused for tea at a charming little inn, Lydia was again in happy spirits and quite ready to engage in verbal sparring with the Earl.

In the days ahead it seemed the front-door knocker seldom stilled. With the departure of the Duke of

Clarence, fewer entertainments offered, and society, having become accustomed to an unending parade of frivolities, was loath to see them end. Lydia, having bidden farewell to the fifth caller in one morning, cast her eyes heavenward and hurried upstairs. She found the Earl in his study at the rear of the house. He was standing with his back to the room in the act of restoring a labeled jar to its place upon a shelf. "If you are busy I won't interrupt," she said.

"I'm quite finished. I was only replenishing my snuffbox. Did you wish something in particular?"

Under his penetrating glance she colored slightly and drew forward a chair. "I daresay you will think me ungrateful, Iain, but I assure you I'm not. It has been quite diverting, in fact, extremely so, but—oh! drat!"

A slight smile curved his lips. "What has occurred to upset you, my dear? I am quite certain that I cannot remember having done anything out of the ordinary."

"Well!" she snapped. "I should have known better than to talk to you!"

"Much better," he remarked. "For a minute there, you had me worried. What have you found so diverting that you come to me in despair?"

She began to twist the ring on her finger. "How long do you plan to remain in Edinburgh?" she said, after a pause.

His brows rose. "Only for so long as it pleases you to do so, of course. Come now, my love. This is not very encouraging. Do you wish to leave?"

"I feared you might not wish to."

"I have been wanting to for weeks."

Lydia stared at him in a good deal of astonishment.

"I wonder I had not guessed as much. To tell you the truth, I have been wanting the same thing myself."

He stood looking down at her, a strange expression on his face. "This is what comes of never being alone," he said thoughtfully. "Well, we will change all that. Run and put on a traveling gown. We leave on the hour."

She recovered in a moment enough to say "On the hour!" in a stunned voice.

"That should allow you sufficient time to pack a valise. Console yourself, my dear, with the reflection that in a very short while we will be beyond the reach of the social whirl."

Still she hesitated. "We have engagements," she murmured, torn between her own desires and their commitments.

"I will cancel them. Have I your permission to invite Robert to visit us at the castle, say in one week?"

Lydia assured him nothing would please her better, and flew from the room. When she at last appeared out front, she found him waiting beside a sporting curricle, his watch in his hand and a frown upon his face. Such a frown, when on the face of a tall gentleman attired in a drab driving coat with no fewer than sixteen shoulder capes, can be very ferocious indeed. Lydia was undismayed. Nor did the sardonic look that swept over her from her head to her feet trouble her in the least. She instructed McTavish in the stowing of her valise, gave her muff into the keeping of a groom, gathered up the skirts of her sapphire velvet pelisse, allowed a second groom to assist her up to the seat, retrieved the muff, and smiled angelically upon the Earl. Other than creating a scene upon a public thoroughfare before his own house, and in plain view of passers-by, there was little he could do but follow her up.

He preserved a stern silence for some minutes—indeed, all of his attention was fully engaged in guiding his spirited team through the crowded city streets—but the moment they were clear of the town his gaze became riveted upon her hat, an upstanding poke-front confection with a high crown adorned with curling ostrich feathers. "How did you come by that monstrosity?" he demanded in crushing accents.

"Mama gave it to me. It was frightfully expensive, but when she got it home she couldn't countenance it."

"I should rather think she couldn't. Whatever possessed you to accept it?"

"I like it, but if you can't abide it, I suppose I could take it off."

"Please do. Nothing could provide me more gratification than having a hoyden up beside me."

"You are vexed with me for having kept you waiting. I am exceedingly sorry, Iain. Really, I had no thought the results would be so calamitous."

The Earl set his teeth and dropped his hands, giving the horses their heads. Since no fewer than four magnificently matched bays were harnessed to the curricle, they bowled along over the ground at breakneck speed. The next miles were accomplished in silence since Lydia, when they swept through a village without a check, had taken one glance at his rigid profile and prudently elected to remain silent.

She bore it with fortitude for as long as she could. "For goodness' sake, Iain," she said at last. "This passes all bounds. Do, I beg you, slow down. You will have us in a ditch."

The Earl vouchsafed no answer, nor did he slow their pace. Lydia turned her head and sat staring with unseeing eyes at the landscape flashing by, and tried to divorce her mind from the scene. From this unsuccessful exercise she was presently recalled by an oath bursting from his lips. They had careened around a corner and were thundering down upon a gig all across the road with a broken axletree. Rigid with fright, she held on tightly and awaited the inevitable crash. It was over in an instant. The bays were swung miraculously to the verge, and in another moment one wheel was in the grass. The curricle rocked alarmingly, righted itself, and the Earl drew the bays to a plunging standstill.

"Good God!" Lydia gasped, weak with relief.

The Earl seemed perfectly unmoved, and only turned his head toward the farmer gaping at them in awe. "Get that infernal contraption off the road before you occasion an accident," he said shortly. "The next driver along could well be a cow-fisted cawker with more hair than wit."

Lydia eyed him askance. "By all means, vent your spleen," she said. "It will make you feel much more the thing than admitting you were in the wrong."

This remark brought a look of amusement into his eyes. "Your bonnet's crooked," he said a trifle mockingly.

"At least I know not to drive about in a hell-for-leather fashion," she replied while setting her hat to rights. "I was sure we would all be killed."

His brows rose. "Trust you to instruct me in how to handle my cattle," he said sardonically. "You are never in the least danger while I hold the ribbons."

"How comforting that will be the next time you

spring your horses," she could not stop herself from saying.

But he only laughed. "How often I have wanted to box your ears for just such a remark as that," he said, setting the bays forward. "Very well, my dear. I will admit to being at fault. We will discount the provocation," he added with a good deal of satisfaction.

"You have only to add that you drive the way you do for my enjoyment and you will have gone your length," she said with a good deal of satisfaction herself. "When do you mean to change horses?"

"There will be no need. There is an inn not far ahead where I plan to stop. We should be there before dark."

They were making good time, and arrived at their destination just as the sun was sinking below the horizon. The village street was broad and lined with great oak trees spreading their boughs over cottages with roses rambling over their gray stone walls. The inn stood at the end of the village, where the street became the highway north, and just next to the church with its burial ground all about it and, off to one side, the Vicar's house squatting in its own garden. The Earl drew his team to a halt before the inn and glanced around. "It appears deserted," he remarked, springing down. "Be so good as to wait here, my dear."

"Iain, what is the time?"

"Around nine. Why?"

"After the experiences I have been through today, I can do without a night on the ground."

Grinning, he turned on his heel and strolled through the door. He reappeared almost immediately with the landlord trotting along beside him, all anxiety to oblige, and assuring Lydia that all the amenities his establishment could provide were at her disposal. Unaccustomed to entertaining the quality at his humble inn, he was round-eyed in wonderment to count the number of capes on the gentleman's coat, and stared in awe at the primest bits of blood-and-bone he had ever beheld. "If your ladyship will but step inside, your chamber will be ready in a very few minutes," he said, ushering them inside. "I'm sorry I can't provide a private parlor, but my wife will set a decent meal before you."

The landlady, casting a worried look at Lydia, murmured that if her ladyship would but condescend to come along upstairs, the largest guest chamber was at the minute being made ready. The Earl turned from watching her go off in the wake of their hostess, and sauntered into the coffee room. Only two customers were extending their patronage at the moment. Putting them down as father and son, the Earl inclined his head in a perfectly civil bow and strolled across to a table by the window. It was abundantly apparent to him that he was being subjected to a thorough and somewhat secretive scrutiny, particularly on the part of the younger man, who colored up and glanced away each time the Earl looked his way. In a short time the landlord set a glass of burgundy before him, and lingered until he pronounced it highly palatable, an exaggeration prompted by the landlord's manifest desire to please. Alone again, the Earl glanced idly out of the window and surprised the landlady running hotfoot toward the vicarage. Presently he saw her come hurrying back with the Vicar's wife, each of them with basket of foodstuffs over their arms. The Earl sighed. Clearly dinner would be late.

Lydia descended the stairs some few minutes later and came upon a scene of chaos. A portly gentleman with bright, angry eyes stood before the Earl, his feet planted firmly apart, and rapped out a question. "What the devil have you done with my daughter?" he demanded in tones of rage.

The Earl fished his snuffbox from a pocket and flicked it open. "I know nothing of your daughter," he replied placidly.

"What you will tell me, sir, is this! Do those bays out front belong to you?"

The Earl delicately took snuff. "They do," he said, dusting his fingers.

"Then where is my girl? Answer me that!"

"I haven't the vaguest notion. Nor, I might add, have I the faintest idea whom you could be."

"The name, sir, is Thinshanks. Ah! I see you know it!"

The Earl's shoulders shook with silent laughter. "On the contrary, sir," he said a trifle unsteadily. "I have never heard the name before."

Squire Thinshanks seemed on the verge of apoplexy. "Think to marry my Sadie, do you?" he said, scowling heavily. "Expect to put your hand in my pocket, do you? Well, sir, I won't have it, you hear?"

"The mystery is solved," remarked the Earl. "Your— er, Sadie has eloped."

"With you, sir! With you!"

The Earl was looking bored. "I fear you will have to hold me excused," he said negligently. "I have a wife."

"Just read this!" the Squire sputtered, waving a paper under the Earl's nose. "My Sadie ran off with a dandy! You, sir, are a dandy!"

"The correct term is Corinthian, but we will pass

over that," the Earl remarked in soothing accents. "You must bear with me while I point out to you that any gentleman could fit the description. If your daughter has left your roof, you will do better to ascertain the name and direction of her amorous friend. I would get right on it if I were you," he added, urging the Squire toward the door. "There is not a minute to lose, you know. You had better run along home and question her friends. She's a female; she's bound to have confided in them." In another moment, the Squire found himself in the hall, the door closed in his face.

Lydia, having by this time succumbed to her emotions, was seated at a table shielding the mirth on her face with a hand. The Earl walked across the room and sat down facing her. "If there is any virtue in you, I have yet to discover it," he remarked, pressing his handkerchief into her hand.

"If you could but have witnessed it," she gurgled, wiping her streaming eyes.

At this moment the landlord came into the room to place a moderately supportable meal before them, and hovered about to wait upon them himself. Lydia nibbled at her portion, pronounced the food delicious, and tactfully declined a rather heavy appearing apple dumpling offered for her inspection, on the score that she was not partial to sweets. She did not appear to the landlord to be overfed, but far be it from him to question the ways of the quality. He merely cleared away the covers and set a bottle of cognac before the Earl.

Half an hour later he came back into the room to inform the Earl the village blacksmith was quartering his team for the night. "When I first clapped eyes on your lordship's bays, I said to myself there's but one stable hereabouts that's fit to house them. I hope your lordship approves?"

"I am sure you did the right thing. If you will be so good as to desire the blacksmith to have the curricle before the door in the morning at ten?"

The landlord bowed and turned to Lydia. "If your ladyship pleases, your bed has been made up, and hot bricks have been put in it to air the sheets."

Lydia rose to go upstairs, but the Earl elected to stroll about for a time, and went out-of-doors to stretch his legs. He very soon went around the corner of the inn and came upon the landlady's flower garden. The air was sweet with the scent of roses, and the moon, peeping out from behind the clouds, cast just enough light to reveal a grass path leading off toward a clump of hedges. He set off down it, and nearly stumbled over a figure seated on a bench. A girl of no more than sixteen years started up and flung herself against his chest. "Sir Charles!" she cried happily. "I had despaired you were not coming."

The Earl went very still for a moment, before holding her off with the steel of his hands. "I am sorry to disappoint you, but I am not Sir Charles," he said in a gentle voice. "No, do not attempt to pull away. You have nothing to fear from me."

It was a very frightened child indeed, and one who immediately burst into tears. The Earl saw nothing for it but to coax her back to the bench and wait for the storm to pass. "Feeling better?" he said when the flow at last slowed to a trickle. "That's a good girl. Sit up now, and dry your eyes."

"W-who are you?" she asked in a pitifully trembling voice.

"I am the Earl of Torquay. And you, unless I am much mistaken, must be Miss Sadie Thinshanks. Your father was here earlier looking for you." When she would have jumped up and fled he placed a restraining hand on her arm. "I will say this only once, Miss Thinshanks. It is not safe for you to wander about alone at night. Little though I might relish the chore, I must put you in my charge."

"You needn't bother," she said stoutly, while glancing at him suspiciously. "Sir Charles . . ."

"I am well acquainted with Sir Charles. Believe me, Miss Thinshanks, it will not do. Where did you meet him, by the way?"

"He put up at the inn en route to Edinburgh. I—I was taking clothing to the vicarage for distribution to the poor, and—and met him."

"The matter now becomes abundantly clear. Tell me, Miss Thinshanks. Are you an only child?"

She looked startled. "Well, yes, I am," she admitted. "But what has that to do with it?"

"A great deal, I'm afraid. Forgive me, but as your father's only heir, you become quite the plum to fall into Sir Charles's hand. Well, come along. I don't mean to sound unamiable, but the night air has grown chilly."

"W-where are you taking me? I must warn you my Papa . . ."

"Kindly refrain from adding insult to my burden, Miss Thinshanks. I am taking you to my wife."

By the time Lydia came downstairs some thirty minutes later and went into the common room, the Earl had sent word to Squire Thinshanks and was awaiting his arrival. He cocked an eyebrow at her and rose to push in her chair. "For a lady enjoying a series of exciting adventures, my love, you look singularly depressed," he remarked, resuming his seat.

"Don't speak to me of adventures," she said, shuddering. "I have never felt so old in my life. I declare I should put a cap on my head and retire into a corner."

The Earl put up his quizzing glass and surveyed her through it. "Now you mention it," he said outrageously, "I'm sorry, my dear—but can that be—forgive me—a touch of gray? Ah, no," he sighed, lowering the glass. "'Tis only a trick of the light."

"That precocious chit hasn't stopped chattering a moment," she went on, ignoring the bait. "Oh, I know you are thinking I should have stemmed the tide. That is very true. I should have, but I was lured into discussing Sir Charles. Dislodging the pedestal on which he stood was no easy task, believe me."

"On the contrary, I believe you very well. He did become dislodged?"

She choked, and went off into a peal of laughter. "Tumbled," she gurgled. "Smashed all to smithereens."

He smiled and said: "May I inquire the present whereabouts of the heroine of this piece?"

"Upstairs bathing away the signs of tears. She should be down presently."

"Sir Charles must be more desperate for funds than I would have supposed, to sink to robbing the cradle," he mused thoughtfully. "He will bear watching."

A disturbance was heard in the hall. A male voice became upraised in anger; a female one terrified in reply. The Earl swore softly under his breath, and strode across to the door. "Have done, Sir Charles," he said in haughty accents. "Miss Thinshanks enjoys my protection."

Sir Charles jumped as though he had been shot, and

wheeled about, staring at the Earl. "You!" he gasped, stunned.

"As you see, Sir Charles, it is I. Indisputedly, it is I. An unexpected encounter, would you not say?"

Sir Charles flushed dark. "I have business with Miss Thinshanks. What right have you to interfere?"

"The right, sir, of a gentleman to rescue a lady in peril of her virtue. It is singular indeed. One wonders where one will run across you next. I seem to have acquired an unhappy—shall we say knack?—of finding you always on the scene."

Sir Charles licked his lips. "I didn't come here seeking your company," he asserted nervously. "What brought you here?"

"But fate, my dear Sir Charles. Fate."

"Go to the devil," Sir Charles spat, goaded.

"I would be happy to do so if I had any assurance I should not meet you there. And now you will unhand Miss Thinshanks and come into the coffee room."

Sir Charles ground his teeth. "It is unlikely I will take orders from you," he said grimly.

"Please do not put me to the trouble of forcing you," the Earl said with bone-chilling coldness.

Sir Charles seemed to experience considerable difficulty in holding his fury within bounds, but a certain logic overcame his anger. He stalked into the room and cast himself into a chair.

Lydia looked at the Earl with anxious eyes. "Are we never to be done with him?" she said.

"One day, my dear, the devil will gather in his own. He always does."

"What happens now?"

"We wait upon Squire Thinshanks's pleasure."

"Oh dear," murmured that redoubtable gentleman's penitent offspring. "Papa will be so cross."

The Squire's home was situated some six miles distant from the village, and it was therefore some time before the clatter of wheels on the cobblestone street heralded his arrival. To the surprise of all, he hurried into the room and took his daughter into his arms, his face wreathed in smiles. "Naughty puss," he said. "There, there. You are safe. I musn't scold."

The Earl, who had been observing the reunion with a sardonic smile, remarked: "I trust that, when we have finished with these affecting passages, we will be able to dispense with your business and go about our own."

"So you shall, sir. So you shall," the Squire agreed affably before catching sight of Sir Charles. "But who is this?" he demanded, a flush creeping into his cheeks.

The Earl waved him to a chair. "You must realize I dislike disturbances of any sort. Therefore, Squire, I will ask you to look to the presence of ladies in the room."

"My lord!" said the Squire, a light dawning in his eyes. "Do you mean to imply— You!" he spat at Sir Charles, surging to his feet.

Sir Charles blinked and subjected one well-manicured finger to a minute inspection. "Really, sir," he said. "What reason can you have for taking such a tone?"

"The right of a father!" the Squire cried with strong feeling.

"You will appreciate my position, I feel confident," said Sir Charles. "To have been restrained in this place . . . "

"You will be restrained, sir. Indeed you will," the Squire returned in a grim tone. "I happen to be the local Magistrate, as you were not to be knowing. What I am thinking, and make no mistake about it, is that you will come to trial for your crime. You will soon see, sir, what happens to dandies bent on kidnapping our local girls. Indeed you will."

"You are making a grave mistake," Sir Charles said, blanching. "I intended using no force. Your daughter . . ."

"Quiet!" bellowed the Squire. "I shan't listen to your lies." Beckoning the landlord forward, he added: "Lock him in the shed."

Sir Charles sprang to his feet, in no disposition to accompany his jailer from the room, but two stout sons appeared at their father's side, presenting a formidable front. Cornered, he could only glare at the Earl and suffer himself to be led away.

"The man's a charlatan," the Squire confided to the Earl the moment the door closed on the prisoner. "Needs to be put away. He should get twenty years, perhaps more."

Lydia and the Earl then heroically endured quite five minutes of effusive gratitude before the Squire took himself off, shepherding his daughter before him.

Lydia watched them go and heaved a contented sigh. "Life has been such fun since we married, hasn't it?" she said.

"I can imagine nothing more pleasant," he replied, smiling down at her.

"Do other people have so many adventures?"

"I devoutly hope not."

"You are quizzing me, of course. You enjoyed your

set-to with Sir Charles. I made sure the fur would fly."

"I mean no offense, but it didn't seem to worry you overmuch."

"No, for the Captain told me you have the most punishing left imaginable. He was speaking of fisticuffs, wasn't he?"

She encountered a cold glance. "Robert is as reprehensible as you, my dear," he remarked dryly. "Boxing cant sits no less uneasily on your tongue."

"You may be as prudish as you like, but I should like seeing you land him a facer," she replied, showing him a look of so much irrepressible mischief that the smile returned to his eyes.

"The Squire appears to be before you, my love," he said, standing aside for her to precede him up the stairs. "He will see him jailed for life. I doubt he will accomplish it," he added thoughtfully.

"Never say so!" she uttered, surprised. "Shall we dispense with Sir Charles and discuss what we will do tomorrow?"

"You bewilder me," he replied, opening the door to their chamber. "I should have thought you had had enough of adventure."

"If I said I had, you would be offended," she twinkled, and walked into the room.

The Earl followed her in and flicked her cheek with a finger. "You talk too much," he said with the glimmering of a smile, and put an end to further speech by fastening his lips on hers.

CHAPTER FOURTEEN

It was a dark night one week later when the curricle swept around the courtyard and drew up before the great front doors of Castle Torquay. Curiously, no light shone forth from behind the shuttered windows. No retainers came hurrying down the steps, and no grooms came rushing from the stables to spring to the horses' heads. The Earl thrust the reins into Lydia's hands and sprang down, a black scowl upon his face. He took the steps three at a time, and jerked the bell-chain beside the door. Hardly had the sound died away within the vast and silent interior when he jerked it again and pounded mightily upon the door. The sound of bars being drawn was faintly heard, and the door opened a crack, to reveal the face of McTavish peering out.

"What the devil!" the Earl swore. "Open up, you fool!"

"My lord!" the butler gasped, relieved, and swung wide the door. The branch of candles in his hand shook slightly and cast flickering light over his drawn face.

"What is the meaning of this?" the Earl demanded. "Where are the servants, and why is the place dark as a tomb. Well? Speak up, man!"

McTavish gained command of himself and bowed. "If your lordship pleases, I will send for the servants. I regret . . ." He found himself speaking to empty air. The Earl turned on his heel and strode back down the steps to assist Lydia to alight. McTavish issued orders in rapid succession, which sent the night porter running, and quickly moved around the hall lighting candles. By the time Lydia and the Earl crossed the threshold, the room was ablaze with light. "I regret the state of affairs and beg your lordship's indulgence, but there has been trouble, my lord. If you will but step this way, the fire in the blue salon is being lit, and I have sent for tea for her ladyship."

"What trouble?" demanded the Earl, casting his gloves and coat down upon a chair.

"A burglary, my lord," McTavish replied, ushering them across the hall. "Lady Flora became distraught and ordered the castle barred and dark. Captain Turbull surprised a man in the yellow suite, but the doctor assures us his wound is slight."

"Wound? Good God! Where is he?"

"I took the liberty of establishing the Captain in the guest chamber at the top of the stairs, my lord."

Lydia could not suppress an exclamation of horror, and turned to follow the Earl, who, having snatched up a candelabra, was taking the stairs two at a time. The Captain lay in a laudanum-induced slumber, his face ghastly against the white of the sheets. A bandage swathed his chest and strapped his left arm to his side, and his curling blond hair clung damply to his brow, but other than an occasional twitching of the right hand, he lay quietly enough. The nurse, a raw-boned woman well into middle age, rose from her chair beside the bed and turned a stern look upon the visitors. "I kinna allow ye to disturb me patient," she said briefly. "I dinna want him wakened."

The Earl strode to the bed and stood gazing down upon his friend. "How bad is it?" he said tersely.

"The doctor says 'twill be all right with he, once the fever breaks. What he wants now be rest."

"Send for me when he wakes, or at the least sign of any change in his condition. I am the Earl."

"Aye, I thought ye were. He dinna be waking till the morn, me lord. The doctor dosed him right good with laudanum."

Lydia and the Earl left the room and went back downstairs. The house was now ablaze with candle-light, and a roaring fire crackled on the hearth in the blue salon. McTavish ushered in a footman bearing a substantial tea on a tray, and supervised its disposi-tion on a table drawn up before the fire. When he would have bowed himself from the room, the Earl said: "Stay, McTavish. You will inform me what has been going forward here."

The butler was unable to tell them much, but the little he did relate was enough to appall the Earl. The Captain had been attacked within the castle walls; McTavish was unable to give a name to his assailant.

"We will discover who it was later," the Earl said. "Go on."

"The Captain arrived just this morning, my lord. His valet tells me he left his chamber to go to your lordship's study, remarking that he intended penning a letter to his mother. The footman on duty in the lower hall claims not to have seen him, but it is my opinion the lad had left his post. There is a downstairs maid who appears to have taken young Colin's fancy, but I won't trouble her ladyship with disciplinary problems concerning the staff at this time."

"We leave it in your hands. Pray continue, McTavish."

"Thank you, my lord. Whether the Captain surprised the burglar in your lordship's study has not been determined, the Captain being in no condition to be questioned due to his injury. We do know from what Johns tells us—he was just in the act of coming along the downstairs hall, my lord—is that the Captain erupted from the rose salon in pursuit of an individual with a mask across his face. Never had Johns—in his own words, my lord—thought to see such a sight within the castle walls. When he recovered from surprise and set off in pursuit himself, he had been left far behind, and by the time he came upon the Captain in the yellow salon, it was too late. The Captain had been stabbed, and of the intruder there was no sign."

Lydia gazed round-eyed at McTavish. "But the yellow salon is on the other side of the house," she said in a stifled voice.

"Exactly, my lady," the butler bowed, his face an expressionless mask. "Close by the west wing."

The Earl broke the silence that followed. "You examined the doors and windows?" he said finally, in his calm way.

"All were securely fastened, my lord," McTavish replied gravely.

"Then how could an intruder have gained entrance?" Lydia said, puzzled.

"We will come to that later," the Earl replied. "You haven't explained the very odd reception we received here tonight, McTavish."

A flicker of emotion disturbed the schooled impassivity of the butler's face. "Lady Flora became—disturbed upon becoming apprised of events, my lord."

"Hysterical, you mean," remarked the Earl.

"As your lordship says," McTavish said, the veriest hint of a smile twitching at the corner of his lips. "Her ladyship only became—calm upon being assured that all entrances into the house were securely bolted. Lady Flora declared a house in darkness is less likely to be noticed by roving bands of rogues than one showing light, and ordered the candles extinguished."

"The doctor should have dosed her with laudanum," Lydia remarked, to the Earl's amusement.

"I believe he did, my lady," McTavish replied, his countenance once again impassive.

A sardonic smile curved the Earl's lips. "What had Lady Cavanaugh to say to all of this?"

"To my knowledge, nothing, my lord."

"I thought not," the Earl mused somewhat enigmatically. "Thank you, McTavish. That will be all."

The door had scarcely closed behind him when Lydia's feelings got the upper hand. "I wish you will tell me what you meant by that!" she exclaimed.

"By what, my dear?" the Earl asked imperturbably.

"You know very well what!" she replied somewhat ungrammatically. "Lady Cavanaugh."

"I cannot at the moment recall my thoughts," came

his maddening reply. "Will you pour, my love? I find that I am hungry."

Lydia knew from experience she would elicit nothing further from him with such tactics, and busied herself pouring out his tea. "Do you think," she began hopefully while arranging sandwiches on his plate, "that the intruder could have escaped through the west wing?"

"I really have no idea," he replied, watching her closely.

"It is quite true that Lady Cavanaugh controls who comes and goes there. Myrna is permitted entry, remember. Do you suppose . . ." She broke off and handed him his plate.

He continued to regard her every expression. "What unguarded observation are you about to make?" he asked, picking up a sandwich.

"I was just wondering if the intruder gained entry through the kind offices of Lady Cavanaugh. He could have, Iain; surely you won't deny it. There can be no other explanation."

"Now you have confounded me," he replied carefully. "I think we should refrain from comment for the time being."

"But what will we possibly gain by ignoring any clue, however slight?" she insisted.

"May I suggest that you not worry your pretty head over it? It will only take your mind off me, and that, my love, I will not countenance."

She snorted. "Those are fine words from a gentleman who gobbles up the sandwiches while his wife goes hungry."

His gaze lazily roamed over her breasts pushing gently against the bodice of her gown. "I shouldn't wish a plump pullet in my bed," he murmured, his eyes wickedly quizzing her.

"You seldom have very little else at all on your mind," she said, thrusting out her lower lip.

"Very little, love, to your great good fortune," he agreed, chuckling softly.

She looked away. "I should think you would one day cease trying to shock me," she remarked, only too conscious of his eyes roaming over her curves.

His laugh rang out. "Not while I can feast my eyes on rounded breasts and tantalizing thighs," he said provocatively.

"There is no talking to you," she shot back, by no means displeased. "If you will excuse me, the hour grows late."

"Don't bother putting on a nightgown," he said, rising to pull back her chair. "I will only remove it."

"I do not go upstairs to play, my lord," she told him in honeyed accents while crossing to the door. "I go upstairs to sleep."

Fifteen minutes later he strolled into her room, and grinned to see her nightgown laid out neatly across the back of a chair. Eyes twinkling, he quickly stripped off his clothing and sank into her waiting arms. . . .

When she awoke the following morning shortly after eight o'clock and found herself alone, she dressed and hurried down the hall to the room in which the Captain lay. The Earl stood beside the bed, a worried frown creasing his forehead. The fever had not broken, and the nurse was placing cloths wrung out in cool water upon her patient's brow. He was muttering in delirium, and although his eyes were open it was obvious he was unaware of the activity going on around him.

"How long has he been like this?" the Earl demanded of the nurse.

"Since just before I sent for ye," she answered crisply. "Dinna ye go getting ideas into yer head, me lord. The surgeon will be along soon. I told yer groom he weren't to tarry."

"Is there anything I can do to help?"

"Ye can hold the Captain still, me lord. We dinna want him pulling the bandages loose."

By the time the doctor arrived, the Captain was groaning and struggling under the Earl's restraining hands, his fever on the rise. The doctor took his pulse, placed his hand on the Captain's forehead, and announced there was scant cause for concern. "His pulse is not too tumultuous, and he has a strong constitution. We will bleed him to relieve the restlessness, and he should do famously." He took a pint of blood, instructed the nurse to force the medicine he left down the patient's throat, and departed, saying he would return by evening.

"Out ye go," the nurse said firmly the moment the Captain ceased his endless tossing and fell into a heavy stupor. "There's naught to do now but wait. I'll send word to ye the minute the fever breaks."

The day seemed to drag on endlessly. The servants whispered about the house as if the family were in deep mourning, and Lady Flora fluttered aimlessly from room to room getting on everyone's nerves. Lord Cavanaugh established himself in the blue salon, and spent the day in relating similar instances he had known to anyone willing to listen to his tales. The cook sent up delicious meals that no one had the heart to eat, and fumed when the food came back again scarcely touched. At around two o'clock Miss Wingate calmly entered the sickroom to relieve the nurse, telling her she would be of little use to the Captain when he woke if she refused to go and rest. Miss Wingate then pressed her fingers to his forehead and, upon finding it not unduly hot in her estimation, lifted up his head and expertly tipped liquid down his throat. Nurse, satisfied, went away after requesting she be awakened in one hour.

A few minutes before five, the Captain groaned and opened his eyes. Miss Wingate immediately bent over him and put a glass to his lips. "Drink," she said firmly.

The Captain obediently swallowed, his puzzled gaze on her face. "Do I know you?" he said faintly.

"You are not to talk," replied Miss Wingate, smoothing the sheets to make him more comfortable.

A slight twinkle crept into his pain-wracked eyes. "An angel come down from heaven," he murmured on a sigh, and closed his eyes.

Miss Wingate stood staring down at him a moment, the tears stinging her eyelids. As she turned away, the Earl appeared in the doorway. She shook her head and crossed silently to his side. "He awakened for a moment and took the medicine," she said in a low voice. "His fever is abating, though he seems in a good deal of pain."

"That is to be expected. Where is the nurse?"

"Resting. I thought it best. She has been twenty-four hours without sleep."

"Go down and have your tea, Miss Wingate. I will sit with him."

"I would prefer to have it here if you will be so

good as to send it up." A faint smile curved her lips. "Should the Captain wake, he is much more apt to take orders from a female."

The Earl nodded. "I will have the nurse awakened in time for you to join us for dinner," he said, and went away.

Miss Wingate returned to her chair by the bedside and folded her hands in her lap, thinking the Captain asleep. When he spoke, she quite jumped.

"You haven't told me your name," he said faintly, but with the ghost of a smile.

She stood. "It is Miss Wingate," she told him primly.

A flash of humor crossed his drawn face. "Will the very proper Miss Wingate give me a drink?" he said with obvious effort.

With his eyes following her every move, she felt flustered, but he didn't speak again until she had slid her arm under his shoulders to raise him up. He drank the water she was holding to his lips. "I shall call you Angie, short for angel," he gasped against the pain as she lowered him down onto the pillows.

Pink tinged her cheeks. "You will do better not to talk," she said, putting the glass down upon the bedside table.

It seemed as though he would sink back into the fretful sleep from which he had awakened, but he roused himself and said: "Where have you been hiding yourself, little wren?"

Miss Wingate's cheeks fairly flamed. There was no denying it was very agreeable to be talked to in caressing accents, but she had, after all, reached her twenty-eighth year, and knew better than to let her head become turned by the flattering phrases of an accomplished flirt. Accordingly she said: "I could more accurately be described as a bird of prey, Captain. I am a distant relative of Lady Cavanaugh."

"Forced by circumstances to accept charity, are you?"

Miss Wingate gasped. "I am—comfortably situated," she said with what dignity she could muster.

"But, of course," he remarked, wincing a little. "It is always agreeable to run and fetch from morn till night."

She looked at him reprovingly. "I was in no position to pick and choose, sir. On the contrary: I consider myself fortunate to be treated with a good deal of consideration."

"It won't fadge, you know," he said in a fretting tone. "I dislike the thought of you being in such a situation. Hold my hand."

She saw that he was becoming agitated, and clasped his fingers in hers. His skin felt hot and dry, but the personal contact seemed to soothe him, for he closed his eyes. She waited a few minutes until she thought he slept, but at the first sign she meant to disengage her hand, his grasp feebly tightened. "Don't leave me," he said, turning his head on the pillow to gaze at her.

The entrance of the nurse at that moment put an end to further conversation, and she could only promise to return immediately she had had her dinner before being obliged to leave the room. By the time she went back upstairs the doctor had arrived and was re-dressing the Captain's wound. His breath came in wincing gasps, but he summoned up a weak smile upon catching sight of her. The doctor's ministrations at an end, he dispensed a dose of laudanum and took himself off, saying the fever should break by morning. His visit left the Captain too exhausted to be much interested in conversation, but he groped for Miss Wingate's hand and clung to it until he dropped into an uneasy slumber.

When the Earl came into the room early the following morning, he found him propped up on the pillows and engaged in arguing with his nurse. The bowl of gruel in her hand was soon seen to be the bone of contention. Nurse was insisting her patient swallow every spoonful, while the Captain, every bit as determined, was stubbornly refusing to do so. The Earl, when appealed to, tactfully suggested that if he would first eat the gruel, then soft-boiled egg and toast could be sent up from the kitchens.

"Oh, very well," said the Captain. "But I will have a mug of ale with it, mind."

"Ye will nae have anything o' the kind," said Nurse.

The Captain frowned direfully upon her. "Then I shan't eat your gruel," he said querulously.

The Earl controled a twitching lip and took the bowl from the nurse's hand. "Eggs and ale it shall be," he said. "Go and order it, Nurse. I would speak to the Captain in private."

"I couldn't have put myself in a worse case had I tried," the Captain remarked when she had hurried from the room.

"That is what I would speak to you about," said the Earl. "Open your mouth."

"There is something I would know," said the Captain, swallowing obediently. "Miss Wingate . . ."

The Earl removed the spoon. "My dear boy, first things first. Do you feel up to telling me what happened?"

"You must know that I arrived—was it yesterday

about mid-morning?—for God's sake, Iain. Must you keep thrusting that revolting pap down my throat?"

"Woe betide you unless you down it before Nurse returns. You arrived yesterday morning, Robert. What then?"

"I went to your study to pen a letter," the Captain began, and pushed away the spoon. "Would you believe I surprised a rogue standing behind your desk? Just as I was wondering what the devil he was about— he was prying at the lock, by the way—he looked up and saw me. I cried out and made a lunge for him, but he shoved me aside and ran from the room. He was quick, I will give him that. To make a long story short, I chased him through the house—almost had him, too—but he whirled on me—the last thing I remember was the flash of metal in his hand. I must be getting old," he finished in disgust. "Stabbed by a pesky burglar, by gad!"

A glint of humor came into the Earl's eyes. "Thirty-one is quite an ancient age, of course. I will also agree that it is customary to anticipate being accosted by armed rogues roaming about in the home of one's friend."

"I had the oddest feeling I had seen him before. Not his face—he wore a mask. It was his shoulders, I think. I have seldom seen a broader pair."

The Earl was suddenly very still. "Would you describe him as rather above the average height, and bearlike?"

"Yes, come to think of it. Do you know him?"

"I rather think I do."

"Now see here, Iain. If you are spoiling for a fight, you will wait on my recovery, won't you? I'd hate to miss the fun."

"You have put me to the blush as it is, Robert."

"Of course, if you had been in my place you would have turned your back while he burgled the place," came the Captain's scathing reply. "Well, enough of your affairs. I want to know about Miss Wingate. Just who is she, Iain?"

"Joshua Wingate's daughter. You may have heard of him."

"I rather think I have, if he is the Winny who ran with Sutter's crowd. Gambled away everything and then blew his brains out, as I recall. Poor Angie."

"Angie?"

The Captain grinned and looked sheepish. "Miss Wingate," he explained.

"But my dear Robert, I cannot believe this of you," the Earl wondered with a perfectly straight face. "You have always been a sensible fellow. Surely you aren't going in the way of the petticoat line at your advanced years."

"I would be more to the point if you would ask her to come and sit with me," the Captain replied, sinking back exhausted against the pillows.

The Earl took due note of the tiny furrow of pain between his brows and took himself off. Calling next in the west wing, he was ushered into a paneled room with an oak-coffered ceiling by a footman who made no effort to conceal his curiosity. The Earl's lips curled as he reflected grimly on the coming changes. To his further annoyance, he was left cooling his heels a good fifteen minutes before he strode to the bell and pulled it.

He had scarcely released it when the door opened and Miss Wingate came hurrying in, dressed for gardening in a large hat, with her hair tucked under the veil. "Do forgive my tardiness," she said, coming forward, stripping off the gloves from her hands. "Lady Cavanaugh is laid down upon her bed with the headache, and Thomisan has just this minute informed me of your call."

The Earl controled his temper with an effort. "I am not here upon a visit of courtesy," he said, recovering swiftly from his irritation. "As a matter of fact, it must be all of ten years since I set foot in these rooms."

"Then we are indeed honored," Miss Wingate replied, looking at him with a hint of surprise in her eyes. "I see the servants have been neglectful. May I ring for coffee?"

"Thank you, Miss Wingate, but no. I have had my breakfast. You must forgive me for bringing you from your gardening at such an early hour."

A slight smile touched her lips. "You did not call to exchange pleasantries, my lord. May I be of service?"

"Perhaps you can, at that. The thought occurs to me you might have noticed, had Angus McDougall been admitted to these rooms in recent days."

The color rushed into her cheeks. "I had made up my mind to speak to you," she admitted. "The thought seems ludicrous, I know, but . . ."

"Nonsense, Miss Wingate," he replied calmly. "The notion is not at all ludicrous. It is quite plausible, in fact. Then he was here yesterday morning?"

"Yes, my lord, he was. He has fallen into the habit of calling often during recent weeks."

"Did he by any chance wander about the castle?" At her flustered look he added: "I want the truth, Miss Wingate."

She sat down upon a chair by the fireplace and

turned a pained look upon him. "Lady Cavanaugh has been—kind. I feel a traitor," she said faintly.

"If she has, it pleased her to gather a court about her," he said levelly. "Pray, do not squander your sympathy, Miss Wingate."

"That is easy to say, my lord. I am, however, aware that yours have been the monies that have supported us all. My debt of gratitude to you is, therefore, by far the greater. In answer to your question: Yes, Mr. McDougall has transgressed severely upon your hospitality. He has come and gone very much as he pleased."

"And Lady Cavanaugh's servants permitted this?" he asked after a moment.

"Abetted is the more accurate term, my lord."

"I wish you would call me Iain, Miss Wingate. 'My lord' sounds devilish formal."

A slight smile curved her lips. "No more formal than 'Miss Wingate' sounds, sir," she said with a touch of humor.

It was on the tip of his tongue to term her "Angie" in reply, but her blushes were saved by a footman coming in just then. "Did you ring the bell, my lord?" the man said.

"I did. Some time ago," the Earl answered with more asperity in his voice than Miss Wingate could remember having heard from him before. "Have the goodness to inform your mistress I do not wish to speak with her after all."

"Yes, my lord," the footman said, sniffing. "What shall I tell the lady, my lord?"

"I have just instructed you—what lady?"

"Miss Myrna McDougall, my lord."

"What the deuce!" the Earl ejaculated, stunned.

"Tell her Lady Cavanaugh isn't receiving. And another thing. No member of the McDougall family will be admitted to the west wing in future," he added tersely.

Miss Wingate turned from watching the footman bow himself out. "How often have I longed to issue just such an order as that," she remarked ruefully.

"My aunt's staff need not trouble you much longer," the Earl replied. "I will instruct McTavish to replace them with competent servants."

"I wish you wouldn't distress yourself on my account," she said, startled. "I don't know what else to say."

"It is only the first of many changes I intend to institute. And now, ma'am, if you will excuse me, I have pressing business elsewhere."

"You will be careful, will you not?" she said somewhat anxiously. "Mr. McDougall has proven his proficiency with a knife."

"You refer, I apprehend, to his attack upon my friend. You are not to worry. Robert was caught unawares, whereas I know what to expect. Speaking of the devil, Robert is begging that you sit with him," he added, grinning.

"Then I will go to him at once," she replied, perfectly mistress of the situation, albeit her color ran a little high. "May I suggest you not wreak complete havoc upon your enemy? I should think a simple lesson would suffice."

"I shan't kill him, if that is what is disturbing you," he said, crossing to the door. "Lydia wouldn't approve."

Twenty minutes later the curricle was before the door, and the Earl was seated at the desk in his study, applying wax to the flap of a folded letter. "You rang, my lord?" the butler asked, coming into the room.

"I am going out, McTavish. In the unlikely event I should not return, you will give this into the hands of her ladyship. Otherwise you will return it to me without mentioning it to her ladyship."

"Certainly, my lord," the butler said, accepting the note, but with his eye upon the small sword lying on the desk. "I trust, my lord—is anything amiss?"

"Nothing at all, McTavish," the Earl replied, picking up the sword.

The McDougall's groom, when the curricle swept up before the house, ran an appreciative eye over the bays and leaped to their heads. "I'm thinkin' I niver seen a bonnier pair," he remarked, shaking his grizzled head.

"Thank you," the Earl replied, springing down. "Can you tell me whether young Angus is at home?"

"I dinna know, though I'm thinkin' he be," the ostler muttered briefly before leading the bays toward the stables.

The butler, only slightly less taciturn than the groom, goggled at the Earl mounting the front steps, and held wide the door. "Master Angus?" he said in surprise at the Earl's query. "He be in the oak parlor, me lord. Ye be sure 'tis not Himself ye be wantin'?"

"I'm sure," the Earl replied, crossing the threshold. At the door of the parlor he paused and said over his shoulder: "My business with Angus is private. See to it we are not disturbed."

The butler cast him one quick glance, and waited only until the door closed behind him before hurrying off to inform his employer, all agog. A gentleman of

the Earl's stature come seeking Master Angus—and
armed—meant trouble. Himself would scarce be best
pleased not to be informed of it.

Angus, meanwhile, when he heard the door close,
looked up from the tankard of ale before him and
stiffened. For a moment they faced each other, Angus
with hatred in his eyes, the Earl with very little emotion at all in his. Angus's gaze wandered to the sword
at the Earl's side, and he leaped to his feet. "If it's a
fight you want, it's a fight you'll get," he gritted
through his teeth.

"You have a charming way of putting it," the Earl
remarked. "Presently you will tell me what you were
seeking in my home."

"What makes you think I will?" Angus spat.

The Earl raised his brows. "You will be perfectly
willing, once you have received an identical wound to
the one you dealt my friend," he said, drawing his
sword from its scabbard.

Angus strode to the mantel and snatched up a
weapon. "Look to yourself," he said savagely, whirling
to face the Earl.

They stood staring at each other a moment before
laying down their swords to remove their coats. The
Earl had just seated himself to pull off his top-boots
when the door crashed open and Himself stood upon
the threshold. "Hold!" he said, moving forward. "What
is the meaning of this?"

"Ask your son," the Earl said calmly. "He may wish
to explain his reason for burglarizing my home. He
may even wish to reveal his purpose in stabbing a
guest of mine in the process."

Himself turned his gaze on Angus, his brow darken-

ing as he considered his son. "I'm waiting," he said
sourly.

"He's lying, Papa," Angus said with a great show of
bravado. "I'll stuff his words down his throat!"

"And what makes you think your skill equal to Torquay's?" Himself said, glaring. "I haven't any intention
of obliging him by letting you stand up against him."

"You know, it really would not oblige me," the Earl
said. "I intended pinking him only."

Angus looked surprised. "I was under the impression you meant to kill me," he said in amazement.

"I should not care for the consequences to myself,
should I do so," the Earl admitted with perfect hon-
esty.

Himself was looking at Angus with a look of sad-
ness upon his face. "It becomes apparent who is
lying," he said. "Apologizing for my son goes against
the grain, Torquay. I fear I must request you to tell
me more. What, for instance, did you mean when you
said a guest of yours had been stabbed?"

"Angus was apprehended while searching my desk,
and knifed my friend in making good his escape."

Himself drew a deep breath. "I fail to understand,"
he said. "Angus may be somewhat wild at times, but—
a thief? You can't expect me to believe that."

"Perhaps he will enlighten you," the Earl said gently.

Angus had been listening with a look of growing
terror upon his face. He well knew the bite of his father's temper, and searched his mind for a way out of
his dilemma. "It wasn't stealing," he asserted. "Balls of
clay haven't any value."

"Balls of clay?" Himself ejaculated, stunned.

"That's what I said to Myrna," Angus said hopefully.

"You dismay me," Himself said with scant control. "To put the blame on Myrna . . ."

"That is just where it belongs," Angus asserted stoutly. "She only wanted them for spite. Helene had told her how much Lady Lydia seemed to treasure them—why, I couldn't say—but it was enough for Myrna that she did."

Himself looked at the Earl with a trace of pain in his eyes. "It appears I must also apologize for my daughter, Torquay. Rest assured you will not be troubled by my offspring in future."

"Say no more," the Earl replied with compassion. "I could not wish to be in their shoes after this."

Himself held out his hand. "My only regret is that Angus has never displayed your strength of character," he admitted ruefully.

The Earl took the hand and gripped it. "The thing I most admire in you, sir, is your own strength of character. There is nothing wrong with Angus a little discipline wouldn't cure." With which statement he bowed and quickly left the room.

CHAPTER FIFTEEN

Upon his return to the castle the Earl went at once to the library, a thoughtful expression on his face. He was not completely satisfied that mere spite prompted Myrna. Avarice had more usually been the motive spurring her to action. He crossed to the paneling beside his desk, slid back the panel, and stood looking at the safe. Feeling foolish, he inserted the key dangling at the end of his fob-chain in the lock and removed the casket containing Lydia's balls of clay. The notion that someone might enter the room occurred to him; he put the box down upon the desk and crossed to lock the door. Returning, he seated himself and picked up one of the balls, turning it in his fingers. It was perfectly smooth and oval in shape. He could discern nothing about it in the least unusual. Laying it down, he picked up another and subjected it to the same minute scrutiny. There seemed to be a slight split in the dried mud. He lifted his quizzing glass. Yes, he decided, it most definitely was a split. His interest caught, he picked up the letter opener, inserted its tip into the minute crack, and applied pressure. The clay coating parted, and a twinkling stone rolled across the desk. The Earl stared in considerable surprise at the flawless diamond sparkling in the sunlight. Recovering from his astonishment, he selected another ball and probed with the knife. In another moment one of the largest diamonds he had ever seen rested in the palm of his hand. So far as he could ascertain, this stone also was without flaw. Grinning, he tossed it up into the air and caught it again. *Well, well,* he thought, and went across the room to unlock the door.

"Inform her ladyship I wish to see her," he said to the footman on duty in the hall.

"Yes, m'lord," the footman replied, startled by the elated expression on his lordship's face. "Now, m'lord?"

"Immediately," the Earl confirmed. "Oh, and tell my secretary to attend me at once," he added, and went back into the library.

Ten minutes later the footman rapped and entered. "Begging your lordship's pardon, but her ladyship's maid informs me her ladyship rode out some three hours ago, m'lord."

"Alone?" said the Earl, brows raised.

The footman seemed to shrink, and stole a furtive glance at his face. "Edward accompanied her ladyship, but he returned about an hour ago. Her ladyship sent him home, m'lord."

The Earl's eyes blazed. "Have my stallion brought around," he said, and turned away to replace the casket in the safe. "Take good care of this, Henry," he added to his secretary.

Five minutes later the horse was before the door. Edward was clinging to its head, endeavoring to control it. The Earl gathered up the reins in one gloved hand and swung aboard. "Where did you leave her ladyship?" he said to the groom.

"Beside Loch Broom at Lookout Point, my lord," Edward replied, coloring. "I begged to remain with her ladyship, but . . ."

The Earl nodded. "Be thankful I believe you," he said, and sent the stallion plunging forward.

The groom watched him out of sight and sighed. "Be thankful your skin remains whole, Edward, my boy," he said to himself, and went back toward the stables.

Lydia, meanwhile, awoke to pain, her eyes adjusting slowly to the flame of a flickering fire, the glow swimming in and out of her consciousness. It was almost impossible to concentrate. Wincing, she touched the lump on her forehead and struggled for recall. The morning had been warm and balmy, pleasant weather for a gallop astride her favorite mare. By eleven o'clock she had reached the hill overlooking the ocean, where the breakers rolled in to join the waters of the loch. Here, under the shade of a tree grotesquely gnarled by gale-force winds, she had dismissed Edward and lingered to rest, and to gaze dreamily out to sea, her back against the trunk of the pine. At the bottom of the hill a grouse paused, instantly alert, its neck stretched long, and eyed her keenly before moving away.

A drumming echo had sounded in the distance, faint at first, then more loudly, borne to her ears on the northerly breeze.

She sat up and stared, her breath suddenly ragged. Horsemen approached at a rapid pace, their mounts fairly eating up the ground. Something in their frenzied stride had caught her notice, urged her to flight. She had jumped up and run to the mare, utterly frightened and not knowing why. Down the hill, past a stone cairn and on by boulders tumbled in disarray, the mare had carried her, surefooted, over the uneven turf. *Do not look back*, had drummed the mare's hooves. *Ride low in the saddle, flee*, had run the promptings of her heart. The head of a stallion drew alongside, its ears laid back, its nostrils flaring: She had screamed in terror, the sound becoming lost in the clatter of hooves over stones on the ground. An arm had reached out, engulfing her, snatching her from the mare. She had screamed again, struggled, had been flung down across a saddle, her head striking a pommel. . . .

A face shimmered into focus, and she was looking up into a pair of sneering eyes. Sir Charles! She blinked and paled.

"Alive, are you?" he said. "Good."

She shuddered. "Why . . ." she began, then paused, feeling nauseous.

"Why?" he repeated, laughing harshly. "Why, indeed. You have a penchant for removing heiresses from my grasp. I trust you understand."

She strove to concentrate. "Ransom?" she murmured, struggling to sit upright.

"But, of course," he replied.

She could not contain a sigh. "Then perhaps you will not deny me water," she said, relieved.

"See to it," he snapped to someone beyond Lydia's vision.

"See to it yourself," came an instant reply.

Lydia recognized the voice, and turned her head, appalled. Myrna's face swam out of focus, cleared. She was seated on a sofa, watching the tableau with the fires of hatred in her gaze. "Let me teach her the meaning of suffering," she suggested, eyes gleaming.

"I will not have my plans placed in jeopardy," he replied, shaking his head. "Your revenge means nothing to me, my dear Myrna. It has no value in the marketplace."

"Value!" she snorted. "Pray, what worth do you place on wads of mud?"

"Enough!" he commanded, silencing her with the word. "There is more at stake here than mere personal gratification. I would like nothing better than to humble our fair charmer as I was humbled, but I will forego the pleasure in favor of the ransom."

Lydia was too benumbed to take it in. The conversation had assumed all the aspects of a nightmare. Surely Sir Charles could not be serious in suggesting her balls of clay sufficient to constitute a ransom; he must be mad. She felt dizzy with fear and uncertainty, so much so that when he poured out a glass of Madeira and placed it to her lips, she found her thirst had forsaken her. She was so sure he had drugged the wine that she turned her head away, and only sipped it when he ordered her to do so in a voice that chilled her to her very soul. Had she but know it, her alarm was wasted. Sir Charles was profoundly indifferent to the frailties of others, and would have felt himself demeaned had he been obliged to allay her fears. Her anxiety, which he was too unimaginative to recognize, passed completely over his head. The Earl soon became her prime concern. She was so sure that he would come looking for her at Brodie Hall once he guessed her plight, that each passing moment became a torment and fretted her unbearably. Sir Charles, whose character was an open book, was not above laying a trap into which the Earl might blunder.

At around one o'clock her worst fears proved justified. The clatter of a horse's hooves heralded his arrival, and within a very few minutes the sound of his voice raised in altercation with the butler smote her ears. A quick step sounded in the hall, the door was flung violently open, and the Earl stood on the threshold, booted and spurred and wearing a heavy surcoat. His gaze swept the room and came to rest on her. "You are unharmed?" he said.

"Except for a blow to the head," she answered with admirable control.

He swung his gaze to Sir Charles, who was just recovering from the shock of his unexpected appearance upon the scene. For a moment they stared at each other, Sir Charles rigid in his chair, the Earl silent in the doorway, but with murder gleaming deep within his eyes. The Earl shut the door and turned the key in the lock. "I shouldn't care to be disturbed," he remarked, moving forward. "I venture to suggest that you defend yourself without benefit of paid assassins by your side."

Sir Charles thought to bluff his way through. "I have no intention whatsoever of dueling with you," he muttered, clearing his throat of the constriction that threatened to stifle him.

"That we shall see," the Earl said silkily, and thrust the sofa against the wall; a chair and table quickly followed.

"No!" Myrna screeched, rushing forward to position

herself before Sir Charles, arms outspread. "You will kill him! He is no match for you!"

The Earl smiled evilly upon Sir Charles. "Hiding behind a woman's skirts?" he said in tones calculated to inflame his quarry.

It was all Sir Charles needed to cast discretion to the winds. "Out of the way," he gritted, rudely shoving Myrna aside. He was in a towering rage by this time, and snarled at the Earl: "If you will be so good as to hand me the sword on the rack behind you, I will prove who is the better man."

The Earl strode to the wall and snatched it down. "You may try," he said, passing it across, hilt first.

Lydia, instinctively knowing Sir Charles greatly outmatched, grasped the Earl by the arm. "This has gone far enough," she said. "Just take me home, Iain."

"Stay clear of the blades," he replied, disengaging her clinging fingers and removing his surcoat. "Nothing you can say will stop me."

"Iain, I beg you . . ."

The Earl removed his coats and boots and shook the Dresden ruffles back from his hands. "You have offered me insults I will presently avenge," he told Sir Charles, testing the flexibility of his sword.

Sir Charles, succeeding at last in removing his topboots, stood and faced the Earl. Both men were in shirt and breeches, both were determined to put a period to the existence of the other. The blades flashed in a brief salute, and the battle was enjoined. From the oustet it was apparent that Sir Charles, mediocre at best, was no match for an experienced swordsman. He had a certain dexterity with which he somehow managed to parry the Earl's thrusts, but he was soon gasping for breath and seen to flag. The Earl broke through his guard again and again, only to check and withdraw, intentionally, the rasp of steel scraping on steel setting Sir Charles's teeth on edge. His gasping breath and the slap of stockinged feet on the floorboards, were the only other sounds to be heard in the room.

The fight went on, the Earl toying with Sir Charles as a cat will toy with a mouse. Repeatedly the tip of his blade darted in, opening a gash on the forearm here, leaving a red slash on the shoulder there. Perspiration was dripping from Sir Charles's forehead, and blood was flowing freely from his wounds. His arm felt leaden, and he thought his lungs would burst. He realized the inevitable outcome of the fight and, gathering his last remaining strength, lunged forward. It seemed as though what happened next would be impossible. Sir Charles, his foot slipping in a pool of his own blood, lurched sideways toward the spot where Myrna was standing, the point of his sword plunging deep within her shoulder. Horrified, he wrenched the blade free, and stood gaping at her lying in a crumpled heap upon the floor.

In two strides the Earl was at Myrna's side, and in another moment had dropped down onto one knee beside her. "Get linen," he said to Lydia, and slashed Myrna's gown with the tip of his sword, baring the wound. To Sir Charles's whispered query, he said: "No, she will not die, but the wound is deep."

Lydia, looking around and seeing no cloth spread upon the table, quickly lifted her skirts and slipped one of her underskirts down over her hips. Stepping out of it, she handed it to the Earl. He slashed the cloth with the sword and tore two strips from it. One of them he folded into a pad and pressed against the wound to stanch the flow of blood, the other he bound tightly around her shoulder to hold the pad in place. He got up then, unlocked the door, and jerked the bellpull.

The butler answered the ring with an alacrity that indicated he had been hovering about close by. "Send for a doctor," the Earl ordered. "Also notify the McDougall his daughter has been wounded." He paused and glanced at Myrna's still figure lying on the floor. "Have two stout footmen carry Miss McDougall upstairs to bed, and send the housekeeper to tend her. And cease shaking, man. You had nothing to do with this."

"I trust not, my lord," the butler said, and went out, shutting the door behind him.

Sir Charles had slumped down into a chair, a pained frown creasing his forehead. "I don't suppose you would fetch me a brandy?" he said, wincing.

The Earl picked up the decanter and poured out a glass. "I had better bind up your wounds," he said, handing Sir Charles the wine.

"Why?" Sir Charles demanded, downing the brandy in one gulp. "A moment ago you swore to kill me."

The Earl bent over him to bandage the cuts. "I rather think the McDougall will appreciate my efforts," he remarked dryly. "If I were you, I would put myself beyond his reach. He might just take it into his head to complete what I began."

"Experience leads me to agree," Sir Charles remarked, his face contorted with pain. "Very well, then. The Continent it shall be. Add to your damned goodness by sending word to my man to pack a valise."

The Earl picked up his sword and carefully wiped

it clear. "Indulge me," he said, sliding the blade back into its scabbard. "How did you manage to elude Squire Thinshanks?"

Sir Charles smiled thinly. "The shed turned out to be an outhouse," he admitted in rueful humor. "I kicked the blasted thing apart, believe me."

The Earl's lips twitched. "Had I known, it would have added a certain—er, piquancy to our encounter," he said, holding out his hand. "You're a rogue, Sir Charles, but I wish you luck, regardless. Banishment from England is punishment enough for any man to sustain."

Sir Charles took the hand and weakly gripped it. "I hardly dare to tell you, Torquay, but had I won, your wife would have fared ill in my company."

But the Earl only laughed and escorted Lydia from the room. She waited only until the door closed behind them before saying: "How will you hush this up, Iain? I should think the servants will put it all about."

"Put your faith in Himself, my dear. He has had a great deal of experience along that line. Where is your mare?"

"I haven't any idea. I was unconscious when brought here."

The matter was easily resolved. It seemed the majority of Sir Charles's staff was gathered in the hall, all a-twitter. The Earl turned his head and issued one brief order that sent a footman scurrying for the stables. A few minutes later the mare had been brought around, and Lydia and the Earl were cantering down the drive, side by side.

She regarded him pensively. "You must be in an uncommonly good temper," she remarked. "You haven't scolded me."

"You are not out of the woods yet, my dear," he replied.

"Then you do intend to scold."

"I haven't said so."

She frowned. "What am I to understand by that?" she asked rather sternly.

"Only that I am in a benign mood, my love."

She folded her lips and took refuge in silence, for she could find no words adequate to chastise him. The thought occurred to her that she had acted more than a little foolishly in dismissing her groom. She had never felt so guilty. She became much inclined to think she had placed his life in danger; a lucky thrust on Sir Charles's part—she dared not pursue the fancy further.

The castle came into sight; very shortly she was allowing him to help her down, ignoring the amusement in his eyes. She swept before him into the house and nearly stumbled over a pile of luggage in the hall.

"What the devil!" exclaimed the Earl.

McTavish, harassed, nevertheless came forward with stately step. "I believe that Lady Flora plans to leave shortly to reside with a friend, my lord," he said.

A look of astonishment crossed the Earl's face. "When did this come about?" he asked.

"Her ladyship informs me she has been considering the possibility for some time, my lord. I understand—a disagreement with Lady Cavanaugh hastened her decision."

"Convey my compliments to Lady Flora. I will see her before she departs. She will find us in the library," he added, and strolled with Lydia into the room.

"I think she must be mad," Lydia remarked, stripping off her gloves. "One simply does not rearrange one's life on a whim."

"Oh, I don't know," he replied, crossing to the wall safe beside his desk. "It has a familiar ring, my dear. She appeared on our doorstep in my father's time in much the same way."

"That is not to the point, Iain. I am thinking of her safety."

"Outriders will accompany her," he replied, unlocking the safe. "I have purchased a quite respectable house on the other side of the village for the Cavanaughs. They should be fairly comfortable there. You appear surprised, my dear. I thought it an excellent notion. Do you approve?"

She did. She had known that something must be done. There would be no peace so long as Lady Cavanaugh remained in the house.

The Earl had one further problem to resolve: Miss Wingate's future. "She is far too intelligent to relish spending the remainder of her days in Aunt Mary's sphere," he remarked, lifting out the casket.

"You are oblivious to everything around you," Lydia said smugly. "For my part, I know what is occurring beneath my very nose."

"Such a pretty nose," he remarked, putting the casket down upon his desk.

She cast him a triumphant look. "You should ask me what I mean, sir," she said.

The Earl, wisest of men, dutifully responded. "What do you mean, my dear?" he said.

"The Captain and Miss Wingate. I felt a romance was in the air, so I thought I would, well, toss out a few hints."

He looked at her half in amusement, half in reproval. "I trust you found no indiscretion on your very unguarded tongue," he said, seating himself behind his desk.

"I was quite diplomatic, thank you. I could tell he is in love by the way he looks at her, and when I mentioned his name, she turned the subject. So I knew she is in love with him. What do you think of that?"

"I think you very properly have love on your brain," he informed her. "I am in a position to recognize the signs."

She ducked her head. "That was not very nice," she said in a woebegone voice.

But he had caught her smile, and grinned. "You are up to something," he remarked. "You have a natural propensity for sticking your lovely little nose into other people's business."

She raised her head, her eyes daring him. Satisfied that he didn't intend hazarding a further remark, she continued: "I gathered from what she said that she considers herself beneath his touch. She spoke of penury and her father's suicide—as if the Captain would care a fig for that!"

"He undoubtedly wouldn't, but it is not your place to prompt him, Lydia. Allow him the privilege of his own decisions."

"Don't be provoking, please. I have told you it is not the Captain. It's Miss Wingate. She has the most gothic notions imaginable. I see I will be forced to reorder her thinking."

She noted the convulsive movement of his hand, and searched her mind for words with which to defend her somewhat indefensible position. Much to her surprise, she found herself spared the necessity of doing so. He merely remarked that it would solve the

dilemma of Miss Wingate's future, should they make a
match of it, and frowned her down when she would
have pursued the matter further.

Lydia belatedly became aware of the casket reposing upon his desk. "It's the strangest thing, Iain," she
said. "Sir Charles expressed his intention of demand-
ing my balls of clay as ransom. Did you ever hear of
anything so foolish?"

"Foolish?" he repeated, grinning.

"I feel sure—you are acting rather strangely."

"I am? In what way?"

"I don't know," she replied, puzzled. "No, I take
that back. If you had whiskers, they would be covered
with cream."

"If I were a cat, my love, I would be purring."

She reflected briefly on the perversity of men, and
changed her tack. "If you are incensed that Sir
Charles held my worth so low, you needn't be. It isn't
as if my pride were . . ."

"That hadn't occurred . . ."

" . . . as if my pride were touched by his miserable
opinion of me. Quite the reverse. I should have been
incensed had he held me in great esteem."

"Are you finished?"

"No, I promise you I'm not. You aren't being very
nice . . ."

"To do so requires an opportunity that . . ."

"Oh!" she stormed. "Of all the insufferable . . ."

"Lydia, come here!"

"Why?"

"I mean to kiss you."

She rose and, bending over him, dropped a light
peck upon his brow. "There," she said.

He knew what was expected of him, and drew her onto his knee. "I shouldn't call that a kiss," he remarked, smiling into her eyes.

"I could do better, given cause."

A bold hand slipped under her skirts and up the soft flesh of her inner leg to the satin smoothness of her thigh.

"Ah," she breathed, wriggling her bottom enticingly against his loin. "That isn't fair."

"Nothing of love is fair," he murmured, lingering long on her lips. "It is the way of woman to bewitch her man."

She smiled saucily and laid a finger against his lips. "I have wretched news for you, sir," she said. "You neglected to lock the door."

"Console yourself with the thought that your enjoyment of our orgies is entirely legal. You do enjoy them, love?"

"Yes, but I shouldn't express it quite like that."

"Shortly we will investigate additional ways in which to express it, but first I have a surprise for you. Up you get."

"Why didn't you tell me," she said, rising in one graceful movement. "Don't, pray, keep me in suspense."

"Take this," he said, handing her the letter opener. "And this," he added, holding out one of the balls of clay.

Lydia gazed in bewilderment from the knife in her right hand to the oval of mud in her left. "I hesitate to sound stupid, but . . ."

"Chip away the clay, my dear."

"Are you saying there is something inside?"

His glance swept her face. "Certainly I am," he said, and took the objects from her hands. "Let me help you."

In another moment a diamond lay sparkling on the desk. She gazed, dumbfounded, and felt her brain to be reeling. "Good God!" she said blankly. "I had no notion . . ."

"I will break them open, and you can put the dirt in the waste-can," he said, emptying the contents of the casket out onto the desk. "I felicitate you, my love. You are now an exceptionally independent lady."

"Iain, however did you know?"

"I discovered it quite by accident. Henry is a prince among secretaries, my dear. He assures me of an interesting theory concerning their origin that I am persuaded will intrigue you. According to him, pirates are much in the habit of camouflaging their jewels by coating them with clay, and often secrete them away in caves along a seacoast."

"I should think a pirate would have returned for them, if that were the case."

"His is a perilous occupation, at best. The fact that he had not done so would seem to indicate his demise. In any event, they could have lain there undisturbed for centuries. It will be a tale to thrill our grandchildren one day."

"Indeed?" she said, smiling. "I was under the impression that children came first."

"You are quite correct. They do," he said, catching her up in his arms. "I am sorry if you object, my love, but—if it's all the same with you, I would like us to have a houseful."

"But I don't object," she murmured, gazing up at him with adoring eyes. "I don't object at all."

THE TAMING

Aleen Malcolm

Cameron—daring, impetuous girl/woman who has never known a life beyond the windswept wilds of the Scottish countryside.

Alex Sinclair—high-born and quick-tempered, finds more than passion in the heart of his headstrong ward Cameron.

Torn between her passion for freedom and her long-denied love for Alex, Cameron is thrust into the dazzling social whirl of 18th century Edinburgh and comes to know the fulfillment of deep and dauntless love.

A Dell Book $2.50

Bonfire

by
Charles Dennis

Alan Farrel was a runaway at age 12, an ex-con at 15, a drifter, a boxer and a man no woman could refuse. Tough, charismatic, he rose from the teeming slums of New York to Hollywood's starry heights. His life was the dream-stuff movies are made of and his Polly was the only woman who lived life as lustfully as he. She loved him and had the power to destroy him!

A Dell Book $2.25

THE DARK HORSEMAN

Marianne Harvey

Beautiful Donna Penroze had sworn to her
dying father that she would save her sole leg-
acy, the crumbling tin mines and the ancient,
desolate estate *Trencobban*. But the mines
were failing, and Donna had no one to turn to.
No one except the mysterious Nicholas Tre-
varvas—rich, arrogant, commanding. Donna
would do anything but surrender her pride, anything but admit her irresistible longing for *The
Dark Horseman*.

A Dell Book $2.50

Dell Bestsellers

- ☐ **WHISTLE** by James Jones $2.75 (19262-5)
- ☐ **GREEN ICE** by Gerald A. Browne $2.50 (13224-X)
- ☐ **A STRANGER IS WATCHING**
  by Mary Higgins Clark $2.50 (18125-9)
- ☐ **AFTER THE WIND** by Eileen Lottman $2.50 (18138-0)
- ☐ **THE ROUNDTREE WOMEN: BOOK 1**
  by Margaret Lewerth $2.50 (17594-1)
- ☐ **THE MEMORY OF EVA RYKER**
  by Donald A. Stanwood $2.50 (15550-9)
- ☐ **BLIZZARD** by George Stone $2.25 (11080-7)
- ☐ **THE BLACK MARBLE**
  by Joseph Wambaugh $2.50 (10647-8)
- ☐ **MY MOTHER/MY SELF** by Nancy Friday ..$2.50 (15663-7)
- ☐ **SEASON OF PASSION** by Danielle Steel .$2.25 (17703-0)
- ☐ **THE DARK HORSEMAN**
  by Marianne Harvey $2.50 (11758-5)
- ☐ **BONFIRE** by Charles Dennis $2.25 (10659-1)
- ☐ **THE IMMIGRANTS** by Howard Fast $2.75 (14175-3)
- ☐ **THE ENDS OF POWER**
  by H.R. Haldeman with Joseph DiMona ...$2.75 (12239-2)
- ☐ **GOING AFTER CACCIATO** by Tim O'Brien $2.25 (12966-4)
- ☐ **SLAPSTICK** by Kurt Vonnegut $2.25 (18009-0)
- ☐ **THE FAR SIDE OF DESTINY**
  by Dore Mullen $2.25 (12645-2)
- ☐ **LOOK AWAY, BEULAH LAND**
  by Lonnie Coleman $2.50 (14642-9)
- ☐ **STRANGERS** by Michael de Guzman $2.25 (17952-1)
- ☐ **EARTH HAS BEEN FOUND** by D.F Jones ..$2.25 (12217-1)

At your local bookstore or use this handy coupon for ordering:

Dell **DELL BOOKS**
P.O. BOX 1000, PINEBROOK, N.J. 07058

Please send me the books I have checked above. I am enclosing $_____
(please add 35¢ per copy to cover postage and handling). Send check or money
order—no cash or C.O.D.'s. Please allow up to 8 weeks for shipment.

Mr/Mrs/Miss_____

Address_____

City_____ State/Zip_____